A LESSON IN BUSINESS ETHICS

"Right," Luke said. "He should know." Luke was rapidly beginning to get a signal now. He didn't like it. He'd heard of this kind of thing but he never expected it in here. Maybe he was wrong.

"And what with the American plane being there to fill the orders, the competitor I mean. The Channing jet…"

Luke put the tumbler down on the glass covering of DeJohn's desk with a crack.

"Why do you keep spelling this out?" he asked sharply. "What are you trying to say?"

"Say?" DeJohn looked flustered, for about one fiftieth of a second.

"What's the message you're trying to pass from Schaum to me?"

"There is no message, Luke. All I'm saying," DeJohn said slowly "is that Schaum would be very relieved, and very much helped in the market—in fact *saved* in the market—if you were to find evidence of sabotage." He paused, Luke waited. "Even if it's not, shall we say, conclusive."

"Even if I have to invent it, you mean."

DOWNTIME

PETER FOX

BERKLEY BOOKS, NEW YORK

This Berkley book contains the complete
text of the original hardcover edition.

DOWNTIME

A Berkley Book / published by arrangement with
the author

PRINTING HISTORY
Hodder and Stoughton edition published 1986.
Berkley edition / January 1988

ISBN: 0-425-10550-4

A BERKLEY BOOK ® TM 757,375
Berkley Books are published by The Berkley Publishing Group,
200 Madison Avenue, New York, NY 10016.
The name "BERKLEY" and the "B" logo
are trademarks belonging to Berkley Publishing Corporation.

PRINTED IN THE UNITED STATES OF AMERICA

10   9   8   7   6   5   4   3   2   1

And now I see with eye serene,
The very pulse of the machine

Wordsworth

1

Day: minus 15

The great jetliner eased itself back into level flight gently, elegantly almost, like a soaring black gull, settling on to an altitude to initial surface pressure of ninety thousand ticks exactly. Exactly was what made the captain cringe, way down deep inside the well of his pilot's guts.

He watched the LCDs hopefully for a few seconds, waiting for a driftdown, but it stayed dead stable, right there. Not eighty-nine thousand nine hundred and ninety, not ninety thousand and ten, but ninety thousand. Not a hair either side, the captain noted despairingly, not a smidgen either way. Ninety thousand exactly.

The autopilots (an old word for it, no more than a hangover really) had governed the climb; they had decided on it, initiated it, timed it, executed it. No member of the flight crew had taken a hand in it, not one of them had put in even so much as an opinion on it. The machines were flying the machine again, and no matter how much you . . .

The captain let it go. He peered out and up through glass fifteen centimetres thick, hoping to spot the satellite this time. It would be close to its perigee as it passed above them, and treetop low by Navstar standards, but it would still be miles higher than this highest flying of all airliners. So much higher in fact that the captain had never really caught the significance of this jump up for the data pass. It had seemed to him a mere gesture, devoid of cause and effect, like a savage climbing a hill to pray because it got him nearer to God.

He looked up into endless dark. Above, his view unimpaired by the scattered light of lower atmosphere, he saw the violet black of outer space. Though they had left the ground only an hour or more ago, and not long after dawn, the sky he beheld was of eternal night, traced and spattered with a million stars. The captain gazed among them, seeking the one that moved from the north-east, but he saw nothing that qualified.

Elsewhere in the plane, other men paused momentarily for a view of things, as if the climb-complete announcement (a machine's voice, faintly female) signalled some kind of pause. Some looked from flight-deck canopies, others from cabin windows, and others from places you wouldn't have thought offered any kind of view at all.

Had it been night, then this arctic route would have shown them northern lights; great green fingers leaping from electric discharges thousands of metres below and out into the heavens along highways of magnetic flux. In daytime there was a different blend of views. Twenty seven kilometres below, the distant, arcing horizon-line of earth shimmered in a translucent halo of mingling colour. Straight down through the thickening void lay the blue-grey, icy solitude of the Bering Sea, forbidding and featureless, prowled by submarines. South of it, the long, broken sweep of the Alaskan peninsula and the Aleutian chain, their invisible islands revealed by rising telltale clusters of puffy cumulus. Beyond them lay nothing but the vastness of the north Pacific, empty all the way to the Hawaiian group, eight thousand kilometres more distant still. Ahead and to the west, tempests raged, silent and majestic. Mighty stormclouds spiralling up ten kilometres in blinding summits and deep ravines of magenta, though at this stratospheric height the plane was above any kind of weather, these monsters included. To the north, nine hundred kilometres remote but clear from this far aloft, they could see the awesome white desolation of the polar cap, its cordons of icebergs discernible only as pinpricks in the haze, though many would tower like cathedrals, a thousand metres and more into the air.

The plane was bearing west by south over the shoulder of the world, knifing towards the date line at more than three thousand kilometres per hour. Few rifle bullets travelled at such a speed, and almost no other aircraft outside the military. Its quarter million-plus kilos of frame, fuel and payload were outstripping the sound of its engines by a factor of three, and then some. The air through which it raced was thin, with less than one per cent of sea-level pressure, and at sixty below as deadly cold as the most hiemal places on earth, but despite that the matt-black titanium alloy skin of the aircraft seared with enough heat to vaporise a hand. Five hundred degrees at the midwings was its coolest, pushing up to a near thousand and orange-white at the engine exhausts. And each time it flew, this infernal bake annealed its every joint like a second weld.

Beneath its great, swept-delta wings, and outboard of its retracting ventral fins, two pairs of giant engines punched the liner forward like a missile. In every second of flight, each of the huge inlets that ringed the nacelle cones sucked in more rarefied air than the combined inhalings of twelve million people, like the single gigantic breath of a whole metropolis. Some of it was fed into combustion chambers deep inside, some drawn around to be injected into afterburners, and yet more hurled into exhaust ejector streams, combining to generate the colossal thrust that held the plane at its Mach three cruise. At such a speed you ran on a turbo-ramjet effect. Eight tenths of your thrust came from your inlets, another one and a half from your ejectors. Your engine pulled only one twentieth of the cruising thrust, and only a third of what it had to supply at takeoff. Nobody had ever made power plants like these before. These engines had consumed thousands of millions in design costs, hundreds of man-years in effort. Men lived who thought of them as their life's work.

Inside the wings, and under some sections of the huge, slender, knife-flat body, bladder-lined tanks held almost a hundred thousand kilos of fuel. It was a high-temperature concoction, this fuel, virtually inert when cold; it had to be chemically exploded into life at engine start-up, and in flight it flowed along mazes of siphons, valves and pipes, balancing the aircraft as she manoeuvred, shifting the weight centre fore and aft as the lift point moved with changing speed. Accelerate and the lift point went back, so fuel flowed aft to the rear collector tanks to compensate. Decelerate and the reverse happened. But as the engines burned it, so the calculation gained complexity. Only computers could do it, and the fuel system had several.

In fact all the systems had computers. If you looked at it one way, this whole big bird was one big computer thing. It was conceived in them, designed in them, built, tested, modified, flown and controlled by them, and many of its components *were* them. There wasn't anybody who looked at it that way though, or hardly anybody.

This flight was a finalising test. Almost the last of many proving tests, before the maiden voyage in service. It was bound for Tokyo out of Vancouver. It carried a flight crew, thirty technicians and a very large quantity of equipment. It was never going to arrive.

Three minutes and ten seconds after rotating into the takeoff, they had crossed thirty thousand vectors and Vancouver had cleared their flight path for Mach three plus. In another forty minutes, eighty thousand plus high and running abeam of the west Canadian coast, they had covered more than three thousand kilometres and were sighting Alaska. Anchorage came in with continued super-sonic clearance for US air space. Then they had requested end-to-end Scout satellite navigation, which Anchorage had acknowledged. They had used it before, and in a sense it was another test.

Scout was a new system, completed only in the late nineties. Unlike the high-orbiting Navstar satellites, the Scout system's radar-equipped tracking satellites performed highly elliptic orbits that brought them close to the earth. In these low passes they detected and tracked aircraft. Given a plane's call sign and desired route, the Scouts could check its heading and relay any course changes direct into its autopilot computers. The Scouts slid by in strings over the world's oceans, bisecting the course of any plane that ventured out. It was a brand new system and few aircraft as yet had the means to deal with it. But this was one, and between them, or so the theory went, the satellites and the autopilots could take her over the Pacific's dome without a human hand to help. Anyway, that was one of the things they aimed to test.

The plane had other navigation systems of course. As well as satellite navigation, it had its threefold redundant INS using laser gyros and computer position-pooling, it had its Omega receivers, picking up the triplet pulses that the earth transmitters sent rolling longwave around the curve of the earth, providing autosynchronised and ultra-accurate fixing, and of course it had the *humans* naturally, as an absolute fallback, so you could say that this plane would need a hell of a lot of losing. On the other hand, you could say that at a kilometre a second, you could get lost quickly.

Ten minutes after their request, American ground controllers on Kodiak island came through with confirmation of Scout tracking, which meant that the satellites had their auto-call sign and would relay it to each other as they handed the plane on, one satellite to the next, taking her over the great circle as they skimmed by one after the other, fifteen or so minutes apart. The captain had acknowledged that and was advised that a Scout was inbound so he could lock in without a wait. He acknowledged that too, locked in his autopilots, and a minute later the plane had risen eerily and unaided towards the passing orbiter. The silent exchange of data had lasted but ten seconds in time. The plane had flattened back five thousand or so, the communications and navigation officers had announced all well, and the captain had taken back control for the turn. One more look at the distant misty peaks of the Kuskokwim mountains and the captain had bidden farewell to Anchorage and Kodiak and brought the liner around towards the open ocean. Autopilots back on, time and vectors noted, transponders off. It had been six thousand kilometres to Japan, she had eight thousand or more of fuel on board. They would vault this ocean wilderness alone, with no human contact until the Russian ground stations at Petropavlovsk in Kamchatka. Their destination had been but two hours and twenty minutes away, allowing for the ballistic descent.

Right now it was about one hour and fifteen, and the event was close at hand.

Already the captain had noted that the plane was holding its height for what seemed a little too long. Deep inside his mind, something moved, very slightly, and waited. Wait, it told him, but tighten up.

As well as the flight crew actually needed to handle this thing, there was a real crowd on board, as usual for the test flights. The technicians, checkers, measurers, observers: they infested the aircraft's guts like termites. Up front here they tried to stay out of the way for the most part. They looked and listened but the actual flying they naturally left to the crew. But further back behind the flight deck it was the engineers' ball.

Through the long and luxurious lanes of the passenger lounges, between the padded velour seats, they studied their recorders and the output of the masses of boxes and wires that squatted and hung there, mimicking the demands and responses of passengers who would soon use this mighty craft in their thousands. Occasionally one of these men would speak to another and the two of them would come together in a huddle, staring at a scope, comparing a note. Over the hum of the plane their voices were muted, like in a reading room.

Further back again, where the trailing edges of the great wings met the tapering fuselage and beyond that, where the huge forty-metre tail fin sloped down to the roof, more specialists monitored elevon drives and gearings, emergency fuel jettisons and brake-chute clusters. In various other nooks, yet more men studied subsystems beyond numbering with equipment beyond ken, fuel transfers and control surfaces, airflows and temperatures, hydraulics, electronics and ballistics, pneumatics, mechanics, radionics and geodesics.

Thirty-seven men in all, counting the crew.

'I'm not getting way point from Scout four.'

The communications officer said it quickly, grabbing an available silence in the crosstalk that had just started in his headphones between captain and copilot. He kept his voice flat and calm because it was no big deal yet. He was aiming his announcement at the captain. The navigator would have the information on his screens by now.

Captain and copilot exchanged a glance. The copilot started into a long inhaling sigh.

'It or us?' The captain still didn't move his hands towards the controls. The plane was still on autopilots, still hanging at ninety thousand vectors waiting for the course change to keep it on the great circle to Japan. A few kilometres above, the Scout satellite was grazing by and theoretically sending the course change now, though *right* now the input looked like nil.

'Evens till I check,' said the comms.

'Check it quick, Ed,' the pilot said. 'I need to turn soon, otherwise we get Russian military traffic ahead.'

The comms officer tried Kodiak first, then he tried for Petropavlovsk. He waited a little while then tried again, watching the readouts roll up his monitors in green and red. Nothing in, nothing out.

'It's us, chief,' he reported. 'Can't raise the ground stations. Looks like all or part of the outboard comms is down. Not getting Omega data in either.'

'Put a size on it,' the captain told him. 'I'll stay on auto for five more minutes and then I'll start driving. Got that, Dave? That's maybe one seven five past way point. Check the air space.'

'Roger that,' came in the navigator. 'One seven five at this speed. Still clear of the Russians.'

As the navigator started to punch up the course change, the communications officer was flicking overhead switches on his control panels. Then he too began to key in commands on the terminal before him.

'Checking out the comms, top down,' he warbled into the log. 'When you've eliminated the impossible, my dear Watson, what you got left . . .'

'Stow it, Ed,' snapped the captain. 'Just get on with it.'

The pilot was trying to think, for which he didn't need the kid being wise in his ear. Should he give it five minutes? Maybe that was dawdling, on reflection. He'd prefer to take her down to thicker air for a hand turn. She'd speed up going down, he'd need time to rein her in a bit. It all took time. Also, the captain had this point of view about Russian fighters.

He wasn't going to get five minutes. None of them were.

The comms man found it quickly enough though. This time there was a real underscore in his voice.

'Oh you fucker,' he announced mildly.

The captain swung around in his seat then and peered back and up into the communications bay.

'I told you to get a hold of your mouth,' he said, and he was going to add some more to it, but the look on the face of the young communications officer stopped him dead.

The captain's back went rippling up and down.

'Sorry, sir.'

'Uh?' The captain blinked. 'Well it goes on tape, Ed. The whole thing's logged.'

'Yeh. Sorry.'

The captain pulled a face again. 'So what is it?'

Comms nodded at his screens, his eyes fixed back on the red lines that stood, emphasised, among the green.

'Computers,' he said, as if it was something they all needed to be alerted to, like a snake crawling round your foot. 'Both the outboard message processors are down.

Online and standby, both gone.' He let his voice fade a little. 'It's crazy.'

'It's impossible is what it is,' the navigator opined suddenly through the static. 'It's impossible is what.'

'Uh? What's impossible?'

'It's billions to one against, Ed,' the navigator purred. So all of a sudden he knew about these things, which was a surprise to the comms officer.

The pilot said. 'What the hell . . .'

'Impossible nothing,' comms said. 'It's up here in red. Status and viability failures, both the machines got a pain.'

'Software,' the navigator said flatly. 'They're hung up on something. No way is it a double hardware fault.'

The point was philosophical, with the navigator arguing that a one in ten to some damn big power event just didn't happen and the comms officer advancing the case for small but finite probabilities. The captain nodded to the copilot to release the autopilots. He pushed down on the column. Air speed began to rise.

'Software bug,' the navigator was insisting. 'They're not down, Ed. They've just got hung.'

'That's your special gift, right?' the comms officer said. 'You're a clairvoyant. Listen . . .'

'No, you listen. What's the odds . . .'

'That'll do,' the captain cut in on both of them. 'It's no use arguing. Dave, I want that course change now. Ed, I want the outboard comms in some kind of shape so I can talk to ATC when we get in range, so fix it. Meantime I'm flying this ship to Japan. Autopilots are off. We're going down for a turn.'

The captain said it tiredly, as if the whole thing was getting to be a bore, what with faults from nowhere and kids talking jive in his lobes, and then, with a kind of sporting fluidity, he violently rammed his head against the thick thermoglass of the cockpit window.

At the same time, the copilot butted him in the right shoulder.

Simultaneously, the communications officer cracked his

monitor screen with his forehead and the navigator prostrated himself over his panel like a pope at prayer.

In roughly the same instant the rest of the crew, both flight and test, by and large either rolled or stumbled or took a hopping jump at the port side.

There had been no warning at all.

In the same microsecond, minutes inside the shadow of the satellite, both online and standby outboard communications computers had struck the programmed jump that had trapdoored them both to remote regions of their memories. Here they found the secret instructions – code that should never have been there – that held them cycling in an infinite and uninterruptible loop, ignoring all inputs, all stimuli, all commands, in a dead, mindless sleep, shutting the aircraft off from the world in a single, instant step.

Deep inside the starboard wing, more machines, masters and slaves, had found more clandestine code and had begun to monitor the scheduled signals from the flight panel, waiting for the instant when the autopilots would be released. When that signal came, they had triggered the servos to the starboard engine nacelle cones before they too had lapsed into electronic coma, announcing, betraying and obeying nothing.

The result was inevitable then. As the cones retracted, the shock wave held captive in the engine inlets had gone unstable and escaped. There had been an inlet stall on both power units, losing most of the thrust on that side. The aircraft had dived to starboard, wrenching the crew like rag dolls at their stations. At that instant the autostabiliser system would normally have intervened, injecting rudder at fifteen degrees in a tenth of a second, but that system was dormant too by now.

And while the protective systems failed to respond, others, usually inactive, began to act. More computers joined the dance of death, in the elevon drive units in the wings and the fuel emergency jettison under the tail. Already yawing hard, the aircraft now began to roll, and as the fuel tanks went out of balance, she began to pitch down. Unstable around all three flight axes, she didn't have any chance left at all.

'Dropping fuel,' came a voice from the tail. It was hysterical.

'Rolling,' the copilot said, very calmly.

The pilot clenched his teeth hard, wrapped his big wiry hands around the column grips, felt the sweat sliding in his palms. He had heard it, his mind was saying, he had heard the rumbling building out in the wing but he had assumed it was boundary layers shifting, a common enough thing in a descent. Would it have helped if he had not assumed it? Could he have stopped this? Forestalled this? Somewhere in the rising, frantic exchanges in his headset he could hear the comms officer moaning over his gashed face. Penetrating the whole row was the whooping of the stability system howling its warning. Before his eyes, lights were coming on and flashing, green and blue, the horizon was tilting as the plane shuddered to starboard, heaving against Mach three airstreams, the small white aircraft silhouette on the pitch dial was going nose down. The captain drank it all in, ground his teeth, and tried to fly. He tried with his very soul but it was no use. It was the stuff of nightmares by now, death a formality, with only the long fall to come. Down and down she fell, end over end along a great lazy southerly parabola, twisting and tumbling like a toy from a roof, made suddenly miniature by the pitiless immensity of the void through which she plunged. Nine endless minutes it took, while men rolled and bounced inside.

She exploded on impact, bursting against the speed-hardened ocean as if made of paper, and all her fragments sank at once, both of men and machine, into a second – time-wise longer – and final descent through the blackening depths of the Aleutian trench, eight kilometres down below the golden day.

The Scout saw it fall, through its passionless radar eyes, computed its vanishing trace as plane blended with planet, and informed Kodiak. They were already moving on it by then, since the satellite had reported no response from its waymark transmission, but this final message that spoke of fading track and descending trajectory left them wordless for a while, knowing but not saying. And of course there was no reply when they called.

2

Maringelli paused for a minute after he came out of the bookshop because the robot with the red suit on caught his eye. He walked over Oxford Street, dodging the traffic that was swishing by heavily in the early evening rush on roads made wet and glistening in the light sleet. It was dark by at least an hour but the Christmas neons and laser lights made the street like midday, at least until you looked up into the pitch black, starless sky.

Maringelli stopped and watched it for a while through the huge plate-glass window of Selfridge's, the last one before the main entrance going west. Others had stopped as well, staring up at the crummy thing as it squatted there on its elevated stage, going through its silent contortions like some manic mime artist. On its stainless steel skull a jaunty red cap with a bell on the end hung down over its moulded, skin-coloured plastic ears. Below the cap, a pair of light-emitting diode eyes peeped out over an optical-fibre beard. From an open sack before it, multiply jointed servodriven arms daintily plucked one parcel after another, waved them about in a lunatic fashion, placed them in a pattern around it, then plonked them one by one back in the sack again.

Steve Maringelli figured offhand that it was about the seventh or so worst thing he'd ever seen in his damn life. Going by the looks of the mini crowd around him, it wasn't the season's number one sensation with them either. Half of them grimaced as they watched it through the big window. The other half wore the slackmouthed expression reserved for watching somebody vomiting. Maringelli gave it one more second and stumped off in the direction of the Arch.

He'd stepped off the tube in the West End this evening, instead of going back to his place, for two reasons. First because he'd wanted to pick up the book he'd ordered. *Stereochemistry of Monoclonal Enzymes* was now tucked under his arm as he hunched along. And second because he'd told his big sis that he'd drop in on her Monday night, definite, so there was this Christmas present to buy. His breath fell away behind him as he walked, little puffs fanning out from his collar and his long, blond hair.

To look at Steve Maringelli, you might have taken him for what they used to call a hippy, decades ago. That long blond hair was held away from his eyes by a black bandana, a wispy mandarin-type moustache looped out from either side of his mouth and dangled below the line of his jaw. In the middle of his face, his eyes peered out owlishly from a pair of circular glasses with steel wire frames. The leather windcheater was covered with stick-on badges from places like Lithuania, and the jeans surrounding his bony legs were faded in the right places and to the right degree, though not patched at all.

No hippy, you'd have got it right second glance. A young intellectual. A chemist in fact, two years out of his university and already valued by the mighty Measons Corporation who, as all knew, had more chemists than chemists had chemicals. The megalith had seen a talent in Steve, paid some big change to get him, and accelerated his pay to keep him. A firm had to do that to some extent these days, though. Ever since ninety-three, when they started making students pay their grants back, what you got to start with had been a big issue. Maringelli had paid back his grant in a year.

Maringelli wasn't thinking about chemistry or salaries or anything hard-edged like that. Just now his mind was coasting in neutral, until that cavorting monster with the diode eyeballs had set him off thinking about how human-looking robots were just gimmicks. Even though everybody knew damn well that human-looking robots (droids, captain, they always call them *droids*) had never been anything but a figment of scifi imagination, it was surprising how many people clung to such a dumb notion. These days they had more robots than people, but none of them looked like people. They looked like the task they were designed to do, that was all. If you wanted a robot to do things with its arm, then you didn't bother with legs and balls and a head, but if it was handier for the arm to have ten joints, you gave it ten joints. Five years ago now, the Japanese had started flooding the world with robots that could mine coal and God knows they didn't look like miners, though pretty soon there wouldn't be any miners to make the comparison. Not that *he* knew anything about robots. All of this stuff he'd picked up from an argument with that new bloke his big sis was knocking off these days. He was a software something or other, or a cyberman or whatever, or so she'd said. Decent enough guy, if a little old, though Steve hadn't got him ironed out yet. Mind you though, old is relative, he reflected, tacking on. *They* probably thought *he* was young, being all of twenty-three. And his big sis wasn't any chicken any longer herself at what was it now? Thirty-two? She must be getting droopy in places, he decided slyly. Why, in places she probably hung out like. . .

That was when his left eye found the new shop.

Using both, and flicking his hair back, Steve veered for it right away. The name had a natural appeal for a man in his line. 'Drugerama'. They shifted non-prescription drugs in bulk, using mass marketing and lowest prices. Drugerama were going to take over Europe by way of the UK pretty soon. Lots of American companies took over Europe by way of the UK.

Nobody worked in this place. The pyramids of packs and bottles were reloaded from below. The whole shelf would descend to a subterranean stockroom, where lurked a *real* robot that would replenish it and zoom it back up.

If products got thrown on the floor by ape-ish joe public, entire sections could tip up, depositing spillages below where the whirring denizen would sort them back up to the shelves. Normally this never happened when people were standing on the floors because *it* knew just when that was happening, which made for a second function after closing, burglarwise. These robot watchmen-warehousemen checked in sales by the hour to some central node and could be reprogrammed with what went on what shelf today and what today's special offers were.

Ordinary everyday folks would often stand outside this shop and watch the shelves disappearing and reappearing, and the floor sections flipping down and up. They would point and smile to see a thinking shop. It was more fun than an unthinking Santa.

The paying end didn't have any liveware either. You put your laxatives and tranqs on a conveyor and they vanished into a chamber where lasers read magnetic dots and you were asked for the appropriate amount of money on an LCD. When you got your goods, the magnetic dot would have changed to say it was paid for, so the sensor on the door wouldn't scream and bawl when you left, which is what it did when you tried to slide away with goods that weren't paid for. As well as taking your picture, that was.

Maringelli wanted to try Drugerama, though he had vague reservations about maybe it was a gimmick. He wandered about inside, hating the softporn music that was oozing out of the walls, looking for the drug he wanted to buy, his grey eyes scanning the shelves for the blue, crosshatched boxes with the familiar curved M for Measons in the corner, like a stylised ram's head. They were there of course, after all the publicity they'd have to be there. He reached out and took a medium box. A hundred should do for grinding up.

One hundred Phenthanol tablets, The modern way to handle *your* headache, it said blandly at the top. Marketing had sworn to all the gods that it was the low-key kind of motto that sold drugs. Horn-rimmed specs and white labcoats in the ads. No smartassed puns in the slogans.

Maringelli didn't give a fart about marketing the damn stuff. His interest and pride was in the fact that he'd helped to make it. His company, Measons of the ram's head M, made Phenthanol, and he, Steve Maringelli, personally, individually and unaided by more senior souls, had isolated not one, not two, but several of the key features of its structure. And the trouble with this soulless emporium, he now decided, was that there was nobody behind a till anywhere that he could mention it to in passing.

Steve flicked his five and two ones into the money chute, picked up his fifty change and his hundred pack of Phenthanol and left. He was not going to get as far as claiming his money back from the company, so you could have said he was paying for this fatal error out of his own pocket. But nobody would have called it that just then.

3

Day: minus 14

'You know what I like about you, Luke?' the gravel voice enquired fetchingly, crackling on a lousy line.

She wasn't looking into the lens of her viewphone camera because her face didn't come square on out of his monitor screen. She was sitting sideways at her desk with her right knee just visible over the edge of it, pretending to be occupied with some cigarettes. Guessing, Luke surmised the only reason she was putting a picture out was so he wouldn't think she was faking her annoyance. She wanted him to see she was annoyed. Anyway, he wasn't into psychology so screw it.

'What?' he said in his deadpan voice which was guaranteed to wind her up even more.

The knee vanished behind the desk and she leaned forward, reaching down out of the viewfield. The picture blinked off, but the voice remained.

'Fuck all is what.'

'Right, right,' he said. 'So I said I'd come over.' Then he sat there for a second at his bureau with his chin on his fist, letting her imagine his grinning face. Luke didn't have a viewphone; his finances didn't run to it, unlike Tanscon TV, whose finances ran to anything. 'So I forgot.'

The line went down with a snap.

Luke waited three point four seconds to see if George would come back. He knew she wouldn't.

Lucius P. Finn. He didn't mind the Lucius, in fact he rather liked it, which was why he had the whole thing, complete with the P, emblazoned on the frosted glass of his office door. It was other people who seemed uncomfortable with Lucius, so everybody called him Luke, without being invited. Or Mister Finn. Either way, Luke didn't mind. The thing he didn't like about his name was the abomination that began with the P. Very few people knew what it stood for, which suited Luke fine. Lucius P. Finn, Technological Investigator.

He eased back in his real leather (you could tell by examining the edges of the cracks) rotating chair and planted his feet on the desk so his knees almost touched his goatee beard. Then he pushed gently to roll himself away from the desk without pushing himself over backwards and breaking his neck. After accomplishing this feat, he was able to deploy his legs across the bureau top.

Wouldn't have her any other way of course, the bad-tempered bitch. Luke extracted a match with forefinger and thumb from the breast pocket of his grey waistcoat and then stretched up to his coat stand to get a cigar from the top pocket of his jacket. A woman without spirit lacked more than beauty in his view, not that George lacked beauty. Well she wasn't drowning in it, no, but she didn't lack it either, and though he made his living by being ultra smart, he was no Valentino himself.

Luke Finn struck his match on the fifties match-striker that he kept among the other baubles on his bureau, and lit up, filling his small warm office with rolls of odiferous smoke. Straight ahead he could see his reflection in the Perspex fronts of the disk drives stacked up by the side of his computer rack. Everything needed a trim by the look of it. Hair (maybe he should drop the Afro look; he had only grown it as a gesture towards the past, a sort of demonstration of his old-world chic), goatee, moustache, the whole curly black thatch wanted pruning. Luke grinned at himself holding the cigar between his geometric teeth, watching the wrinkles form around the corners of his mouth and eyes. You've got bags under your beautiful brown eyes, he told his reflection, and your tan needs topping up. Otherwise you're perfect.

Lucius P. Finn creaked up from his chair laughing in soft self-mockery. He had no tan, and his teeth weren't all that straight, and he had a little more of a weight problem than usual for a man of his years. Otherwise he *was* perfect. Luke slouched over to his monitor, sat down in another revolving thing without arms on it and stabbed a button marked 'Network 2'. Then he folded his arms, locked his feet behind the stem of the chair, dropped his chin on his chest, and watched the screen. The first one was a circular.

'Wipe it. Gimme the next,' he muttered irritably. The advert vanished from his monitor and its encoded image from his maildisk. The speech recogniser only needed 'wipe', or 'erase', and 'next', but you could add more if it made you feel more comfortable. The next one was from the Government: 'On His Majesty's Service'. It was all about renewing his licence, which seemed like he should possibly read it.

All technological investigators had to be licensed, and that was where the similarity to Philip Marlowe stopped. The old-time *private* investigators spent most of their time hunting for missing persons or digging up dirt for divorces. But that was before the national identity tracking systems came into operation and since then it had become more of a feat than before to go missing in most of the countries of Europe. As for divorces as a source of work, well that got screwed by a lack of marriages. Or at least, a lack of unstable ones. It was the same with all that kind of work, an ex-private eye had once moaned to Luke, it just got programmed out by events.

The technological investigator, conversely, had been programmed in. By a phenomenon now called technocrime.

Ten days to renew it, Luke noted, but he'd need time to argue if OTC wanted to be difficult, not that there was any reason they should. Leave it for now, but get reminded.

'Run this again tomorrow,' he said, enunciating the words clearly after removing the cigar from the corner of his mouth.

A confirmation of his verbal command to put this piece

of mail before him again when the Julian date had stepped on by one was whipped over the screen. Some systems gave you tellbacks in a sexy voice (sex of your choosing) but Luke ignored such fancies.

'OK,' he said, which was a neutral command to this speech recogniser. Just one of lots of things you could say if you felt like hearing your voice without having it obeyed. 'Next,' he added.

The next one was a coffee bill. A coffee bill?

Technocrime had appeared in the early seventies in the form of computer fraud. It was so breathtakingly easy then, even easier than now to manipulate the machine systems of the western banking world that the historians had always said, in retrospect of course, that computerised monetary fraud had been the natural place for technocrime to start. By nineteen ninety (a year whose statistic stuck in Luke's memory, he knew not why) that particular felony was running at two hundred billion dollars a year in the USA alone, though that figure seemed small by now.

Because that kind of thing had only been the beginning of it. Since then, technocrime, as well as being christened, had grown with the technology that had spawned it. Now it was more than financial fraud involving computers, *far* more. It was many things now. It was also financial espionage and financial sabotage. And it was also industrial espionage and industrial sabotage. Then it was commercial and military and agricultural and educational and institutional. It was everything and everywhere. Whatever the environment, whatever the scene, there was technology and there was technological crime and there were technological criminals. And of course there were technological investigators. There had to be really.

Luke was on top of the coffee bill by now. He and the several other small fry who shared this floor of the block had come to an agreement over the coffee dispenser in the corridor, as a party to which, the rental company had agreed to rig it to dispense its filthy attempts at coffee, tea, chocolate or soup on numbers only, without the actual input of coins, and then send each of them the whole tab by turns, changing each month. This month it was Lucius P. Finn.

'Bank that,' he told it, which would whisk this thing over to his bank disk to be dealt with by the software which handled his bank account. Mentally he made a note to review his membership of the coffee club. Some of those people must be drinking it in buckets. 'Next.'

You were bound to end up with technological investigators, for several obvious and not so obvious reasons. Firstly, the other kinds of crime – like, shall we say, rape – had retained their quintessential popularity with the felon fraternity, so it wasn't as if the police didn't have plenty on already without this newcomer. The police functioned primarily as preventers of crime and hunters of criminals. For that, they needed to know what the crime was, or even if there'd been one, which is not a matter for debate if you're a shopkeeper and the front door's been kicked in and your stock's gone and your alarm's ringing. But if you're a multinational and somebody has deciphered the prime number encryption codes that were guarding your computerised marketing plans, then the situation isn't quite so clear. The problem with technocrime was that, as often as not, it just couldn't be identified up front as a palpable crime at all. Perhaps there's been a crime here, you would say. Somebody cracked our codes and maybe they read our plans. If all you know is that a code's been broken – and, hell, you might not even have known *that* – then all you could say was that there was a possibility of a crime. You couldn't trigger much of a police investigation with that, so you either ignored it, or you tried to dig it over yourself, or you hired an expert to do it for you. You hired a technological investigator.

No more mail, the monitor had been insisting. Did he want the mailbox wiped or stacked? Which were a couple of its birdbrained software notions for what used to be in-trays and out-trays, dealt-with and pending. Precious little of this day-to-day stuff was actual paper these days, so the desktop bits and bobs had become rare, and with them, their terminology. This crap didn't sound any better though.

'Wipe it,' Luke said.

Luke drew on the cigar while his computer cleaned up. Over to his right, a disk light winked on and off again as files were file-handled. Luke stabbed 'Network 3' this time. Catch up on the news time. He blinked as the smoke found his eye. Grimacing, he pulled his lips back from his teeth. 'Aaah.' He should stop using these things. He should get more exercise. He should try abseiling maybe, like that damn fool down the PO tower yesterday. His belt felt tight again. . .

This stuff came up in screenfuls. First thing you got was headlines. When you'd read the headlines, you could order up the articles. That was the basic idea, though of course there were the usual tricks you could play if you wanted to learn them. All the channels ran these news-sheet generators on one net or the other of the compgrid. BBC and independents, even the cables had till they spiralled down into struggling near oblivion. Some people regarded the news-sheets in much the same way that hifi buffs used to look on that stuff in the old days before the technology got so good and so cheap that there was nothing to be a buff about any more. System first, purpose second. Luke just wanted to watch the news.

Three p.m. he told himself, she'll be back on the line by three, begging my favour, beseeching my attention. He consulted his watch. Pushing ten a.m. She'll be taking it out on her minions by now, she paraded them before her at ten most days. He bared his teeth again in another down-at-heel grin.

Luke snorted his way out to the coffee machine. One three seven was his combination, black no sugar. It smelt and tasted like the stuff they put on fences to keep the rain out of the wood, so he decided right then and there that he was going to get a percolator that very day, and some beans, and a grinder, and set up coffee-wise on his own and the club could go to Fiji. He was going to bring some style back to his coffee-drinking. Some charm.

Well, this week anyway.

Luke had this fad for ancient old-fashioned charm. Most people took him for a slight freak on account of it. The door on which his name and function were emblazoned in arching gold letters looked like something out of a thirties film. Luke had found the door in a junkshop, reglazed it with the frosted glass, stripped and revarnished it himself with a craftsman's care. Behind the door, his almost Dickensian office continued the theme. Luke had scoured many dusty shops in derelict and remote corners of London for his furniture, paying biggish bread to various educated spivs to obtain it, and restoring each piece with loving devotion. His desk was of Brazilian mahogany, no less, and the matching bureau with its let-down, leather-inset flap was of the same. He had a set of matching chairs around an old table with fold-down sides that had once graced somebody's sitting room. He had a red, velvet pile carpet that he had rescued from Harrod's when they had been about to destroy it for want of warehousing, and he had a teak fireplace with an electric fire with mock coals that glowed all red when it was on, as if they were real. Now *those* were like gold dust.

Luke chewed on some coffee.

Nothing much today yet. No natural disasters, no fires, no famines, no savage outbreaks of ideological conflict.

'More,' he droned, and the screen scrolled up.

By his side he had a morning paper as well, two hundred pages of it, to compete with the news-sheet services. So far Luke hadn't opened it.

Somebody blew up a barge in Amsterdam, killing all twenty head of prize cattle on board, and there was our abseilling friend again. God, you could weep. Shadow foreign secretary apologises. . . There's a novelty.

'More,' he gasped. 'And more.' It went by almost in a blur, so he damn near missed it.

'Stop . . . back one . . . Again . . .'

30

Luke read it very slowly. It had to be in print. He snatched up the paper and found it one page in. Again he read slowly, taking it all in at one pass.

'SUPERPLANE VANISHES IN ARCTIC' it said by way of a headline. Then it went on:

The plane regarded by many as the world's most advanced airliner disappeared yesterday deep inside the Arctic Circle. The British-designed Schaum AX–9 vanished without warning over the region of the Bering Sea, an extreme distance from land, on a proving flight from Vancouver to Tokyo. A test crew and more than thirty scientists and technicians are presumed dead.

The AX–9 is due to be offered for service with commercial airlines within a year. Advance orders are believed to total over fifty aircraft. Its only competitor, the American built Channing V5, is due for service about the same time.

This is the first loss of an AX–9 during the plane's development. The Channing airliner has so far suffered no accidents.

Spokesmen for Schaum Aircraft Corporation today declined to give any. . .

'Shhh. . . !'

Lucius P. Finn considered his reflection again and started to toy with the notion, lacing it with spurious trivia, so it went in and out of his mind like random discharges of some kind. Was there anything in this? Should he really change his Afro style, shave his beard, lose some weight? Should he ring Sandy? If he didn't poke into this plane thing, then would someone else? Or did this grey suit look shabby all of a sudden?

'Break,' he told the screen, planting his feet on the floor. His cigar had gone out.

'Phones. Sandell. Ring it.'

There was only one Sandell in his directory. The number came up at once. It announced that it was dialling it for him. When the light appeared on the receiver and the phone buzzed, he picked it up. The company was a long time answering, but then their switchboard was probably under siege.

'Schaum. Good morning.' A mature woman, about fifty, but well preserved at a guess.

'Hello.' Luke put on his charm tones, slowing it down some. 'I wanted to speak to Doctor John Sandell. He used to be on extension five seven four.'

'Hold the line please.'

There was a hissing and a faint bleeping as the electronic exchange signalled the extension (the last clicking of relays had been heard in the UK in nineteen eighty-eight) and then a louder bleep and the line went very quiet. Luke sniffed and decided on a strategy. He would consult George over the question of his change from Afro, deferring slyly to her opinion after a suitable pretence at discussion.

'Five seven four. Sandell.'

Luke could have anticipated the deadpan Yorkshire voice before he heard it. He could picture the expression too. It would be equally bland, and it would remain so after Luke intro'd himself, as if all the surprises had been had already.

'Guess who?'

'Lucius Finn.'

'Stroll on . . .'

A chuckle. It would be dry and mirthless at a glance, though Luke could imagine the dark, mischievous eyes in the crinkled, puckish little face.

'How's things, Luke?'

'I'm breathing in and out. You?'

There was a pause, and though no discernible sound filled any part of it, Luke knew that the man was helping himself to another knowledgeable snigger, because Sandy was sharp. But sharp.

'Well now,' he said when he was ready. 'Shall we say I'm fine, or shall we talk about why you rang?'

'Why I rang is why you don't feel fine today, is that right, Sandy?'

'That's right, Luke.'

'Can I come and talk about it? Unofficially, right? Off the record. I mean it said in the news you weren't talking.'

Sandell let out a long heavy breath, almost a sigh but without any real voice to it.

'We aren't,' he told Luke. 'We definitely aren't. But I would have rung you before the end of the day.'

'So let's meet,' Luke said.

Lucius P. Finn stayed in his office until after three because he had things to get out of the way. He didn't *have* to get them out of the way, but he had a feeling – nothing reliable or hunchy or sinister or anything, just a feeling – that once he turned this plane thing over he was going to be busy for a while.

Anyway, George hadn't rung back by then after all.

4

Georgina Maringelli worked for a razor-toothed organisation called Transcontinental Television – Transcon, or just TCTV, they often called it. Both she and it, you could see, were a reflection of the times. It's probably best left at that.

Sooner or later, inspired pundits had contended, TV companies were going to have to give up trying to be all things to all men. The world was shrinking, which meant there were going to be more types of TV programmes, from all over it, than a single TV company could effectively cover. Conversely, they'd gone on to say, companies were expanding, TV companies included, and multinationals were proliferating. Sooner or later you were going to get cases where one TV outfit would reside in several countries and then it would be able to produce and transmit programmes from nation to nation using its own resources end to end. The old idea of complex, inter-company collaboration across frontiers would fade. No longer would a French company use its production facilities and its transmitters to beam a feature into England where a British company would use *its* receivers and *its* facilities to show it. The multinational would control it all, organise it all, minimise the cost of it all, and maximise the profit from it all.

And groupings within these multinationals, the pundits had reiterated, would centre on programme types. One arm would handle news, another features, another documentaries, another light-E, and so on. The shrinking world would provide material enough for all, and only by these means would all the material be encompassed.

Although nobody much had realised it at the time, because TCTV played its preparations very close, it had been gearing up to go multinational as early as eight-seven or eighty-eight. The gearing up consisted of manoeuvres towards the takeover of a string of foreign independents, plus the laying of plans for the future. It had moved in nineteen ninety-one, seizing control almost simultaneously of target companies in all five continents. In Europe, it took over independents in London, Paris and Bonn. In Asia it planted its feet in Tel Aviv, Delhi, Bangkok, Singapore, Hong Kong and Tokyo. Below the equator and in the antipodes, it appeared in Rio, Cape Town, Perth, Sydney and Auckland. Then, still hungry despite the massive sums laid out in this rash of acquisitions, and in a home move subtly delayed to avoid signalling its intentions, TCTV had expanded sideways from its New York base to set up in Montreal and Mexico City. As an exercise in fast but controlled corporate expansion it had required and used the direction of geniuses (now ultra rich to a man) and as a corporate phenomenon, its boldness was unprecedented. Books had been written about the rise of TCTV, countless documentaries screened, many by the company itself. And many of the pundits marvelled at it still.

George worked for the London arm of the TCTV corporation, and had done so for more than four years now. She made it up a fair way before anybody noticed she was a woman, but even then she had continued to do pretty well. She liked the company and had read all of the books. Without harbouring the slightest shadow of doubt, she figured that the firm was going much further yet, and she was going with it.

Right now she wanted a reaction from this parcel of pricks around the conference table, and she wanted comments. What she wanted was inputs. Her idea needed feeding. Also AD 2001 was getting pretty close for comfort.

'Lasers would be the classy way,' Technical agreed. 'But

I don't know about that kind of scale.' Technical was male, about thirty, with pimples. One of a set of three, with the other two much the same. 'It's the time factor, that's the thing,' he added.

'We've done it on this scale in the States,' George said. 'Well, nearly on this scale. They did the World Trade Centre in New York. It doesn't take long to set up. They'd give us advice.'

'We know where the World Trade Centre is, darling,' Artistic said.

George didn't like Artistic, basking like a crocodile at the other end of the conference table, displaying his flowery shirt and his ridiculous velvet bow tie, and playing with his gilded locks. She'd have liked Artistic to go down with herpes.

'You shut your mouth, you,' George hissed.

'Lovely.'

PR looked worried. PR was a little man in his middle age. All the production team except George were men, which accounted for the brickbat relationship most of them enjoyed with her. PR was untypical in being (a) newer to it than the others and (b) less involved with the nitty gritty and (c) quite nice.

'Let me get this straight,' PR said, slowly, attracting a silence. 'You are proposing to cover the entire face of Centre Point with television screens. The whole skyscraper?'

'About the top two thirds,' George said.

'With television screens. Yes?' PR looked dazed.

'Not tubes,' George said. 'Not TV tubes. Sheets of light-sensitive laminate. It, like, glows when you shine laser light on it. Shit, I don't know. It works, right? All bolted together to make one huge screen.'

'And you want to project live TV pictures on to this screen from the street? Actual live pictures.'

'Right,' George said. 'Oxford Street. Or maybe we'll need to project from the top of Selfridge's or somewhere. That's a detail.'

She wagged her hand to indicate a mere bagatelle and Artistic imitated the gesture with an accompanying roll of the eyes. George glared down the table at him and considered smashing out his brains with one of the massive stone ashtrays that lay along its polished top.

'And you project the pictures using laser beams?'

'That's it,' George said. 'We sweep the live stuff up on to this big screen with lasers, so the whole city can see it.'

George flashed up an enthusiastic smile, displaying incisors as even as dominoes. Her big, brown eyes narrowed into slits. 'I *know* it can be done,' she assured them, still showing both rows of teeth. 'It's been done before, dears. All it needs is team work. Remember team work?'

The work production team just went on staring at her like a school of fish. Technical, Artistic, puzzled PR, Video, Sound, International, the whole crew just sat and struggled with it. Or in Artistic's case, scoffing at it because it was clear he regarded the whole idea to be too vulgar by half, the blue-rinsed bitch that he was.

They were a good team, when they functioned together. Most of them were experienced in the kinds of things they did. And in Artistic's case, the lousy truth of it was that he was as good as they came.

One of TCTV's many channels was dedicated to the mounting of international television spectaculars around current events. The group company was called Real Features, and like all of TCTV's organs, it spread its net across the world. Whenever an event of momentous or spectacular nature was scheduled, TCTV-RF would mount a feature, piping it around the TV screens of the globe as it actually happened. They were experts at it, with many memorable and breathtaking productions under the belt.

Georgina Maringelli had been a member of some of the teams that handled the London end of the earlier extravaganzas. Now she was in charge of one, for the first time, and the event that was to be covered had to be about the biggest ever. It needed big ideas to do it justice, bigger than ever before. Her ideas.

George decided to address the troops.

'Look, you turds. Just listen to me,' she began demurely. 'I don't think I'm seeing the right kind of enthusiasm for this job, if you want it straight.'

'Oooh,' the fag started. 'Well if . . .'

George hurled a pen. It clattered and bounced end over end along the table, skidding off somebody's wrist and on to the floor. Artistic shut his mouth with a pout.

'The fact is that it's the best ever,' George continued a semitone lower. Then she softened her face to a diplomatic leer and tilted her head to one side, like a shark about to take off a sailor's leg. Her brown, shiny hair fell forward over the stems of her horn-rimmed glasses (for business only, more imposing than contacts) and her lips parted into a half-smile. In fact, George was a very considerable lady both from the neck up and the neck down. In many situations that was an asset with a herd of men. And George knew all about that, too.

'Just imagine it,' she purred on. 'It's going to go on all day, right? At twelve noon here on December thirty-first, New Zealand will go into the twenty-first century. We'll get it live. Then Australia will go into the new century a couple of hours later.' Her hands fanned out in front of her face like she was pulling apart the last vestiges of the twentieth. 'We'll be pushing it out over the transworld link by satellites. Crowd scenes, live interviews with politicians, reactions from people in the streets, celebrities, the lot. Then it'll be Japan and Singapore. Then India and Israel and we'll be pouring it out live as they go through midnight, one after the other. Then it'll be Europe's turn and we'll bring in Italy and Germany and France. Only it'll be dark by then and we'll only be an hour away from it and our crowds'll be out by the million, teeming in the streets . . .'

They were gawping again.

'Just *imagine* it!' she went on. 'We put it up live on to a skyscraper for them! Can't you just *imagine* that! The whole

38

world going into a new century? Live? On the biggest screen on earth?'

She was getting excited at the idea again, waxing a trifle breathless. One or two of them were nodding and tilting an eyebrow here and there, starting to go with it.

'Well it's a new century, dammit!' she exclaimed yet again. 'A new frigging *millenium* even! The biggest thing ever. Bigger than the coronation, bigger than the prospectors landing on the moon' – she'd been in on both of those, but she'd enjoyed the coronation of King Charles the best – 'bigger than *anything!*'

They were almost agog. Like she was insane.

'It's only a couple of weeks away,' she said, winding down. 'A lot of the plans are laid,' she added after a sinister pause.

Pep talk over, she subsided and reverted to threat mode. They went down with her and started breathing again. Artistic put on his finest unimpressed smirk and twisted a strand or two at his collar. George adjusted her glasses, pushed her hair back behind both her ears and flashed her deep brown eyes around the table. A wicked smile adorned her luscious wet lips as she licked them like some kind of canine.

George was what you'd call a handsome woman. She wasn't Sophia Loren or any other of the famous classics that they had footage of in the archives, but she knew how to optimise what she had. What with a million laps of the park every week, she went in and out where it counted, more or less. Anyway, she had outstanding legs.

George sent her gaze boring round the table at each of them in turn, so they'd know she meant this for all of them. They'd had this thing boiling for weeks now, clearing all the basics like theory and methodology, practicality and publicity, so half the world knew about it and already there was a torrent of money flowing and a lot of people on the move. What she had here was the core team, the cream. Apart from the new PR, they all knew damn well what was what.

George clasped her hands flat on the table in front of her and leaned her face forward so her mane lay flat down over her neck. She looked straight at Artistic.

'Well, you'd better get with it from now on,' she informed them in a warm motherly tone, 'or I'll castrate the fucking lot of you.'

5

Working weekends was strictly an occasional pursuit for Steve Maringelli, because the company no-overtime policy wasn't for bending. Whenever he did put some in, he generally took it fairly casually. This particular day though, he'd found plenty to do, so he didn't get around to the check until early evening, coming up to seven when he came back from the selectasnack with two polystyrene-clad hunks of salami on cut roll and a can of soda. The stuff was OK on the whole, and subsidised price-wise. Steve often dined out at the selectasnack.

It was dark outside. Across the car park that separated this building from its twin there were lights at random windows, but mostly in the upper offices. Maringelli knew there would be other weekend work freaks upstairs in this block too, here and there, hardening up some point in a plan or poring over their damn memory dumps (machine floor only). Down here in the main chemlab he was alone, the pool of light over his desk the only light in the huge room. From where he sat and munched, rows of benches, glassware, cupboards and instruments stretched away until they disappeared in the gloom.

Steve put both his feet up on the chair bar and leafed at his new book again. Monoclonal enzymes had a future, or so an increasing number of research prophets kept on saying. Biochips was the coming buzzword. Put your dough on it in time. Brain cells cultured in their own organic environment, linked to integrated circuitry to give truly thinking microprocessors. Living electronics, if you liked that term. The dream and the nightmare and all that crap. It was all too far off, anybody could see that, but the way to it was with monoclonal enzymes and Steve was into brain chemistry at present. Hence this new book he'd been perusing on and off all day. Often he had underlined things, like many people do, and many people hate to do. With Maringelli a book was a tool.

He took one more throw at the soda, pumping it around his mouth so it fizzled all through his teeth, and put the book down. He would do the check, clean up all his gear, and be in bed by nine or ten for an early night. Tomorrow he'd take a lazy day and *really* get into his book.

The Phenthanol tablets were about a centimetre long and shaped like a flat cylinder with rounded ends. He used about a third of the tablets in the pack. Thirty of them made a handful. Maringelli poured them into the hopper of the grinder on the nearest bench and gave the on-button two or three quick bursts. Using a cup-shaped spatula he took out a generous amount of the powder and tipped it into an analyser's separation chamber. Powered up, this would take the granules apart, reducing them to their constituent chemicals, hanging in space. Beams of sundry radiations would lace through this chemical gas. The radicals would absorb the rays, the way they absorbed would identify them, the extent to which they absorbed would reveal their concentrations. A computer would be fed the information, would perform the calculations and would reveal all in spike-laden graphs on a VDU screen. The VDU sat blank on Maringelli's desk, awaiting commands. Steve ran up the multi-analyser, went back to the desk, and touched a softkey labelled 'f5' on the VDU keyboard. A line appeared, in reverse black on white video, announcing the Phenthanol suite ready. Maringelli watched the console of the multi-analyser. A minute passed, then two. Halfway through the third, a blue light came on and an LED display said 'ambient'. Maringelli pressed the 'f6' key and sat back to watch.

The graph built up rapidly, the peaks growing like small

mountains until some became razor sharp and narrow, whilst others stayed flat and squat. They shuffled side to side, like soldiers on parade, arranging themselves tidily across the screen for an optimum presentation. There were twenty-two of them in all. Enclosing them in a kind of frame were the axes that gave quantity to their size and spacing. In seconds the whole thing had settled down.

Steve Maringelli did not move for a while. Only his eyes danced back and forth across the now familiar image. These mysterious bumps and troughs were by now old acquaintances, seen many times before and etched on to that part of him which recognised the things he knew. Except this time.

Because this time there was a surprise.

One of the peaks was far bigger than anything in his memory. The fifth from the left. *Far* bigger.

For a long time it didn't register. Then it came up as puzzlement, then scepticism, then disbelief. Was it a newcomer? A glitch? No, it was. . . (pause). . . it was the fucking active ingredient! That was all, only the damned Trinax. Maringelli checked the abscissa point on the screen again. No doubt of it. Again he ran his gaze up the high shimmering green spike and then along the ordinates. The concentration looked huge, far higher than it was supposed to be. Maringelli played tunes on the keyboard. A crosshair sidled across to the peak, settled, an enter key went down, a column of numbers swept down the side of the screen.

The chemist jumped his finger down the list. Twenty-two constituents, twenty-two concentrations. His other hand groped for something to scribble on and found his book. He hacked the numbers down inside the flyleaf in pencil, taking care to transcribe them accurately from the screen by keeping his finger up there and pointing. He needed this hard copy because he was going to have to rerun this, and right now he couldn't be bothered to go and online a printer.

It took Steve Maringelli another ten minutes to change the hopper on the grinder and the separation chamber on the analyser to keep the samples apart and rerun the test with another third of the tablets. The picture was the same, and the numbers.

Staring at the list scrawled inside the book he wondered if he was having some kind of hysterical aberration. Dammit, it *couldn't* be that far out, could it? Well, *could* it? He scrabbled about in a desk drawer and fished out a typed list of numbers headed by the words 'design concs. mass. Phenthanol'. There were twenty-two numbers on this list also. Whatever any sample test said, this was what the concentrations were supposed to be, this was the official definition of the drug. This was what they'd told the Drug Commission was in the stuff.

Now Maringelli saw that it was not only the Trinax number that was wrong. The matrix was wrong also. That one was too low, though not by the same factor. That didn't matter. It was the Trinax that mattered. It was this chemical, structure jealously guarded by the company, known only by its trade name, that was the active ingredient of the analgesic pill now known as Phenthanol. This was the substance you needed to handle your headache the modern way. What it did was not unrelated to, but by no means identical to the action of the old barbiturates and other hypnotics. It constricted nerve cell membranes, slowing down the alkaline ion transfer and lowering the energy output of the cells so they couldn't respond to stimuli as readily, so the nervous system was suppressed. It did all that and a damn sight more, and in the wrong quantities it was a damn sight more dangerous, and what you had here was the wrong quantity.

What you had here, in this packet, from that *shop*, was a concentration that looked about a hundred times over the design level. Maringelli started to get a sick feeling in his belly.

This time he left the numbers painted on the screen, because now he remembered seeing Jim Pruett earlier. Pruett had to see this. *Somebody* had to see it. There were still some tablets in the box for another run if necessary.

Maringelli started dialling an internal number. It rang six, seven times before the voice came on. Maringelli relaxed a little and started talking.

Jim Pruett did not strictly work for Measons. Pruett was a consultant, by which you meant a specialist, by which you meant somebody who was regarded by other people as a specialist. In fact Pruett's speciality was process control software, in other words he was a computer specialist. If a machine made a pill, or in fact a whole chain gang of machines made a pill, they did it not on their own initiative but by being programmed. It took a very special kind of programming skill and Pruett was an expert at it. The Meason Corporation had upgraded its London manufacturing plant recently, with new machinery, new techniques, new everything. They had wanted the whole thing online fast so much of the skill they bought in ready made from the consultancies. That was how Pruett had appeared. How much longer he'd be around Steve had no idea. As long as he was, he was Steve's boss, in most things anyway.

Pruett listened from the machine floor as Steve went through it from the top. He didn't interrupt exactly but whenever Maringelli went for any kind of pause, he'd put in with a 'fuck me' or a 'shit', to demonstrate his continued presence on the phone and the range of his vocabulary, as well as his ongoing concern over what was pouring in his ear. By the time Steve had finished he sounded really bad. He stuttered, he sighed and stumbled, and he finally said he'd better come down and stop trying to discuss it on the horn.

Coming down, as it turned out, took him all of twenty minutes. Maringelli thought maybe he'd been having a cry or something but when he turned up he gave Steve a surprise because he had this smile all over his face, as if he'd spent the twenty minutes in a cathouse.

'You want that printed out?' Maringelli pointed at the VDU. 'We could print it out to show 'em.'

'Nah, leave that. Wipe it off,' Jim said. 'We'll run this check again from scratch with what's left of the pills when we've got an audience. We'll use a different analyser, do it a few more times just to be sure.'

'Sure? What's to be sure about, Jim? You mean you aren't sure? Well I'm fucking sure.'

There was that grin again! Hell's bells, what the hell was funny about this? I like you Jim, Steve was thinking, but don't you try and cover this up or go closing ranks on me, Jim. Don't you . . .

'We're both sure, Steve,' Jim said, still grinning his wooden grin, like Pinochio. 'Now I'm going to tell you what I intend to do, right.'

'Right.'

'First, I'm going to take these pills and lock them in my desk for tomorrow. Then I'm going to make a lot of phone calls. I'm going to get the plant manager and a distribution manager down here and we're going to trace that batch right through from when it came off the line down to where it went and we're going to make a list of every retail outlet that's holding it. That'll take half the night. Then I'm going to ring a bunch of directors and get them here, by eight a.m. tomorrow morning, before the shops open. Leave all the pills with me so I can rerun the check for them, so they'll get the drift. Then I'm going to give them the list and tell them to warn the retailers right then and there or I'll do it myself. You feel better about that?'

Steve was impressed. 'They'll go apeshit.'

'They can go where they like. I don't work here, remember.'

'I do, though.'

'Then stay out of it.'

'Come on,' Steve laughed. 'I didn't mean that. Hell, I'd *pay* to see their faces. He stopped then, for a beat or two, caught up in it. 'Listen, I could stay and help with that list.'

'No. It's their job. I'll just be here to push them on and make the calls afterwards. Go home, Steve, or better still go get a few drinks.'

Maringelli switched off the VDU, watching it blink and

shrink as if reluctant to go, and then picked up his book and his remaining salami roll. He finished the soda and threw his jacket across his shoulder.

'You'll call me, right?'

Pruett touched his arm, lightly, with just one forefinger. 'Listen, don't mention this to anybody tonight, all right? I don't need to say that, do I?'

'Am I that stupid?'

'Go on, beat it.'

Pruett watched him all the way to the swing doors of the lab. After he had gone through them, Pruett watched them ease back on their hydraulic hinges until they stopped. And after they stopped, he watched them some more.

Then all at once he stopped smiling.

6

Day: minus 13

In a shaded office very high above the street not far from the very centre of central London, a man replaced an elegant white phone on its cradle and then settled himself deeper into the padded velour armchair. He glanced at the luminous hands of his wristwatch. It was six minutes before two p.m.

The fingers of his left hand began to play with a large jet-stone ring on the third finger of his right. It gleamed in the dim light, like a huge malignant eye. The hands had long fingers, almost abnormally long, and the nails and cuticles at the end of them were manicured to perfect symmetry.

When he spoke his voice came circling out of the dark, coiling around the room like a snake.

'Interesting, Bruno, as you say.'

The man called Bruno stood against a far wall of the room. He was liveried like a real winner, though no more expensively than his companion in the chair, but Bruno always preferred to stand and that made him more observable – had there been anyone else present to observe. Hanging from his massive frame was a grey overcoat with a matching silk scarf. Beneath it he wore a black suit and waistcoat and a regimental tie over a white shirt whose cuffs and collar displayed accoutrements of solid gold. Barely visible in the pile of the carpet were a pair of black-stained real crocodile-skin shoes in a slip-on style, made in Switzerland.

Above this ensemble, the owner's face was tanned and

bland. His pale eyes did not form the contrast they should have done with the long, black hair.

Bruno got bored with waiting.

'You're the front man. Are you going to put it to the client?'

The man in the chair was called Constantine, though Bruno never used his name, even though they had known each other for many years. Constantine was in charge and Bruno knew it, even approved of it. But Constantine knew that there was a limit to Bruno's manageability.

Constantine had seen Bruno's limit just as he had seen that of many other people. For Constantine was by training a psychologist, though he had not practised his science in earnest for some years now. But his lush apartment (almost nobody knew where it was) was lined with every research journal in the field. Constantine subscribed to proceedings of everything. And he read the papers, too, often far into the night.

Five years back, Constantine had given up his academic career in psychology and entered industry where the ferocious world of high technology consultancy had long since identified the need for psychologically skilled management and valued it at a premium. Constantine had moved from one outfit to the next, allowing himself to be made offers he pretended to be unable to refuse, rising all the time. Now he was about as high as he expected to go, short of owning a company of his own. Officially owning one, that was.

People make machines, he would always say. People write programs, meet schedules, don't meet schedules. The trick is driving the people, not the machines. Man-ipulating them.

Constantine was an expert at manipulating people. But he was always just that teeny weeny bit careful with Bruno.

Constantine gestured to the phone. 'No problem apparently. We need certain data and then it can be done from just about anywhere. Extraordinary, isn't it?'

49

Bruno found hardly anything on earth to be extraordinary.

'What data?' he said, uttering the word as if it were obscene.

'Just a few codes. Commands, of some kind. Our little man at Pureflite can supply them.'

'Then what?'

'Then we don't need him any more, do we, Bruno?'

'So?' Bruno wanted it decided. Always Bruno had to have a decision.

'So I'll put it to the client,' Constantine told him. 'It would have certain conveniences for us, would it not?'

'Conveniences?'

'It could be done from right here, or so I am assured. That's convenient. Also it has a certain ah . . .' Constantine smiled again '. . . theatrical flavour.'

Bruno had no interest in whatever Constantine was talking about. He was more into practicalities. As a professional killer, Bruno made a habit of practicalities.

'The point is, it gets it done,' he said. 'It's as good a chance to do it as any. Why wait for another?'

Constantine considered that. Again he made Bruno wait a while. Like all predators, Bruno could become restless when he was made to wait too long. Constantine never made Bruno wait very long.

Constantine ran through it in his mind. It had always been his plan to execute all three commissions as close together as possible. He alone was visible and therefore most vulnerable to complications, and although the first had gone perfectly as far as could be judged, there was already a complication with the second, what with this stupid boy. Bruno would deal with it of course, nevertheless it had irritated him. In fact, he had considered abandoning the third commission altogether and starting the pull-out immediately. Dispose of the others, dismantle the operation as planned, and go now, while the going was good. But then . . .

'It needs clarifying,' he announced. 'If it can be done

easily, well and good. If there are any problems we forget it. We forget the whole deal with the French.'

Bruno hesitated and then said, 'What about the others?'

Constantine shrugged and pursed his lips. 'Nothing changes as regards the others, Bruno. You and I will decide, after I've gone into it a little more. If we proceed the others will agree. If not, well . . .'

'Nothing changes,' Bruno said, with about a tenth of a smile on his face.

'Nothing,' Constantine said soothingly.

Bruno relaxed. Soon he would slay again. Bruno was a very good slayer, with gun, knife, wire or hands. He had majored in it in the army. And Bruno liked slaying though he didn't consider himself a psycho or anything. It wasn't as if he went around with his tongue hanging out for it, he could leave it alone any time he wanted.

Bruno licked the tension off the roof of his mouth like an aftertaste.

'Let me know then,' he said as he pushed himself off the wall. 'If there's nothing else for today, my plants need attention. Also I have a woman waiting.'

He found himself looking at the palm of Constantine's hand. Wait, the gesture said, just one more thing.

Bruno watched the other man produce a box, a small white box a little larger than the kind of box you get a new wristwatch in. Bruno had seen little boxes like this before.

'There is something more, Bruno,' Constantine said as he opened the box. 'It needs your special attention. It's quite urgent.'

Bruno peered down at the hypodermic. The taste was back in his mouth again.

7

They clattered through the door like a bunch of conventioners, with Luke and Steve spilling on the floor and George heaving to against the wall. She kicked the door to, swiped on a light and then stepped on Luke's back as she went on into the living room.

'Crash down, you pigs,' she said warmly as she ditched her poncho. 'You want coffee?'

Luke and Steve followed her on all fours, following the lines of the pattern on the carpet as best they could.

'Smooth with it, ain't she?' Luke wheezed, grinning like a baboon.

Steve burst out guffawing again. 'Always was,' he gasped. 'She used to beat up the old man every night. Right after she came in from the . . .'

'Get him under control, Luke,' George called out. 'Kick him in the rocks, right?'

Luke was hauling Steve to the sofa by the scruff of his shirt. 'Hear that, you young pup? Get a grip, see.'

George was only half plastered, though more so than Luke, who seemed to be able to drink beer like water. She missed the tub of the percolator a couple of times, splattering coffee grains all over the floor before she decided on instant. All the time she was giggling like a kid. She could hear the two of them heaving over her style in the bowling alley now. They'd been screaming about it all the way back. Out of the corner of her eye she could see them with their foreheads together, mimicking her crummy action and then pawing each other as they tried to breathe.

When she edged in with the coffee they were spread-eagled, sucking in air.

'Jus' saying, we were,' Steve told her, 'how you'd have made a good tenpin not many years ago.'

George jumped on her brother and started digging her nails under his ribs. His feet came up a mile. 'Sis, get off, don't, sis. That kills me . . .'

Luke smiled stupidly as they wrestled, pulling the scalding coffee into his mouth, feeling it burning the roof. Later he'd be licking the skin off. His eye fell on the book lying by the sofa.

George rolled off her brother's big wiry body and sat beside him. She kept her hand on his cheek and let it slide up into his hair. She looked right into his eyes and then kissed his nose and kept on looking at him.

'You should come and see me more often. Why don't you come more often?'

Steve let his hand fall on her hip. His eyes dropped their gaze to the rug. 'Busy life, sis. Got to get on. You don't want me round here all the time.'

'No. Just more often, that's all.'

They both laughed softly, as if it didn't matter, and waited for Luke to say something. He was riffling through the book on enzymes one-handed.

'I could never get on with chemistry,' Luke announced, as if that was a very significant historical fact. 'Too many long words in it. No laws, no rules. Just things you've got to learn.'

Steve shook his head. 'That's for schoolboys, Luke. It's not like that these days.'

Luke nodded. 'I wouldn't know, I guess. It's been a long time since I was at school.' He shut the book.

George made more coffee and they talked till midnight. She thought it was the best thing she'd had with her brother for maybe a year or more. Maybe this should have happened earlier, she told herself, maybe she should have got it going with a scientist like Luke a long time ago.

Maybe a scientist could touch her brother for her, pull him back for her.

When it went quiet again she stretched her arms out and yawned.

'I'm going to throw you two bums out now,' she sighed. 'Give him a lift home, Luke?'

'OK.' Luke tossed Steve his book. 'Let's go, Einstein.'

'I can take a tube, it's OK.'

'No sweat. 'I'll give you a ride.' Luke stood up. 'It's on my way.' Which it wasn't.

Steve Maringelli had his book in his hand when he left his sister's flat, and tucked inside his windcheater some laserdisks that George slipped to him while Luke was out taking a goodnight leak. Pink Floyd albums they were, going clear back to the eighties, and if Luke knew she'd parted with them he'd have gone relatively ape. In Luke's car he slid the book down by the gear housing while he jabbered about one thing or another. It was still there when he got out, but Luke didn't spot it till he got all the way back to Oxford Street. Luke didn't think much about that; he just dropped the book on the passenger seat so he'd remember to hand it to George some time.

Steve wasn't thinking about much at all by then, though.

Steve was still thinking about his big sis when he got in.

Maringelli didn't get on all that amazingly well with his big sis. Sometimes he wondered why he bothered to keep in touch, and truth to tell, most of the initiative came from her. They'd never been close. He was an academic with a social conscience and a taste for the esoteric, she was a ball-biting businesswoman who saw everything and everybody (it seemed to young Steve) in the same can-you-sell-it, can-it-sell-you, percentage-point terms. But Maringelli needed his big sis. Maybe it was just that she was all he had by way of family. Maybe he was as primal and as scared as that.

Also, *also*, she was promiscuous by his standards. She had no intention of ever settling with a man, far less marrying one. She'd screw them and all that, she'd have long things with them that went on for years, but when they finished she'd just float on to the next. Young Steve was fairly shocked by that, not that he was a prude, but it didn't accord with what he considered a tenable theory of proper social behaviour. He had a lot to learn, young Steve, and not just about his big sis.

On top of all that, he decided as an afterthought, she was devious, or seemed to be. That was why she'd lent him the Floyd disks; it was so he'd have to go see her again to return them. Steve was no fool.

Maringelli knew his flat would be cool when he entered because unlike other parts of town, this neighbourhood was not heated all day at this time of year by the electricity from the twin AGRs sixty kilometres east on the north Kent coast. By the time twenty rolled they said they'd have the whole metropolis online, but until then he had to shove money in a coinbox, just like the cavemen used to do. It was degrading.

He crossed the living room in darkness, switched on a table lamp and saw it immediately. Not that you can easily miss a suitcase, even a small one.

Steve Maringelli stared at it quizzically, with his back to the open bedroom door where, in the shaft of light that streamed in from the living room, a pair of black-trousered legs stretched languorously from an easy chair. The legs crossed at the ankle above brass-buckled crocodile-skin shoes. A black-gloved hand dangled from an arm rest.

When the figure started to move it was noiseless.

Steve was still considering the suitcase. With instinctive care he stretched out his hand to the name tag. The name was Steven Maringelli. Since this wasn't his suitcase, nor any suitcase he had ever seen before, something deep inside his intelligent mind started telling Maringelli that whatever was happening, or had happened, or just might be about to fucking happen, wasn't right.

He was crazily starting to wonder if it was real – not a

55

real suitcase, a real event — when a voice behind said, 'Hello, Steven.'

Steve jumped and turned like a startled duck. The figure in black was standing in the bedroom doorway now, leaning on the jamb, looking at him, arms folded.

'What?' Who the hell . . .

'I don't want you to be alarmed, Steve.'

'What are you doing in my flat?' Fair question, absolutely to the point.

The man seemed concerned about it, as if his intrusion might cause offence. He also seemed . . . what?

Maringelli added, 'How did you get in?'

'It doesn't matter, does it?'

Maringelli let out a little yip of a laugh. 'Well it might. I mean it . . .' he saw the arms start to move then, because they were uncoiling themselves and fanning out like bits of a huge spider and Maringelli was suddenly thinking some very bad things that didn't have any form of words to them '. . . I mean . . .'

'Don't be frightened, Steve.'

The big man was coming out into the light. He was vast, like a zombie. He seemed to go up about twelve feet.

Maringelli backed off a bit, till he touched the table. 'What's the case for? Who're you?' he whispered, and that was an interesting combination of questions because the first one had been all set to be asked when along came the second one unexpectedly and sort of shunted it out ahead.

'It doesn't matter. Just relax, Steve. Try not to be frightened. I won't harm you, if you behave.'

Well for the love of God, you could put it any way you liked, but this man looked like he could harm a gorilla. So far about six seconds had passed since Steve had first begun to think he was in for some harm and that hadn't been long enough to consider any kind of action. Now he started thinking maybe he should do something, like bolt for it. Or at least scream.

Forget that, though.

A large pistol — well it looked large from just outside

your focal point – had materialised in the dark man's fist and was hanging rock steady at the end of his outstretched arm, with its open end pointing into Steve's face. It had a fat thing with vents in the side on the end of the barrel, which looked about as wide as the muzzle of a tank.

The voice changed. Now it had menace, lots of menace.

'This won't make any noise. It will kill you instantly. If you start to shout I'll pull the trigger while you're drawing breath. Cooperate. Anything is better than being dead.'

Steve was buying that, no argument.

'Shut your mouth,' Bruno said. 'Keep your hands where I can see them and sit on the table. Slowly.'

Keen to oblige by now, Maringelli slowly sat down on the table. The gun followed him.

'The case is for you,' Bruno said. 'We need to take a few of your things. Clothes mostly, starting with those you have on.'

Steve went, 'Uh? Why?'

'It doesn't matter why. Take off your jacket and then roll up one of your shirtsleeves.'

Maringelli thought, Do what?

It was then that he spied the hypo in Bruno's other hand and all at once he was cold across the forehead and his hands were up beseechingly and he could hear himself babbling, 'Aw no, look, come on, please . . .' though Bruno just went on watching.

8

Day: minus 12

Luke and Sandell didn't throw themselves into the Schaum
AX–9 crash right off because going right into business had
struck them both as unseemly, especially after not seeing
each other for so long. A year was it? Perhaps a little less.
Just a few generalities was all that Luke and Sandell had
touched on before they fell to mixing the drinks and talking
about the old times and times since.

That had lasted an hour or so, two perhaps. Now it was
down to business time, with coffee brought in on a tray by
the girl they'd hauled in to take any notes that might be
needed later on.

Later on being when the others arrived. Half the Schaum
executive that was, from golf courses thronging, with
chequered and tartan trousers and gloves on their hands
with holes at the knuckles. They would not be amused.

'Yes, I *was* going to ring you,' Sandell said, pouring the
coffee. 'I know you're good, Luke, and it's a job for a mate,
all right?'

Luke was nodding, watching the hot brown stream.

'But I've got to say it, Luke. What you are is a straw to
grasp at. That's the way they see it.'

'You too?'

'Me, too,' Sandell said. He shrugged, with both hands
still around the coffee pot.

John Sandell was a physicist turned aircraft engineer.
Finn, though now an intellectual bum, had once been a
computer scientist. Sandell and Lucius Finn were the same
age and had gone through postgraduate together with

differing results. Sandell had taken his doctorate with ease in eighty-five, while Luke had flunked trying to write his thesis without the excuse of any distractions at all. They had remained good friends over the years, though they so seldom met, and when they did they mainly got methodically drunk.

John Sandell had remained steadfastly in research, clinging to the urge to produce things and make them work. He had changed only infrequently from one carefully chosen niche to another until his present, very senior position with Schaum. Luke Finn, on the other hand, had slithered rapidly from one ill-fitting function to another until a couple of things he didn't talk about made him quit the research scene altogether and drop into his current, and probably final, peculiar role. Luke had reactionary views about science these days, and scientists. Sometimes he would say that science was a sham and scientists were corrupt and Sandell would bite on it and they would quarrel as they teemed in the booze. Luke had a complicated thing about it.

Schaum did all of the avionics work for the AX–9 program at their vast complex thirty kilometres west of London. Sandy had told Luke that. He also knew that his friend was close to the work, because Sandy told him that, too.

Luke picked his words so they came out sounding donnish and crummy.

'What you mean is,' he said, pointing with his little finger, 'that I, or somebody of my ilk, represents to you the possibility that your plane is not defective.' He hesitated over 'defective' before deciding it was adequate.

'That's the straw,' Sandell said, without nodding.

'Suppose it isn't.'

'We'd prefer that,' Sandell said.

'Right. So suppose it isn't. Then it went down because it was screwed.' Luke poked the air with his finger. 'That's a generic term for the moment, right? Like . . . uh.'

'How screwed?'

'All right,' Luke went on. 'She was either screwed from inside or outside.'

'Knocked down or sabotaged. That's if we discount a suicidal crew.'

'Yeh, discount that,' Luke said. 'So let's give it a throw for a minute, Sandy. Start with outside. What could get a plane that high? How high does it go? Eighty thousand?'

'More than ninety when it happened, if it was flying to plan.'

'So what could get it? Not a fighter, I shouldn't think, unless fighters have changed without me catching on.'

'Not a fighter.' Sandell seemed definite on it. 'Not that high. And unlikely that far out over the Bering. Anyway the satellite that saw it go down would have tracked the fighter.' The research man paused. 'There was no fighter, Luke.'

Luke knew what the pause was for. It preceded the statement of fact and the statement of one fact revealed others, like the fact that Sandell had been talking to the American ground stations all the way over in Alaska for much of the previous day. And they'd told him definitely no fighter. OK, fine. Luke waited for whatever else there was then prodded.

'And?'

Sandell sniffed. 'And no missile either, probably.'

'Why not?'

This time Sandell shrugged again. Why not indeed, he reasoned inside. Luke could keep his mouth shut, he had an operating licence to say so, and he was going to be in on this stuff anyway, so he could be told things. Sandell decided he could justify this conversation, if he ever had to.

'It's possible that a missile could get it, or a salvo of them at least. There are many types that could have reached it, either Russian or American, from launch sites in Kamchatka or the Aleutians. And small, steep-rising sprinter missiles could be missed by the satellite. But . . .' His eyebrows went together.

'But what? You said it probably wasn't a missile.'

'The fact is, Luke, an anti-aircraft missile that operates at that kind of range can't rely on just knocking a plane down with a proximity burst. There's no such thing as proximity at long range. You go for direct hits, using ultra-accurate homing systems.'

'So?'

'So when a missile hits a plane direct it blows it to damned shreds is what I'm saying. It turns it into a cloud of bits and they spread out as they fall, over hundreds of square miles.'

'Ah, right. And the satellite could have tracked the cloud, right?' Oh yes, very cute. Now he remembered seeing those radar films of things being splattered like that, when blips turned into sudden, hazy little patches that floated and fanned across the screen.

'Yeh, I get it. The satellite could tell you if it blew up.'

'Correct,' Sandy said. 'It didn't. There was no explosion, no missile, no fighter and no rotten bloody Martian saucers either. The damn thing just fell out of the sky.'

'No screaming for help? No mayday . . . ?'

'Nothing.'

Luke sucked on all of that for a moment whilst the other man sat across the big desk from him and blinked periodically.

'Seems to come down to one or the other then,' Luke finally said. 'Sabotage or. . . hum.'

'Or we've got a loser,' Sandell said. 'Spell it out, why don't you? I have already.'

'So tell me,' Luke asked lightly. 'If you've got a flaw in the design of your plane, where's it likely to be? I mean, what kind of flaw can knock a plane down without warning?'

Sandell didn't like that 'your plane' much. 'I guess you'd have to bet on either engines or airframe. If an engine failed it could flip out very fast, but failures get caught in advance, no matter how quickly they start to happen.'

'You hope.'

'Right, I hope. Maybe there's some failure mode we missed. Something we didn't test for. Something to do with high altitude, temperature. It's unlikely.'

'And what made you say the airframe was a possibility?'

Sandell shrugged. 'An aircraft moving at Mach three behaves in all kinds of strange ways. Aerodynamically, I mean. It has a stability envelope – a safe range of speeds, attack angles, climb rates, turn rates, rudder, all kinds of parameters. If it moves outside the envelope then it's unpredictable. The envelope has to be computed by design studies, optimised in tests. You've got computer simula- tions, tunnel runs, all kinds of tests. Maybe we made a mistake. Maybe there's a kink in the envelope we don't know about. Maybe it found it.'

'You don't believe it, though.'

'I don't want to believe it.' Sandell threw up both his hands. 'Dammit, Luke, you don't thin!: we take things for granted, do you? We *assume* it's going to lose an engine, two even, *three* even. We *assume* it's going to get flown outside its limits. So we put in failsafes. We put in so many safety systems it looks ridiculous. The thing can practically fly in two halves it's so damn dual-redundant.'

Luke nodded. Ah yes, yes. Always so sure.

'So how do you sabotage a plane that's so tough and failsafe? How do you do that?'

'I don't know that either,' Sandell said, without hesi- tating over it. He gave a weak, brief smile, and picked up one of the phones on his desk because it was showing an intermittent orange light.

'It looks bad to me, Sandy,' Luke told him softly. 'I mean, it does look bad.'

Sandell said something quietly into the phone and put it down again.

'Straws to grasp at is what I said,' he replied airily. Then he slapped his hands together and stood up. 'You want to see them now? They're all waiting. Everybody I could think of.'

Neither of them had touched the coffee.

First off, Luke was put in with a selection of very top brass. Schaum had its own list of titles like any other outfit so you wouldn't expect to recognise any of them. Luke met a controller of this, and a director of that and senior somebody or other of the other. What they told him in as many words was that they'd be pleased to retain his services on Doctor Sandell's recommendation, to be given a regular report accompanied by some hopeful signs of something or other that they could pin their hopes on, with a tidy it's-all-right-really line at the end, at all and every cost. Else, no dice.

Luke knew that speech off pat. He just agreed to the whole thing, like always.

Next, he was taken around to various locations by various and appropriate guides. Sandell took him around software development floors where big computers sat roosting behind floor to ceiling walls of glass. A chief test controller had him peering in wind tunnels and great engine beds and God knows what else. A senior somebody or other hauled him around about twenty aching acres of electronics labs pointing at instrumentation by the ton. A personnel supremo took him into personnel and batted VDU keyboards as if he knew what he was doing so Luke saw people's names and jobs and rates of pay on the screens, all prisoners of the machine as they ought to be, though you had the hard copy too, cabinets full of it. A techpubs librarian led him around the documentation centre where he was skull-dragged down shelf upon shelf of AX–9 manuals ranging in flavour from *Flight Communications Subsystem* (*FCS*) to *Fuel Dispersion Subsystem* (*FDS*) and *Control Panel and Tellback Subsystem* (*CPTS*) etcetera, all of them at least as thick as your frigging fist, all of them diversified and replicated under *Hardware, Software, Design, Test* and others, each edition being bound in a different colour so you could spot it in the crowd . . .

You'd have to say they heaped it on somewhat, though anything more realistic would have taken weeks. What they did do that was sensible was to devise some threats for issuing to their minions about cooperating with this goatee'd guy in grey, whether they thought they wanted to or not. This wasn't a defence job, the AX–9 had no MoD money in it, so they only had their own rules to answer to, their own decision to make, and they had made it. Mister Finn, all minions would be told, was a company confidant, here on recommendation. He was to be assisted, told things, given things. If he wanted a paper copy of any document whatever he was to have one prepared. If he wanted a diskette copy of anything that was on computers then one was to be prepared, formatted for his own machine, using as many company-supplied platters as it took. If he wanted to grope a secretary, then that secretary was to be groped. Luke was fairly impressed by all that.

It took until some middling hour in the afternoon, Luke didn't quite catch which one, and he left for London right away. Before he took off he pumped a good few hands and looked into a good few pairs of eyes.

Worried men, every one. They'd give anything to hear the right conclusion, but they'd have to pay the fee either way.

Bruno was deadly thorough, though he attended to his various details with such a natural slick that you would never have noticed half of them, or if you did, you'd have just taken them at face value.

Like the plank for example. Bruno was very strong, and he could have hefted poor Steve's corpse on to his shoulder with ease, prior to tipping it into the mine shaft. But then, as Bruno's mind had already decided, anybody can slip, and a body's weight on the shoulder unbalances a man so it was better not to stand too close to the edge. So Bruno had cast about for an old plank which he placed with one end a little way over the hole, and it was on this that he rolled Maringelli's stiffening remains.

All ready, Bruno stood and listened and looked slowly about. He had moved cautiously as he worked, keeping his position in the shadows, so anybody watching from the trees or the road below would not have seen him unless they knew how to look. Bruno knew how to look, patiently and carefully, one small arc at a time, alternating the quarters rather than a continuous sweep. There was nobody there, nothing human anyway. Only the things that came out in the moonlight.

Bruno had dispatched his already drugged and unconscious victim with care equal to that he now devoted to disposing of his cadaver. A single silenced bullet through the open mouth and out through the top of the neck into the soft earth, with a pillow behind to stop the mess. The pillow was lashed with string to the head, the bullet would never be found.

Bruno gripped the end of the plank and drove it above his head in a dead lift, as if he was working out in a gym. There was no grunt, no sign of exertion from his massive chest, only the hiss of breath as he locked up his arms and then the faint sliding of the body as it left the plank and the odd satchel thump as it disappeared into its thousand-metre drop to the flooded workings far below. The coalfield was long dead, the mines long abandoned. Bruno had always thought that open holes like this were a public menace, however remote.

9

Day: minus 11

George spent most of the morning deciding not to call Lucius P. Finn. Then, after a couple of early pints in the pub outside the firm she picked up Artistic and together they tubed across the river. They were going to see an organisation called the Pureflite Corporation.

George was worried about the Pureflite thing. She'd seen their ships floating around over town before now (who hadn't?) but apart from the preliminary contact a couple of weeks ago it was a new element in the arrangements. Artistic had been doing most of the dealing with them and he was all for it, which was why the shithole was tagging along now, but George still wasn't all that sure. She soon would be, though.

Pureflite had a big block on the South Bank. Before they got ushered into the meeting, George and Artistic hung around in a reception area for a while being given expensive tea and coffee and watching the publicity films on the viewers there. George was impressed.

Pureflite started some time in the late eighties and could now claim to be just about the leading maker of rigid airships in the world. Dirigibles was the name they preferred for their products, so whenever they hit the news, dirigibles was what you heard about.

The pubfilms showed it all in easy stages. Starting in eighty-seven, Pureflite had pulled together a flight tech-nology that had been developing in the shadow of winged aircraft for over a hundred years. Its first ships were heavy lifters used for timber hauling and firefighting in Canada and South America. Proving their designs and theory, they moved into more special-purpose airships for construction and bulk-cargo hauling.

By ninety-three, Pureflite was into the cargo business in a big way. Its natural targets were the short-haul routes inside continental America and Western Europe. Within five years its North American division had carved huge slices of business away from airlines and rail and road hauliers alike. Already European markets were falling to it as well. The reasons were simple enough. A ship only went port to port, a plane only went from airport to airport, a truck had to wait at frontiers and it carried but a couple of containers a trip. The airships went from supplier to customer direct; they needed no airstrips, they could hover over loading bays, land on buildings, moor to pylons. At 150 m.p.h. they ran on cheap fuel and with helium production up five thousand per cent in a decade, they were filled with the cheapest gas on earth. While that greatest of all aircraft hazards, pilot error, was eliminated by computers on the ground being able to fly the ship remotely should the need arise, a failsafe beyond imagining with an airliner. In a dozen years, Pureflite had experienced not a single incident, lost not a single life.

Pureflite had made billions out of freight and were now developing plans for a prestige passenger service. George had entered their life at just the right moment.

There were four of them altogether. What looked like a secretary, plus their European general manager, their PR man and their chief engineer. The meeting went straight to business, with Artistic swanning at the table-end as usual.

'Our main interest is in publicity,' the PR man reiterated. 'We note your assurance that we will receive plenty of comments from your talk-over.'

'Guaranteed,' George said. 'We can put in plenty of shots of the ship from our ground cameras.' George was pretty warm to it by now, after seeing the films.

'Excellent,' the general manager said. Then he added:

'In fact, we propose to supply our latest dirigible, a passenger liner. Not much bigger than the one you're used to seeing over town but with more passenger space. Perhaps we can agree a description of it for you to use.'

'No problem,' George said. 'Just tell us what you want us to say. You're proposing to put this into service for regular passengers? Like holiday-makers even?'

'Eventually, yes,' the general manager said coyly. 'It will take a while of course. Unlike our business service, a full-blown passenger service will need terminal buildings before it can go operational. Right now we are seeking exposure.'

Hell's bells, thought George, this outfit doesn't play games. 'The airlines must be fairly unhappy about you,' she said.

'They're worried sick,' the PR man told her with his eyes gleaming. 'We're going to be better and cheaper. But that's their problem, don't you agree?'

They jawed for another couple of hours before they wound up. Artistic wanted to know if he was going to be able to operate from up there OK or if he had to know about any restrictions on his unbounded imagination by virtue of being in the sky in a steel cocoon. The engineer told him they could put mountings in for his cameras if he wanted. Artistic said he'd use minicams with the right range. But did he have a good field? Sure, they said, the ship's built for viewing. Ground relay equipment? Standard, they said, this is a high-tech aircraft. Artistic looked like he couldn't wait. George had a different query.

'This new version's got to be safe,' she said. 'Otherwise the council and the police won't wear it. This event's going to go mostly in the dark, see. Can you operate in the dark?'

The chief engineer just smiled at this dumb TV person's incredible ignorance. 'This aircraft is far safer than anything else in existence,' he said. 'It's equipped with ground control.'

'Ground control?'

'Our computers here communicate with its flight computers on board. They will monitor its entire behav-

68

iour. If necessary, our machines can override any pilot control and fly it down. You couldn't do that with a helicopter.'

'You can do that?' George was by no means uninspired.

'Certainly. Just like a model aeroplane, only better. We can rotate its engines, twiddle its tail, fly it up and down and sideways. It can be in our hands at any time.'

'Actually,' the general manager put in, 'we've dealt with the council many times as I need hardly say. Perhaps you would like me to deal with them over this? I'm sure it'll be clearer if just one of us talks to them.'

George liked that. That was a task off her back. George just hated those swine on the council.

Coming out into the street, Artistic was practically coming off on it. This could be amazing, he warbled, just amazing. Good, George said, so make it amazing. No end to the possibilities, Artistic said, they're absolutely amazing. Right, George said, right.

She tried getting hold of lousy Luke a couple of times when she got back, without any success, and that put her in a pique. George in a pique was no joke. She'd rung his office number and also the number of the pigsty he lived in next door to it that he called an apartment. No reply. Well she wasn't trying it any more. The hell with that.

Over her coffee and five fags, George concluded that the thing to finalise next was the technical side of it. In particular, what she planned for Centrepoint. They only had a certain time to do these things in by definition, so it was important to reaffirm that it was time enough. If whoever was going to do it said it was then there were go-aheads to be given. If they said it wasn't then there were arms to be bent until they said it was. George was good at arm bending.

TCTV had a very large and well-equipped division for doing this kind of thing. George knew for a fact that they'd handled some pretty heavy jobs in the past because she'd been involved. That didn't necessarily mean they wouldn't balk at covering half a skyscraper with laminated screens, but then again it might. By the same token, George knew exactly who to go at with the problem, and that was a big ugly Scot named McEwen. McEwen lurked in a big dirty office in TCTV's engineering division building further upriver, where he planned the impossible and ate steel nuts. George was there by four, and caught him on a flyer.

'Where are the screens?' he had wanted to know. 'Are they glass or what?'

'Plastic,' George said. 'Heavy-duty plastic. They'll be covered in some special stuff on one side but that doesn't concern you.'

'It's glass that's yer problem,' McEwen said. 'Glass is a bloody pain in the arse.'

'These are tougher than glass, don't worry,' George emphasised. 'And they'll have fixing brackets or whatever. You just have to fix them to the building and join them together.'

'Where you going to get them from?'

'My technicals have sorted that out. They can get them any time. I checked that already. I just need to know you can put them up.'

McEwen shrugged.

'Sounds dead easy. Case of working our way either up or down in cradles. We can cramp the scaffolding on to the office window corners. We've done similar things before in the States.'

George liked to hear talk like that. Very positive, leave-it-to-me kind of attitude. Not like those stupid shits she had for a team. She could go places with McEwen.

'You'll have to clear it with the authorities,' the big ugly Scot observed. 'I'm no flying up any skyscraper till I'm clear.'

'I've done that,' George said, 'They're as good as sold on it. Also the outfit that owns the place.'

'What about the occupiers?'

'Occupiers?'

70

'It's an office block, isn't it? It's got offices in it. People use them.'

George went 'Uh. Shit.' She could see a long trail in front of her on that one. How many firms could there be in there? Fifty? A million?

'I'll get on it,' she said, meaning that she'd put that squirt of a PR on it. That was a PR job if ever. She bade McEwen farewell, promising to get pissed with him again some time.

George reckoned she could roll this along now. She had a definite go on the permission, a definite go on the can-do. Now it was a case of kicking butt to get it done on time. Just up her street, that was. She started to feel very good about it, even better than she had before.

10

Day: minus 10

DeJohn put down his phone and pulled a switch on his desk.

'Yes, Mister DeJohn?'

'Get me the profile on a TI called L. P. Finn, will you? That's F-i-n-n. And bring in my appointments list for the next day or so.'

'Yes, Mister DeJohn.'

DeJohn's desk was already piling up with the day's tasks. The Office of Technological Crime generated many tasks for the senior fish, every single day. This particular one had jumped the queue by phone. And it looked as if the others might have to wait a little while.

The Technocrime Office started out as a small wart on the nose of the Serious Crime Squad of the London Metropolitan Police, back in the late eighties. Before the turn of that decade, however, it had already been clear that the job lay outside the compass of the police, and definitely went beyond the metropolis, so by eighty-nine you had a brand-new Home Office department lurking embryonic and determined in Lupus Street. It was, as they say, small but dedicated.

Today two hundred or so 'executives' of the OTC broke their balls in their three floors in Lupus Street, while technocrime raged outside like a plague. Ten per cent of reported cases they pursued, and ten per cent of those with any venom. They stuck to the biggest, dirtiest, most irrefutable and most spectacular when they moved in force and then, it had to be said, they occasionally hurt somebody and prompted a TV special. As for the rest, well the TI's report would be sent to the police who would make some kind of show in the labs or the machine rooms or the factory of the victim firm and then fade out. It wasn't much but it usually sent the felon back under his trapdoor so the crime went away, and as often as not the police managed to pin something on some hapless jerk, guilty or not, so it kept the victim's hackles down, it got the investigator paid and it kept the system going, just. Going where, was what some cynics said, what's with one per cent after all? To which you could always point out that one per cent was better than the hit rate on muggings and you've got *real* people on the end of that, not some damn conglomerate.

The thirty-odd men who went down in the AX–9 were real people, though. It had to be admitted.

Carl DeJohn had to admit that. In fact he had just admitted that, or something very much like that, to the chairman of the Schaum Aircraft Corporation not one minute ago. What that considerable person had told him, in no mean manner and in no particular order, was that he had known some of the missing-presumed-dead men personally, that his company's plane was a production-state machine that ought not to have and damn well had not malfunctioned, that Schaum was now on the edge of a market hypercatastrophe, that a technological investigator had been retained, and that if the said dick came up with anything, but *anything*, then he personally would 'require' the OTC to step in and hard. DeJohn had replied that the incident had already been noted by his department, and thank you for calling.

DeJohn was one of three deputy department chiefs of the Office of Technological Crime. At forty he had risen swiftly to his position, though he now sensed that any further progress would not be easy with two other capable men of comparable age running alongside. Nor was his future all that far-reaching in other directions for he now perceived that a function so specialised as his did not lend itself easily to a sideways move either. Deep in his guts,

DeJohn was beginning to wonder about his prospects in the world at large, and for an ambitious man with two decades of career ahead, such speculation gave pause for thought. Bad thought.

DeJohn was a lover of luxury. His middling salary he spent on eating well and loving well and dressing and driving well. About his department he would appear untypical in his expensive suit and shoes; more in place in a boardroom than in a crowded civil service rabbit warren. Secretly, and subconsciously almost, DeJohn had enjoyed the Schaum chairman's call because of the closeness it had given him to such an important man of the world.

I need to move out, DeJohn would often say to himself. I need to score.

Carl DeJohn leaned back in his chair and took the chin of his solarium-tanned face between his forefinger and thumb. His blue eyes narrowed at the name on the pad in front of him. Lucius P. Finn. Of course he had heard of this man before. Who could forget such a name?

Luke and his machine between them had saved DeJohn's secretary a job with that appointments list.

'DO IT NOW' it had railed at him that morning across the screen. That was how he'd programmed it to remind him of something the fourth time. The reminders would get ruder the longer they were ignored.

Luke decided OK, right, fine, he'd do it now. He'd leave his first pass through the Schaum AX–9 job till later, after he'd done it. He took a cab to Lupus Street.

He trudged up the stairs (Luke always used stairs, he thought half-killing himself on the goddamned stairs did him some good) to the topmost of OTC's three floors, where dwelt the licensing section, and turned left and left again to a swing door with an invitation to 'enter and wait' on it.

Luke entered and waited. During what seemed like about nine hours though it was less, a dozen or so different women came in and out of the room. They all ignored him with an effort, looking at potted plants, the VDU in the corner, the view through the window, the phone, the floor, the ceiling, anything rather than Luke, who just leaned on the counter with a hand on a hip, pulling his way thoughtfully through his cigar as if he had all night. He ignored them right back.

Finally one of them re-emerged from a door across the room smoothing down her exterior garments as if recently raped. A redhead, well stacked.

'Can I help you?'

It's a start, Luke thought, we can build on this.

'Renewal.' He tossed his licence on the counter.

'You're an operative. Ah.'

Quick, Luke thought. Like a whip. Straight to it. He continued to smile bemusedly, as a cat might at a small dog.

'Just a moment. I'll consult your file.'

Once you could do this by post, only these days it took for ever. They'd still retained it of course. Electronic mail flew by the megabaud every hour of every day, but you couldn't ram a licence down a wire to get it embossed, and there were a few other things you couldn't do like that either, so you still had a postal service. You still queued for an hour for a stamp, you still glued it on and you still dropped it in a box. Only usually your legs were quicker.

She was tapping things on the monitor and checking off readouts as they appeared. They were telling her that Luke was a good boy still, a fit person as it were, so he could have another year in the game, hopefully. Today they told her something else. Something DeJohn's secretary had punched in to a different machine an hour or so earlier. A program called Network Manager found it, by interrogating another one called Namecheck, which had conned it out of a big bastard called DBMS.

She came flying back.

'Mister Finn?'

'Hum?'

'I'm glad you popped in. Apparently Mister DeJohn would like to speak to you, fairly urgently.'

Luke went on the alert. What the hell did DeJohn want? And what was *fairly* urgently? Like every other TI in the history of the OTC and beyond, Luke neither liked nor trusted Carl DeJohn. It wasn't fear, he wasn't afraid of the man, but he didn't like having to answer to the guy.

'Your licence is renewed, by the way.'

Ten seconds later Luke was gazing down at Carl DeJohn while the deputy chief finished something he was scribbling.

When he had finished, DeJohn dropped the pen with a clatter and focused on Luke's face. Luke saw him taking in the Afro and disapproving of it. A lightning tour of the rest of him came back to Luke's face; the eyes logged up a lowish score, about four out of ten.

'Want a drink?'

'It's a little early, but why not?'

'Scotch?'

'That'll do.'

'Neat?'

Luke didn't care for this one-shot style of conversation. He decided to come to whatever the point was.

'Neat's all right. Why did you want to see me?'

The deputy chief grinned as he poured. He didn't reply until he came over and put one of the glasses in Luke's hand.

'You've been retained by the Schaum Aircraft Corporation to poke around that AX–9 business, I gather.'

'Yeh,' Luke said. 'I put in a notify to the Department this morning.'

DeJohn swallowed. 'I knew already. I've had their boss on to me first thing. Can I call you Luke? I think that's what your friends call you, isn't it?'

'If you want.'

DeJohn looked at him in a queer, sideways fashion.

'The fact is, Luke, they're worried sick over it. They're also very adamant that there has to be some kind of sabotage involved. If they can't demonstrate that, they're in big trouble with that plane.'

'I know,' Luke said, rolling his glass between his hands. 'That's obvious.'

'Good, good.' DeJohn said, before a pause. 'The thing is, Luke, they can't afford an event like this, they really can't. Airline confidence doesn't come easily for them, it happens slowly and it takes a long time. This kind of thing destroys it. You understand me?'

'Definitely. I wouldn't want to buy it either.'

DeJohn winced.

'Well, that's right. And now with this production aircraft disappearing only a few months from going into service, well . . .'

'Cancelled orders,' Luke said, taking a cheerful belt. 'Lots of them. All of them maybe.'

DeJohn winced even harder.

'That's a disaster in their terms,' he told Luke with what looked like genuine concern, though Luke couldn't figure out why. 'Their chairman spelled it out to me on the phone in those precise terms.'

'Right,' Luke said. 'He should know.' Luke was rapidly beginning to get a signal now. He didn't like it. He'd heard of this kind of thing but he never expected it in here. Maybe he was wrong.

'And what with the American plane being there to fill the orders, the competitor I mean. The Channing jet . . .'

Luke put the tumbler down on the glass covering of DeJohn's desk with a crack.

'Why do you keep spelling this out?' he asked sharply. 'What are you trying to say?'

'Say?' DeJohn looked flustered, for about one fiftieth of a second.

'What's the message you're trying to pass from Schaum to me?'

'There is no message, Luke. All I'm saying,' DeJohn said slowly, 'is that Schaum would be very relieved, and very much helped in the market – in fact *saved* in the market

– if you were to find evidence of sabotage.' He paused, Luke waited. 'Even if it's not, shall we say, conclusive.'

'Even if I have to invent it, you mean.'

'I didn't say that, did I?'

Luke put on his I-am-disgusted face. He wasn't though. This kind of thing really did happen. Obviously it happened. It was an obvious thing *to* happen.

'What do I get? A bonus?' What else could he possibly get?

'Dammit, Finn, nobody's said anything to me about you getting anything. Schaum have made no such overture.'

Oh nice. No such overture. Goddamn, they'd probably pay the fucking earth for a pseudo-sabotage to pull them out of this shit.

'So what's your beef?' Luke was starting to sneer now.

'I have no beef, as you put it,' DeJohn snapped back. 'This is a major European company, that's all. I am concerned for it, and for its prospects being damaged in this way. I simply wanted to underline our concern so that your diligence . . .'

'Don't worry about my fucking diligence,' Luke snarled. He began to head for the door. 'I'll be diligent. And I'll report what I find, and nothing more. That's nothing, right. Absolutely nothing more.'

The door slammed.

Bruno had a place by the river, not too far west to be central. Maybe Constantine knew where it was and maybe he didn't. Bruno didn't much care. In any event, he could leave when he had to without much of a hassle or a warning. Bruno had always been mobile.

Bruno lived alone and he existed alone. He had been alone since he was a teenager when he ran away from the care centre and took to the streets. In the army, in Indo-China, in Africa, surrounded by other men, Bruno had been alone.

Some day, Constantine had told him, there would be a time when Bruno would not be alone. Bruno wanted that, but first he must change his life so that he was free and independent and able to choose. They were arranging that between them, Bruno and Constantine.

Bruno went back to his plants. The message had been brief, simple, just a name and a description. To Bruno that was a great deal though, far more than he had been used to with enemies he had faced before.

Most of Bruno's plants were just green things, with a few flowers or splashes of colour. Easier to tend, Constantine had tried to comment once, but for Bruno the appeal was deeper than that. The shades of green reminded him of the jungle.

He examined his pair of araucaria first, stroking the fronds to test for leaf-drop and finding they were firm and strong. Last winter there had been red spiders to deal with, but today there were no signs. Bruno decided against watering for now. He moved on to the cyperus, peering at the tips of its sharp radial leaves and deciding on some moisture. Also it needed food, though it was bearing up well. Beside it, the saw-like leaves of his dizygotheca were waving coyly as if pleased to see him. Bruno smiled and put his fingers on to its compost, keeping them there until he was sure of the temperature. It was warm enough, though a check with a thermometer would do no harm. Fifteen degrees was as low as he cared for with dizygotheca.

Bruno had been broken up when he came out of Laos. Wounded only slightly, his mind was paralysed by savagery – mostly his own – and, like all the other men with him, he had gone into treatment like a sheep, neither knowing nor caring what it was all about. Detraining, they called it. It had lasted a month or more, and Bruno had come out of it just as he had gone in.

. Bruno rubbed the flat leaf lobes of fatsia japonica between his fingers, measuring their glossiness and spring, trying to sense any sign of brittleness. It was growing big enough for cuttings. He did a similar test on his tall hedera variegata, admiring its purple twisting stems and the way they coiled up their pole, reaching beyond it to the light from the window. Next to it, philodendron scandens climbed densely, its pointed leaves gleaming healthily. Bruno noted that its neighbour, the bushy rhoicissus, was reaching out to overgrow it, and he carefully nipped off some tendrils with the nail of his thumb. The rhoicissus needed spraying, he noticed, for there was a clear edge curl to the leaves and, here and there, the shiny green was giving way to a dull yellow.

Bruno knew that Constantine had merely studied him to begin with. After his return to England, he had taken a job as a night security guard in a firm where Constantine was some kind of wheel. It had been a while after that when Constantine found him again.

Bruno bent down to admire the leopard spots of his maranta leuconeura. It was his special favourite, his Brazilian beauty, the one on which he lavished his most particular care.

This guy Finn sounded like a pushover.

11

'This is a hell of a way to hold a conversation,' she gasped, undulating her back.

George was kneeling doggie-style facing the foot of the bed, with her face up and her neck straining. Through the open bedroom door she could see right into the living room. Judging from the light in there it was a bright morning.

'So what you want to talk about?' Luke said, thrusting. He had his hands about halfway down her thighs.

'That's not what I said.'

Luke gave it to her in long slow pushes, coming out a good three quarters of his available length before sliding in again and holding it before starting again. The bed was too damn soft for this one, he reckoned; his knees kept sinking from side to side unless he concentrated, threatening to tip him off balance.

'Oh, aaah,' she panted. George heaved her buttocks into his belly, gripping him rhythmically, pulling at him now. 'Nnnnn . . .'

Luke kept his eye on the line of her back where it sloped out to her shoulders, looking for the shudder-signs of climax. His hands slid forward to cup her breasts. Dammit, if she didn't get there soon . . .

'You . . . are . . . really . . .' he started to say as she squealed '. . . something . . .'

George came off like a tug-of-war team, with a whole long fanfare of sighs and groans. With infinite relief, Luke let go and slumped forward over her back, his face in her hair.

'Gimme a pillow, you sod.'

Luke dragged a pillow to her and she slid it under her chin and settled forward on to her chest, pushing her legs out behind her. Luke lay on her back, but with his weight on his forearms.

'Nice?' Luke was like any other dumb male; he had to ask.

'More often would be nicer.'

In the living room Luke could see the remains of the breakfast they had eaten. Fruit and wine, her idea, something to do with the Romans she said, better than toast and eggs and goddamned crispies. Among the detritus of orange peel and sliced apple was the book, lying there where he'd left it on the floor.

'Do you really like him, Luke?'

'Like who?' Her hair smelled heady, a mixture of conditioner and female musk.

'Steve. Do you really like him?'

'Brought his book back, didn't I?'

'No, really. Could you be friends?'

'Yeh, sure I like him. There's a bit of an age gap but that's OK. Why? What's with Steve anyway?'

George just smiled with her eyes closed and buried her cheek in the pillow. 'It doesn't matter. It's important to me, that's all.'

'If it's important it matters.'

Luke ran the tips of his fingers down her spine, watching her skin twitch on its own, feeling the coolness of it as the sweat of their lovemaking evaporated off.

'Tell me something, Luke.'

'No.'

'Tell me.'

'What is it?'

She smiled again, mischievously this time, but he couldn't see it. Her eyes were still closed.

'What does P stand for?'

'I told you . . .'

She craned her neck around and mocked him with her eyes. 'Aw, gowon! Tell me.'

'Never.' He bit the skin of her neck, slid down away from her, drawing his teeth into the small of her back, nipping at the tiny blonde hairs there. She squeaked and slapped at him, her buttocks plunging into his chest, perfume filling his head. . .

12

The chief executive of the Measons Corporation had always
been able to devote a condescending moment or two to the
activities of his numerous chemists. After all, as he was
wont to say whilst flashing his caps, they're our bread and
butter. What they actually did, and even more so, how
they did it, was a closed book to the chief executive. Those
little boffins had the ideas, probably, and they invented all
the formulae and diagrams, more than likely. But he knew
damn well they were only a small part of the overall
commercial endeavour. A very small part. Compared with
the development strategy, the marketing and the product
testing and the field trials, a downright minuscule part. In
fact, almost *incidental* . . .

The amount of development money that you're going to
lay out for a new headache pill is colossal. It must cover
the year-in year-out funding of the efforts of many scientists
and technicians. It must pay for the pursuit of hundreds
of false alternatives. It must take in years of complete,
exhaustive and neurotically repetitive laboratory testing of
the final choice, on everything from a hamster up to a
horse. It's got to pay for market research, production facilities, advertising and a host of nameless and unnumbered
items that lack headings. All of these factors have to be
driven to exhaustion because you're not going to use this
stuff just here and there, you're going to push it at entire
populations, from billions of bottles on millions of shelves.
You're going to make this pill by the shipload, and you're
going to *compete*, face on, with lots of others. And you have

to get it all right because you're laying all this effort and bread out in advance, before a single pill is sold.

The chief executive of Measons had been carrying all that around his neck for a long time with the Phenthanol product, because it had been a complex and a lengthy project. Now that the live field-test reports were in he felt relieved, especially when you considered the results. Rabbits and rats were all right, you could listen to people going on about rabbits and rats till doomsday for all it actually meant, and if human volunteers didn't keel over either, well that didn't leave you really settled because there was something unwholesome about human volunteers. It was as if a human who would volunteer to test a drug, albeit for a fee, couldn't be a normal human, so maybe his reaction to the drug wasn't a guide to the way normal, non volunteer-type humans would react. That was the way the chief executive's stunted mind saw it anyway. Live field tests though, they were different, they gave you results about *real* people, with real headaches, swallowing your pill in real circumstances, on their own, doing it in all the unrecommended ways, like with whisky and on empty bellies, without anybody breathing down their necks in a lab. For all the care and dough you lavished in developing and testing and proving, this was the only true and valid statement about your *product*, gentlemen, as the chief executive was partial to saying to his senior minions, the *only* one.

Well these live field tests had turned out a glittering success, sure enough. The reports had all said it, and his marketing director had been over personally to make damn sure he'd read them, beaming like a fat cat and talking loud, so naturally the chief executive was pleased. Push it out the door? Of course we push it out the door, he'd said, of course we do. Release it. Sooner the better. That had been some days ago now . . .

The cab driver swallowed three of the oval white pills, with a mouthful of tea, just after gnawing his way through a

French bread sandwich with beef in it. The headache had been escalating all morning, ever since he took an early ride out to Heathrow and then sat in a long fuming queue back into town. In his job you couldn't stop for a headache. Not for long. The driver finished his tea and then slid back into the line outside Paddington station and waited for a pick-up. It turned out to be a big woman who wanted to go somewhere in Victoria. Registering the address almost subconsciously and affording his passenger not the slightest indication that he had even heard her, the driver flicked on his meter and took off. Down Praed Street, Edgware Road, Park Lane was what he reckoned, traffic was thin enough for it at this time of day, though in a rush hour he'd have gone through the park.

He got about as far as the Hilton, or maybe further if you count the skid. The sudden blackout came on him and then went off again like the operation of some kind of shutter, terrifying him with the sheer, pouncing suddenness of it. Instinctively he had slapped his hand to his forehead and dragged the wheel around before he even knew what he was doing. He wiped a Mercedes on his left and another cab on his right before they backed away behind him and amidst the wails of his passenger he passed out altogether and the cab slid over into the crash barrier and started zig-zagging down Park Lane . . .

The chairman of the Manchester Watch Committee often got headaches before meetings, probably in anticipation of what was going to be wreaked upon him. He had downed a couple of these new things his wife had bought before submitting himself yet again and vowing for the tenth time this year that he was going to fuck this job and let somebody else take the fucking Watch Committee into the new fucking century. Sod it, was one of his last conscious thoughts.

They noticed he'd passed out after they'd been yelling his name for a minute or two. At first his fellow committee members assumed he had nodded off, so cherubic did he look, but after raising their voices and prodding him and finally pulling him about by his limp throat, they realised that . . .

As for Fanny (it's a stage name, dear, *please*) well, who could do her job *without* getting a splitting head every night? A girl could of course remove her clothes without having the bass drum banging out of the speakers behind, with the bass channel wound up to the top, it wasn't the only accompaniment for a stripper. Cowgirl peeled off her rawhide smalls to the attendant strains of a banjo, and Jasmine had a sort of oriental flute or whatever it was to go with her rubber python and her tassels, whilst Compass Rose, a rising star of the show, did her jaw-dropping routine with pegleg and plastic parrot to the jolly rhythm of a sea shanty. But with Fanny the image was old-time burlesque, all bounce and bum, and her music and her handle were meant to fit. Hence the big drum and hence the rotten headache and hence the three pills which, she had politely informed Cowgirl, who had given them to her, had better bloody work.

They did work though, with all the precipitous energy of a guillotine, somewhere after suspenders and approaching bra, catching Fanny with both hands up her back. She tottered, pirouetting slightly, into the shiny curtains behind her, fouled her feet in them and then hopped unconsciously forward and toppled headlong on to the sweating little regular in the front row, all but smashing the life out of him with the touchdown. 'Hell's bells,' a voice not his own was heard to exclaim, 'that's new . . .'

And others were less fortunate, like Ron from Hull. Ron from Hull was an electrician, heavy-duty stuff, nothing fancy. Ron's fateful day arrived when he and a mate were checking the cabling high above the seaward side of the Humber suspension bridge. They were working near the centre, absolutely nowhere near the shore, and a dizzying way up in space. Ron's headache crept up on him just before they broke for lunch. It was his mate who had the pills, a new unopened bottle bought that very morning, and Ron unwisely dropped a couple on an empty stomach, not that it would have made much difference.

Ron's mate didn't see him go, having paused to contemplate the South Yorkshire shoreline, and it struck so suddenly that a glance away was all that was needed to miss it. Having blacked out already, Ron didn't sound off as he toppled backwards into oblivion, he just went feet up and over in a single fluid movement. One instant he was there, the next he wasn't. After he'd plummeted a hundred and fifty metres or so, the steel grey waters of the Humber estuary met him like a concrete wall . . .

13

Day: minus 8

They hadn't exchanged any words at all. The message from Luke had been taken by his computer and hung on a streamer tape. George didn't know and didn't much care how it worked, but somehow Luke could *talk* to that thing and actually tell it to ring her number and play her the tape. It had tried, over and over, till she answered. Considerately it didn't start till about seven a.m., which was early enough to catch her before she took off for work, but not unsocial. Although she felt faintly degraded by it, and maybe was betraying her sex or something, George had this girlish glow all of a sudden.

He took some fathoming though, the tight-lipped sod. Sometimes George felt that Luke told her just enough about himself, as if he was letting himself out by degrees, without paying out too much of his personal slack. It showed in small things mainly, like with his job. Like that time with the gun, when she'd asked him if he had one. He'd never volunteered it, and God knows it was a casual question, but he'd surprised her when he'd said he kept a weapon. Just a last resort, he'd said, though Lord knew what that could have meant; he only carried it when he went for an arrest and that was about once every three years or less. Most of the time it lived in one of the secret drawers in his funny old writing desk. George had asked to see it and had been surprised at how small and harmless it looked but Luke just said it was the bullets that did the damage not the gun. George couldn't argue with that.

Now in her own office, with a definite go on the whole

thing, George started to form some definite plans towards the wayward Luke. She decided to bolster her shifting mood with a few vodkas from the bottle in her desk. George had her various poisons fairly well charted in their effects. Vodka was the one to make her feel sexy, whereas gin had generally the opposite effect. Whisky was for fighting, provided she didn't take so much it slowed down her reflexes.

That list of firms coming in was going to be a whole day on the phone, so George decided to try her kid brother again first. She wanted to chase her Pink Floyd disks. Steve was not very OK about bringing back her laserdisks. In fact, he was so non OK about it, he was more than capable of selling them to a girl, anything. Luke was keen on the sound, and if they weren't around for long, Luke was going to know. Anyway, she liked Pink Floyd too.

She tried his flat again. No reply. She tried his work number again. Same reply. Not in today, sorry. A message? No. She tried his flat again.

So where the hell was he, dammit?

The secretary took her mind off it when she came mincing in with the list. Well thank God for that, she decided, giving God some credit for there being but fourteen firms operating in Centre Point. Fourteen was manageable.

Luke made it out to Schaum by eight, maybe eight fifteen. He had been there all of the previous day, breaking his back and his feet just looking at the place, walking about, trying to catch some glances. There was nothing though, nobody cared much that he was there, or so it seemed.

He took a fast breakfast and coffee in their restaurant so he could catch their techlibrarian before he shoved off for a break. Luke kept the man a good two hours, taking him right around the maze of AX–9 documentation again, and showing him how to access the computerised stuff from the techpubs database. Then he shut himself in a study booth with a VDU and started to browse.

This was a reconnoitre of the plane itself. Luke had to know as much as he could about the aircraft that fell without a sound or a sign or a trace or a tear. Of course there were people lining up to be asked, and ask them he would, but a good preliminary laid-back look at the thing would help him form a view as to whether or not he had a chance in hell of getting anywhere near the bottom of this.

Luke started with the easy manuals, the ones labelled 'Introduction' and 'Overview' and 'Fundamentals'. These gave him cutaway pictures of the plane. On a screen the computer did all the archive legwork, Luke just had to type 'engines' (or 'powerunits', or 'thrust generators', or a whole string of other things you could call an engine, it knew them all off pat), and then press a key marked 'search', and it would give him the whole list of every reference there was to engine, in one second flat. If he wanted to be shown a reference he only had to touch it on the screen with his finger and up it came, just as if he had searched it out and had the manual open in front of him. If he wanted a hard copy of anything, he only had to hit another key and one of the dozen printers and flatbed laser plotters in the library systems room would hurl it out in a blink. It was even cleverer than that. If Luke was peering at a diagram showing how an engine sat under a wing he could order a blow-up on the screen. He could point to something in the diagram with his finger and a block of information would appear in a screen corner telling him the part in question was a twin output elevon drive controller. If he then pressed his 'search' key he was into a whole list of references on elevon drives which were part of the configuration control system and nothing to do with engines at all. You could leap about like that, and you could do it in seconds. In a couple of hours you could have a real good root around.

Luke was still rooting around when the techlibrarian cleared off at three thirty. As the darkness closed in outside he went on punching the keys and scanning the screen.

The plant control system dimmed the library lights for the night but Luke was too absorbed to notice. He just rooted on, sitting there in his dimmed-out cubicle with the main light coming out of the shifting coloured images on the screen. Reflections of them danced across the window nearby, and from there across Luke's intense face and eyes. Search, expand, next page, back page, touch, blow-up, show, save-it; the commands became his only thoughts, controlling his hands directly as his mind fought to soak up as much as it could.

Hours went by on tiptoe.

'Hello again.'

Luke squinted up towards the cubicle door.

'Hello, Sandy.'

John Sandell came over, with his hands in his pockets. For a while, he watched Luke's virtuosity on the keys. Luke had been dabbing at VDUs for more years than he cared to think by now. Funny thing, but keyboards had never gone away like the prophets had foretold, they were still here, going strong. Smarter yes, bigger screens yes, higher resolution, more colours, more buttons yes, but basically the same beast as you'd had for thirty years and more. Oh it'll be all voice input, they had said, that and mice and finger-touch screens and rollballs and God knows what else. Well they were all here as well, all those gismos and gadgets were around, all reliable, all useful, all selling well, but between them they still hadn't added up to the death of the keyboard.

'You've had a long session today. Busy yesterday too, I believe.'

Luke kept his attention on the screen.

'Machine told you that, eh.'

'Oh. I keep in touch.' Sandell sat down on a spare chair. 'Any first impressions?'

'I don't believe in first impressions. I never get any anyway.'

'Theories then,' Sandell said after some thought. 'You

like theories, Luke. You're always saying "try this". So try one.'

What are you fucking talking about? Luke thought. He leaned back to watch the effect of his latest command fill the screen. They both watched. A diagram appeared. The form of the AX–9 began to take shape in the wire-frame outline, as if stripped of its skin. Its insides were revealed as logical units of hardware, with information routes drawn as coloured highways along wings and fuselage, tail plane and underbelly. It rotated this way and that, words and pointers dancing about it.

Luke pointed with his free hand.

'Control system,' he said, assuming Sandell would recognise it anyway.

'Right. What about it?'

'It's computers, Sandy. More computers than any other airliner ever built. The whole thing is computer controlled. Everything talks to everything else. If an elevon moves up, it gets moved by a computer that checks with another one that adjusts the fuel distribution. Every other damn thing on board does the same. The way the computers work together is the control system. I didn't know things had come so far, not in civil aircraft.'

'Oh I don't know,' Sandell said, with what could have been an air of deferential modesty. 'There could always be better aeroplanes. They take so long to design, see. By the time you're ready to operate with a plane, half of it could be improved. Don't be too impressed.'

'I'm never too impressed.'

Sandell said, 'I know that.' There was another pause and Sandell added, 'Is this a theory? Why the control system?'

'Why not?'

There was nothing anybody could say to that.

'It didn't blow up,' Luke said. 'You agreed with that. It just fell. How long does a thing take to fall that far? What are we looking at here? Terminal velocity in thin air? What is it?'

'It takes a while,' Sandell said.

'Maybe. Even if it dived nose down with its power behind it at two and a half thousand let's say, it would take half a minute. It didn't do that, did it? Didn't the satellite watch it fall for longer than that?'

'A lot longer.'

'So why no mayday?'

'Maybe they were too busy trying to survive.'

'Come on, Sandy, I've been through the comms system. It's one switch, that's all. One switch is all they need to touch and the mayday and their position go out automatically, non stop, every tenth of a second.'

'OK, OK,' Sandell said. 'The comms must have been out, maybe.'

Luke nodded hard, like a boxer watching from behind his guard.

'Right, the comms system was out. But that wouldn't knock it out of the sky, would it? That just happened at the same time. I get the feeling that a lot of things went wrong on your plane, Sandy, all at the same time. What could do that?'

Sandell waved at the still-moving screen. 'The control system? Fine. So could several small bombs.'

Luke nearly laughed. 'Oh sure, that's very good, John' – it was John now and again. 'Somebody gets these several small bombs and he somehow fits them with timers which he miraculously knows how long to set for – either that or he wires them together – and he smuggles them aboard, let's not worry about how, it's only surrounded by a bloody small army whenever it's not in the air, and then he somehow plants one in the flight deck – you agree he's obviously got to put one of these several small bombs in the flight deck – and he plants the others inside fuel tanks or somewhere really simple like that, and then he figures out a way to set them all off when the plane's out over the middle of the Bering sea and then . . .'

'It was only a thought, Luke,' Sandell cut in. 'They're not paying me to come up with the thoughts.'

'Fine. That's fine.'

'It's not going to be easy to sabotage the control system either, Luke. It's going to be a damned clever trick to sabotage computers.'

'You don't need to sabotage a computer. In fact there's no point in sabotaging a computer. You know that.'

'And you know what I meant, you fucking clown. I meant it's got to be a very neat patch to the software. In fact a lot of large, neat patches to the software.'

Luke sighed like a dog. You half expected him to flop down with his chin between his paws and his eyes rolling about and his tongue out.

'I'll buy that. But then I didn't say the control system was sabotaged, did I? That was just a theory, remember. Another theory is that it just doesn't work properly.'

Luke noticed then that Sandell was sweating. Well, sorry pal, but it had to be said. Sandell got up stiffly, lit up with a weak smile for about a third of a second, and then left. Luke went back to his probing, feeling cold inside his stomach. He was going to firm this line up some, then he was going to try talking to human beings instead of this bag of bolts. Not that they'd be anything like as friendly.

All of a sudden, within a second or two, he felt bone weary. Thirteen hours wasn't his limit in fact, but it was good enough for day one, with a half-baked theory thrown in. He stood up, flicked off the monitor and walked out. Behind him, doors closed softly and automatically, and the big machine silently put away its files.

14

George didn't know he was in till she started catching the odd TV noise through the bathroom door. She stopped slithering up and down through the bubbles and cocked an ear. It sounded like one of her videos. One of her adult videos. George grinned and took another throw at the vodka bottle on the side of the bath.

'Luke?'

No answer. He'd heard her, though. She took another swill. The bathroom door clicked open and Luke leaned in, propped against the jamb. His jacket was open, his waistcoat was open, his tie was loose and his shirt was open too. He looked like he'd been dragged through a hedge.

'You sexy hunk of beef, you,' George said.

'You drink-sodden whore,' Luke said.

'Get in the bath,' George invited.

'No.'

Luke went back into the living room.

When George came out he was stretched out like a pole at one end of her big plush sofa. He had a huge scotch in one hand, full to the brim with crushed ice. He was waiting for it to melt. The glass was dripping with dew.

His free hand was thumbing through the book he had found on the floor. His lips were pursed and his eyebrows raised, the whole effect coming from having his chin buried in his chest.

George sat naked on the other end of the sofa and tucked

one ankle under a knee. For a long time she studied him unwinding.

He held up *Stereochemistry of Monoclonal Enzymes* for George to look at. 'Bit heavy by your usual tastes.'

'Steve'll be around to see me again. He can pick that up when he comes.'

'Which is when?'

'When he brings back my Pink Floyd compacts.'

'You lent him *those*?'

'Relax. He's OK. He'll bring them back. Or he doesn't get his book, right?' she added. For about half a minute, Luke stared at some numbers he had noticed jotted in the flyleaf. Then he snapped the book shut and tossed it aside.

George watched where it landed, then went back to watching him. He just looked dead ahead.

Great prospect you are, George thought.

'So what is it? A case?'

Luke pulled off his tie, flung it to the floor where he'd already dropped his jacket. Then he toed off his shoes and downed half the whisky and water in a swallow.

He just looked at her and she smiled. George could break a man's neck, but she had a beautiful smile. She could have sold things with her smile.

'I'm not good for much tonight, kid,' Luke told her.

'Come on,' she said, meaning who cared.

Finally he said, 'Yeah, it's a case. Did you hear about the plane going down in the Arctic?'

'Yes. Everybody's heard of the plane, lover. The AX–9 jetliner, it said in the news.'

'Yeh, right. The frigging AX–9 jetliner. Best thing in the history of aviation. Best thing since bloody Bleriot.'

'Since what?'

'Not what. Who.' Luke drank again. 'They'd like it to be sabotage, of course.'

'The makers, right?'

'Correct. Schaum. Oh, and my bosses in the Home Office, I nearly forgot them. The fuckers practically told me to make it up if necessary. Plant the evidence or something. Screw them.'

'I don't get you, Luke,' George said. 'OK, I get the bit about Schaum, right. It's their plane, so they don't want everybody thinking it's got something wrong with it. But where's the political interest?'

Luke Finn gave his sneaky smile.

'Government's a major shareholder in Schaum. About thirty per cent. Schaum use a lot of government money – that's public money, right. Protect your investment is the game. It makes me throw up.' Luke drained his glass. 'How'd your grand plan go down?'

'OK,' she laughed.

'What about your own people?'

'They're OK. They're very cool about it – now.'

'Too big a concept, right?' Luke said. 'They can't deny it's going to be good.'

'They're not trying,' she said softly.

They looked at each other for a long time, conversation unnecessary. Luke already knew he was going to give it a try whether he was good for it or not. That was going to be fine with her. Neither of them had any illusions about being Olympic-standard lovers. Neither of them considered humping to be life's number-one priority either.

He thumbed the TV remote to line. The undulating buttocks vanished in favour of the late news. Luke picked up the phone from the floor by his sofa and started to get his office number.

'I have to check my mail,' he told her. 'I haven't been in since this morning. Then we'll go and fuck, if we can.'

'Right,' she said. 'Right.'

'What's your softnet number?'

'How the hell should I know?' George knew she had one. Everybody who had the right TV could have one as long as they subscribed, and TCTV subscribed to all these crazy things for her, so she had one. But that was as far as it went with George. Softnet numbers were for game-playing computer buffs, which she wasn't.

Luke was using the remote, filling the TV screen with information, finding out. He punched in the number to his waiting machine.

Almost immediately his mail started to appear on George's TV screen. He glanced at each item of mail in turn, then put in the code for 'next', 'save', 'erase' or whatever.

'I thought you could actually talk to that thing of yours?'

'I can. Also I can phone it. Tonight I'm phoning it.'

George just shrugged. Why ask?

Suddenly Luke gave out with a big meaty laugh. Something on the screen had pleased him. George just had to read it.

PIG IS READY AGAIN was all it said. There was no return address, no sender ID, but Luke seemed to be delighted by it. He cleared the rest of the mail, sent his computer to bed and put down the phone. George was headed for bed already. She wasn't going to ask about pig.

They forgot to turn off the TV as they staggered out of the room. What they left behind was the rest of the news.

What the rest of the news mentioned was an incident that had occurred that afternoon in a naval dockyard in Portsmouth. A dockyard worker had suddenly blacked out while handling a giant crane that was hoisting smart shells for a one-hundred-and-eighty-millimetre gun on to a destroyer, and ended up smashing the whole lethal load clean through the ship's bridge. They weren't supposed to explode, and they didn't, but some people did some ducking and running just the same, and a few went over the side. One man died on the bridge, another was mangled by the crane and a third drowned in the dock. It was ugly as hell and the Admiralty didn't seem amused by the event so they were going to find out why it happened. Exactly why, they said.

15

Day: minus 7: Christmas Eve

As far as the Brass at Measons was concerned, Christmas Eve went totally sour at about seven thirty in the morning, London time. For it was then that the chief executive, having just consumed a splendid English breakfast, was in receipt of a phone call from some big noise in the Drugs Commission. This phone call informed him of a note from the Admiralty, of all people, concerning one of his products, the ever so recent, ever so marvellous Phenthanol. The navy doctors had put their finger on it with remarkable speed, by the simple but courageous expedient of taking the pills from the crane driver's pocket and trying a few. Four doctors had keeled over, on doses from two pills upwards to four, and with alarming speed. Not exactly a controlled experiment, but it took some ignoring. They had analysed some of the pills because it was easy, and the results were undeniable. Therefore, whether Measons liked it or not, the Drugs Commission was ordering its immediate withdrawal. All medical institutions, all doctors, all directly contactable retail outlets were to be notified immediately of its prohibition. Since the drug was generally available, warnings would be issued on radio and television to all persons holding the drug to refrain from its use and either to destroy what they had or take it to the police. In the meantime, Measons were ordered to undertake sample analyses of all stocks immediately, to cease all further production, and to prepare trace-backs of all batches already released to the market for correlation against returns from outlets. The phone call also mentioned that somewhere along the line, at some later stage, somebody had better be ready with some kind of explanation.

The chief executive went apeshit, naturally. He sent for his production director, his marketing director and his fiddlers three, and together they climbed up the wall. How could it happen? What about the field tests? What about the human volunteers, the rabbits and the rats? Somehow they just couldn't seem to console each other.

In the meantime the word had gone out to the nation. *Don't take Phenthanol* was on every pair of lips. Within hours the reports were coming back, mainly from the police and family practitioners, of victims of unexplained blackouts, many of whom weren't in a position to relate the tale themselves. There was a mangled cab driver from Paddington and a stripper from Soho who now gallantly performed her spot in a surgical collar. There were council officers, mates of death-leap electricians, mothers, husbands, teachers, soldiers, sailors. All kinds of folks had plunged horridly and unexpectedly into a sudden and comatose void, emerging with luck some time later, in the fortunate majority of cases.

The way it was shaping up, the chief executive and his senior board members were looking to take some of the damn stuff themselves. However, they were not permitted such a luxurious solution.

With every lab going full tilt at the job, the first random sample was in fast. The culprit was the Trinax of course, way over design level in what looked like one production run following the primary release just after the live field tests had been declared a success. Batch-wise it looked bad. As feared, the rogue production run went into a number of packaging batches and thence into a whole multitude of major distribution loads. In short, it had got everywhere geographically, except possibly the south-west tip of Cornwall and the sodding Isle of Mull, and it meant that the chances of ever selling one more single solitary pill out of the billion zillion they'd made, or of recouping one single sou of the mind-bending pile they'd spent on development, were about minus nil.

The air in the boardroom was heavy.

'Somebody's going to pay for this,' the chief executive stated, with total sincerity.

The various directors involved nodded in unison.

'You want an enquiry?' Production said.

'What I want is blood,' the chief executive told him. 'Lots of blood.'

There was a director of security there as well on this occasion. He hadn't said much yet. His plate looked pretty clean for the moment.

'It sounds like incompetence to me,' he opined, to nobody in particular. 'I can help in talking to people if it's a question of finding out just who.'

'Anybody's blood,' the chief executive added. He didn't seem to be hearing anything. He just stared into space, a man gone mad.

'Why assume incompetence?' Production said. 'We have some very fancy machinery down there in the factory. It's got the new auto-assay rig on it. It's not easy just to slip up. We can't afford for it to be easy in this game. Incompetence is something we prevent from being an issue.'

'Well what the hell does that mean? You're incapable of being incapable?'

'I want somebody hung up by the balls,' the chief executive muttered softly.

'What I mean,' Production said, 'is that we might have been sabotaged. It could have been deliberate.'

'Oh, I don't think so,' Security got in quickly, sensing the threat. 'That's a thing I very much doubt.'

'A breach of security is what I'm talking about,' Production emphasised. 'A deliberate penetration of our security procedures.'

'I said I can vouch for that,' Security hissed.

'I know you can,' Production went for it.

'Vouch for what?' the chief executive suddenly asked. 'What's that?'

He looked about somewhat wildly as if he had been kicked about the kidneys whilst asleep, his face a mixture of pain and surprise. So utterly paranoid did he appear that his board members beheld him as one would a satanic vision, surrounded by abysmal fire.

'Sabotage,' the chief executive said. 'Did you say sabotage?'

'For my money it's the most likely thing,' Production argued. 'It's a damned uncanny piece of bad luck otherwise.'

'Luck?' Security repeated incredulously. 'If it's not sabotage it's bad luck? What the hell happens to good old incompetence?'

'I just told you it's not an issue in a streamlined modern plant with hardly any fucking people in there . . .'

The chief executive told them both to shut their mouths. The plain fact was that sabotage was a possibility and it had to be investigated. Was it not the case that there were experts in this kind of thing and a Home Office department which controlled them? Get one in here, he commanded; turn one loose in here. I want blood.

That took another five hours or so. The board members had recovered and were awaiting what they imagined to be their avenger. He was late.

Their avenger turned out to be a very scruffy and diminutive fellow with a beard like George Bernard Shaw. Heavy horn-rimmed glasses sat like a giant spider across his nose, magnifying his merry little eyes so they seemed to consume most of his face. His teeth were bucked at the top, and his hair was all over the place, sprouting out and down like the foliage of a weeping willow.

The chief executive and his Savile-Row-clad entourage examined the avenger with amazement. His trousers, drainpiped and totally creaseless, hung a good four inches from the top of his safari boots, which were of pale brown leather and seemed to be the newest thing about him. A fairisle sweater blazed its iridescent message across his torso. He looked like one of those loons that pranced about near theatre queues on Coventry Street.

'Mister, er Wyke? How do you say that, if I may ask? Is that Wyke, as in candle?'

'As in dyke,' Mister Wyke said. 'But please call me Douglas.'

'Thank you,' the chief executive said. 'But we would prefer to stick with Mister Wyke – I'm sorry, *Wyke.*'

The avenger looked hurt. 'As you like,' said Mister Wyke.

'Please sit down, Mister Wyke.'

Douglas parked his butt in the nearest and most comfortable-looking chair. Now he crossed his knees, displaying a pair of chequered socks that made the directors' eyes smart, and laid one arm over the back.

'What I know is that your latest mass market product has been dealt a death blow.'

'That is correct,' Production said.

Douglas continued, 'What you are facing is a confidence disaster that affects not only this product – which is probably not redeemable under any circumstances, you realise that?' – they said they did – 'but also future products, and possibly even other products already on the market.' Douglas waited a mo, his perpetually gleeful face revealing nothing. 'A most unenviable position, gentlemen. If you have been sabotaged here, if what happened to Phenthanol was deliberate, then it's vital for that to be discovered and made public fact.'

'Yes,' the chief executive said. 'Yes, definitely. Yes, that's it.' What the hell else should he add? What's it worth to make something up? Name your price? Hell's bells, no; this tramp could be an honesty freak, he could react badly and land them in even deeper shit. He could even be a plant – a plant? The chief executive's mind lapsed into a kind of mania. What the hell kind of plant for God's sake? Was he going insane?

'There's no doubt of it,' Douglas said.

'Pardon?'

'I said there's no doubt of it,' Douglas repeated. 'In my own mind, I mean. I'm quite sure that something irregular is going on in this case. It's just a matter of finding the proof.'

The chief executive's soul leapt for joy.

'You're that sure? How can you be that sure?'

'Instinct,' Douglas told him. 'Honed by years of experience. Of course, proving it may be almost impossible.'

'Impossible?' The chief executive plunged back to despondency.

'Proof, as such, may not exist at all,' Douglas said lightly. 'It all depends on what you call proof.'

'Uh?'

'Yes,' Douglas said. 'If there is none, you sometimes have to provide it. Or at least, the next best thing to it.'

None of them had a clue what he was talking about by now. He was impressing the hell out of them, though, at least for the time being.

16

The man was on the defensive. Not surprising when you consider his age; he couldn't have been more than twenty-five, which struck Luke as pretty young to be that far up in his department. Sandell said he was a flyer. The way people talked, the whole world was lousy with flyers.

Also, Sandell had intro'd Luke as 'the investigator', which didn't exactly make people want to throw their arms about you at the best of times.

'Right,' Luke said. 'I get the business about the star net. Let's see if I can recap.'

Sandell leaned forward to listen, as if he intended asking questions to make sure Luke really did get what the senior designer in the AX–9 control system team had been saying.

'Sitting in the middle are the host processors. They're dual redundant with a hot standby tracking the online. Spoking out from that is the star highway out to the satellite subsystems. They hook via their communications processors, all dedicated I/Fs. Every subsystem that does I/0 to every other has a dedicated line servicing the link. OK so far?'

His hand stopped moving over the big whiteboard. A picture like a spider's web had appeared, but with crazy criss-crossings that no arachnid would construct. At the cross-overs, there were boxes with legends like 'FSS' and 'CSS'.

'Fine,' the young control expert said. Sandell just crossed his legs. Luke went on:

'If one subsystem needs to get another one to do something, it asks it direct. It also asks the host pair and the host pair pass on the message to verify the direct request. That means the host machines know all about what's going down, right? Question. Can the host machines initiate commands as well as underwrite them? Let's say subsystem A is something like the propulsion system and it's slowing the ship down so it wants the fuel system, that's B, to distribute fuel forward. So it sends this request to B to start pushing fuel around, and it sends the same request to the central host machine and that tells B it's OK to do it. That's the usual case. What I'm asking is, suppose the host machine just ups and tells B to do it off its own bat? A hasn't said a word. Is B going to obey that, or does it need two messages every time?'

'You got me,' Sandell said. 'Hell's teeth, Stan, he's got his nose into this. I'm impressed.'

Stan was impressed too. He looked at Luke suspiciously, as if he didn't want to say any more to this man, who appeared to soak up technical knowledge like a sponge. But Sandell gave him a reassuring little nod.

'It's going to do it provided the message from the host has a priority code in the frame,' Stan said eventually. 'The host machines can drive the satellite subsystems direct. They have to be able to for a number of reasons. Your A system might go down. That leaves your B high and dry. The host can sense that a system's down and take over its I/F to the others. Also your A might go nuts and send garbage. The host can overrule by not passing its dual message on and substituting its own commands with priority set. There are other reasons too. The host can handle crew commands centrally by this mechanism, for example. All kinds of reasons.' He shut up again.

Sandell said, 'Listen, er, when he said about a subsystem going nuts or going down, I don't want you to think we're designing around any suspect performance here. It's just a multi-level fallback mode, that's all. Safer than safe, right Luke?'

Luke thought, Multi-level what? Fucking hell, Sandy, if

it screwed up it screwed up. But his face was a mask, suffering all gladly, Sandell included.

'Maybe you designed something in though,' he said, 'or is this just too fanciful?'

'Is what too fanciful?'

Luke took a deep breath. 'Suppose you code a lethal scenario into your host. Say fuel feeds off, reversed elevons, a string of things like that. I don't know right, there must be any number of crazy things a pilot could do if he really wanted to lose a plane. Only you want the host to do it, so you arrange for the host to send out the orders with that priority stuff set, in response to some stimulus that you can predict. Something that's going to happen over the ocean, let's say. You could do that, couldn't you?'

The two men looked at each other. Sandell said, 'You'd have to reprogram both the central processors to be sure of that.'

'You'd have to reload the satellite processors too,' the control man said. 'At least some of the processors in some of the satellites. Otherwise they'd try to correct. If one started doing bad things, the others would start telling it to behave. That would happen fast, I should think. Odds are they'd control it.'

'But they've got to be OK'd by the host machine, haven't they?' Luke said. 'The host is the bad apple here. It could be coded to refuse to sanction their requests when they tried to correct each other.'

Stan gave a shrug. A slow, reluctant shrug.

'I suppose so. But it's a lot of fancy code in the host.' He started sucking his fingertip. 'I dunno. I still think you'd want to spike some of the satellite subsystems. Otherwise it's going to start fielding a lot of complaints from a load of pissed-off micros.'

John Sandell seemed to have sunk into a private reverie. His eyes watched Lucius Finn craftily. He was weighing it, on one side of his brain and the other.

'You seriously proposing this?' he asked quietly.

'Why not? It's a line of thought. What the hell else is there? Your small bombs?'

'There's the question of proof,' Sandell said. 'I mean a theory's fine, but it gets us nowhere.'

Luke pushed at the air with his flat hands, fingers spread out. 'Let's not jump to anything, Sandy. Let's just firm up on the theory first. There must be others we can come up with. We've got to pick the best one before we spend any time trying to prove it.'

Stan suddenly came to life again. It was as if he'd been in a tick-over mode and some fuse just ran out.

'Well I don't think this one's all that crazy in fact,' he blurted. 'I think Mister Finn's got a hold of something here. It's a possibility at least.' He started getting excited, visibly, as some other notion struck him. 'I mean, look at the prom seats, yes?'

Luke went, 'Uh?'

'That's just our term for it,' Sandell said. 'He means the eproms weren't glued in on the plane that was lost. The technicians might have wanted to try a few in flight tests with replacements. They would be fixed on a production machine, of course.'

'Of course,' Luke said.

What Sandell was gabbling about was the way the tiny microprocessor bugs were attached to the printed circuit boards of the computers in the aircraft. Normally these chips would be flow-soldered firmly into place. However, there was another way of mounting a chip, which consisted of just pressing it into place on a female hole array which for test purposes made it easy to pull the chip out of the circuit, just like pulling a plug from a socket. It also made it easy to plug in a different chip instead.

All very fanciful? Sandell had a doubting look.

'All right, suppose there's something in this,' he began. 'Let's look at the logistics of it.'

'There's no need for that yet, Sandy,' Luke butted in. 'I told you, there's other theories to be thought of first.'

'Sure sure,' Sandell said. 'But let's just run with it for a minute, because for me it sounds like small bombs, right?'

'How's that, Sandy?' Luke could taste a little tension here. Sandy hated to be on the fringe of a discussion, always had. He hated to be the one who wasn't contributing anything. Old Sandy just didn't like Luke and this Stan kid having all the ideas. He must be getting old, like all of us.

'Well listen,' Sandell said. 'Whoever did it, did it the way we said, yes? That means he or she's got to program a lot of little killer proms. He's got to develop the code that goes in them and he's got to blow them in. That takes time and it takes kit, yes? That means a risk. Also he or she's got to plug the damn things into the plane's computers. He's going to have to do it before she takes off, otherwise he has to go with it and do it in the air and then he kills himself. That means his sneaky proms have to pass all the pre-flight checks. It's a hell of a tall order if you ask me, Luke. In software terms it's a hell of a job.'

'It's still easier than the sodding bombs,' Luke said. 'I'm getting a pain over the bomb business, Sandy.'

'Not from a technical point of view it's not,' Sandell insisted. 'I'm sorry, Luke, but it's not. Maybe you've been in that job of yours too long.'

The control system expert began to protest, but he was wary of Sandell's seniority.

'Oh I don't know . . .' he started to say.

Sandell turned to him instead.

'Listen, Stan. Don't you think I'm keen to grab on this? Don't you think I want a sabotage theory? You don't *know* how much I want a sabotage theory. But it's got to be plausible, because there's no way we're going to prove anything with all the evidence at the bottom of the Bering sea.'

'I don't agree,' Luke said. 'I don't think it's that bad. If you said that you'd never prove any of the technocrimes we have to deal with.'

'So how do you prove a thing?' Sandell said quietly.

'It's like you said, Sandy,' Luke told him. 'People do these things, people. Whatever the technique that's used, it's always people in the end. That's why you have to get the theory right because you go from the right theory to the right people. Then you talk to them. If they're the right people, you'll find out.'

'How?' Very soft. Yeh, how, both pairs of eyes said.

'That's my business,' Luke said, and it looked as if he meant it.

17

Day: minus 6: Christmas Day

If you've bullied/persuaded your team to come in and work on Christmas Day then maybe you should go easy for once. You could well think that. It would be natural. Not George, though.

By the time a few days had slipped through her claws without much by way of actual results, George got the message that maybe she was pushing this a little hard. After all, there had to come a point, if you pushed people too hard, when they just pretended to do things so they made you think they were on the move. There had to be an optimum level of push where you held your lackeys at peak productivity.

Then George thought again and decided that was all balls. The problem was that people needed pushing harder. That was *always* the problem with the dickheads she had working for her, always would be. George decided to push harder.

First she had a real good scream at Artistic. She owed that shitkicker one, and this was as good a time as any. She took Artistic apart in front of the rest of the team so they'd know what to expect when it was their turn. She demanded to know what his ideas were for making this event look good. 'Look good?' he'd said, plaiting his hair. 'That's out of the question, darling.' George growled things about ideas on how to make it visually exciting. 'Ideas?' he'd replied. 'I thought ideas were your department, lover. You're the great one for concepts, hahaha.' George threatened death, Artistic sulked, George told him he could walk.

It lasted an hour and then he came to his cake with a few fancy ideas about the commercials. George reconvened so they could all watch him squirm, all anxious to please, *look how I'm trying*. My, but they were embarrassed by it, George noted with glee. Things would speed up a little now.

While they broke their balls, George started reviewing the reactions of the firms in Centre Point. Oh sure, it was really PR's job and she was sharing it, but George knew she was good at this. One or two MDs had listened to the walk-through on the phone and then OK'd it right away. No, that's fine, they said. There's no need to come and spell it out. But others went all suspicious, guard up right away. You want to do what? You mean we'll be, like blacked out or something? What cables? To power what screens? Well, if they've got to run through the office, I don't know. There weren't that many awkward ones, but it only took one to get really sullen about it.

She had spoken to about six of them (all brought round in the end). After checking this off, George succumbed to her growing suspense over Steve. All right, it was dumb, she'd never chased her kid brother around before. But she was speaking to him one night and then she couldn't raise him at all. He's not at work, he's not been there for days, he's not on his own number, so where is he? And where's the frigging Pink Floyd?

George stepped out of her cab and felt the sharp bite of the tiny snowflakes on her face. It had started on her way round there from Cambridge Circus, little pinpricks on the cab windscreen that didn't wipe out for the blades, they just congregated in two lines on the side, and they crackled as they got shovelled off. It was damn cold, that was what. George pulled up her fur collar about her face, breathing into it as she walked, so her breath warmed the tip of her nose. As her knuckles began to ache, she wished she had some gloves with her.

Steve's flat was in a huge old house which was one of a Georgian row, decaying and peeling on the outside but very comfortable within. A lot of rich folks bought these terraces en bloc and then knocked out adjoining walls to form suburban mansions. George had always had a yen to do that some day, a suburban mansion was all she'd ever have, you wouldn't find her rotting in some country pad.

The caretaker said he hadn't seen Steve in days, though he himself wasn't here all the time, only six till six.

'His flat's at the top, isn't it?' George said, starting up.

The caretaker followed her arthritically, resisting an urge to grasp her rump. George had a graspable rump, even with a heavy topcoat cladding over it.

'It's a long day is six till six,' he wheezed. 'I generally see everybody some time in a day.'

'You know the lad I mean, though?'

'Who, Steve? Yer, I know Steve. He's a scientist is Steve.'

'Right. He's my brother,' George told him, rounding a landing.

'Oh yeh. Well, he's all right in't 'e. Mind you, there's some rum lads in this place, I can tell yer. He's all right though, he's . . .'

'Up here?'

'Yeh, keep going. Right up till there's no more stairs. I was sayin', he's not a loud sort, your brother. I never had no trouble with him.'

They were right at the top of the house, on a long dark landing with a skylight in the ceiling and an old red carpet. Several doors led off it. The caretaker shuffled past her and down to the end one.

'I suppose you want to go in?'

'I want to go in, yes. But we might as well knock first.'

So George knocked. Four times. And then she waited and knocked four more times.

'OK, let me in.'

The way she was talking to him, he'd have been out of his mind to argue. She sounded like a bailiff.

The caretaker stood outside, peeping round the door, as George went into her brother's flat and looked around. Immediately she felt strange.

The place was dark, because curtains were drawn, both here and in the bedroom beyond. She stooped and switched on a table lamp. Then she stayed where she was for a while, just looking around.

It was cold in here, she realised now. Colder than the landing, colder than the rest of the house. There was a meter behind the door which drove the electrical central heating, and it had a coin slot in the top, one of those things that allows you to shove the same coin in over and over again so you're never stuck for one, but it counts how often you use it. It read zero, unfed, ungiving. The gas fire in the elegant old fireplace was dark and cold. The place had not been heated for a while, obviously.

A coat lay over the settee by her side, but it wasn't the windcheater she usually pictured him in, the one Steve was wearing when he borrowed her Floyd disks.

They were there. On the coffee table by the lamp. All of them, just as he took them from her. In her mind's eye she could see him going out of her door with them under his arm. The one on top then was the one on top now. In his bedroom the bed was unused. In his wardrobe a few clothes hung neatly. But not enough of them, not enough shoes, not enough clean shirts. She dived into the bathroom.

The sink was dry, the soap was hard and crusty, the bath was chalky to the touch.

His toothbrush hung from its rack. Very slowly, feeling a little sick, she reached out and touched it with the very tip of her forefinger. Then she let her hand move over it and rubbed her thumb against its bristles. There was not a trace of dampness on it.

George stood there in the bedroom of her young brother and listened to the little snowflakes ticking against the window pane and began to feel something tightening up inside her.

18

Luke was over at her place again when she got back, drinking her booze again. She was really glad he was there. As he sat and sipped and watched her TV, she had tried to put words to it.

'You never worried about him before,' Luke said, still watching the TV screen. 'Not since I've known you.'

George was wringing her hands in an uncharacteristic way. She had her elbows on her lap, her knees together and her feet on the floor, like a matron suffering from some minor chill.

'I know. Yes, that's true. I just wanted to tell him to take care of those Floyd disks. Only I couldn't get hold of him. And then it just went on.'

'What went on?'

'Well . . . not being able to get hold of him. I kept trying and he just wasn't anywhere.'

Luke started fishing for a cigar.

'He's just gone off for a few days. So what?'

'Well they don't know about it at his firm. They don't know where he is either. Neither does his landlord. And if he's gone off somewhere he didn't take his toothbrush. And his soap. And his overcoat . . .'

Luke frowned now.

'How do you know that? You've been to his place?'

'Of course I've been to his place.' God but he could be slow. For an intellectual giant, he could be damn slow. 'I was there a couple of hours ago.'

Pause. Mutual wait. Luke said, 'And?'

'And it's like, well . . .' She put her hand over her eyes for a moment, and in that gesture Luke saw the real extent of her concern. 'It's horrible, Luke . . .'

Luke turned to her now, moving along the sofa a little way. He remembered to bring an ashtray with him. 'Listen kid, just relax. What is it that's horrible?'

She told him as best she could about the sick thing that welled up inside her in that cold flat with the snow whispering at the window, and the feeling she had that her brother had dissolved into its very walls like a captive ghost.

He didn't speak after she ran out of steam. He just watched her, as he often watched people after he'd let them talk themselves to a standstill. It was one of many interviewing-cum-interrogation techniques; see what else is there. There's always something else there.

'I must be losing my fucking grip,' was what George finally offered. 'You want some rotten bloody coffee?'

'Yeh. Get us some coffee, kid.'

She practically ran into the kitchen. Luke wasn't overly concerned about her. Being a hard case, George would surface pretty quickly, swearing and spitting. But this thing about Steve looked odd . . .

His eye fell on the book again.

She hadn't moved it from the spot where he'd placed it the other night. Luke picked it up again, opened it one-handed as was his way with books. Forgotten by chance. Never reclaimed. *The Stereochemistry of Monoclonal Enzymes* . . .

Twenty-two numbers. Luke counted them out of habit.

Quantities of what? No units to say.

Meaningless.

He put the book down again.

She came back in with the coffee as the late news started on the TV. Luke sat with his mug in his hand, the cigar between his teeth, and said nothing still, not until she went for the switch.

'Leave it on, George.'

'What? You want to watch TV? You don't want to talk about little me and my kid brother? Well, that's very . . .'

'George. That's not it. Just leave it, please. I want you to watch something.'

She worked for the biggest and flashiest news-gathering machine on the planet but somehow she didn't know. Well, maybe she'd been busy, what with her brainstorming extravaganza in the making. Maybe he should just let it come on again and keep quiet till it did.

And then, maybe not.

'George, you haven't heard about what happened at your brother's firm?'

'What?' She looked distracted, about to panic maybe. An explosion? A riot? Was *that* what had happened to her brother? 'What happened?'

'Measons released some new pills,' Luke told her. 'Some kind of headache pill. I don't know. Anyway, it's some terrific new drug, big thing and all. It turns out they made a mistake with these pills. Or maybe somebody did something deliberate to them. It turns out they're dangerous. People have been killed, they don't know how many yet. The pills are being withdrawn. They've had warnings on radio and TV, regularly, at peak times.'

George Maringelli went white. 'Oh my God. He was working on that pill. I mean he'd finished working on it. I mean . . .'

'I thought so,' Luke said quietly.

'He was really proud of what he'd done. It was the first thing he did when he came out of college. It gave him a big kick, seeing something he'd helped with going out in the shops. It was . . .'

Luke wasn't so much listening to the content of what she was saying as the style. All those 'was doing this' and 'had done that'. As if he was dead. It was the way you'd talk about somebody if you were fondly remembering them after their funeral. Luke was bothered by that, and so caught by it that he didn't fully realise she'd stopped in midstream and was glaring at him with her lip up, like a cornered bitch.

'What the fucking hell do you mean, you *thought* so?'

'I didn't mean anything but that.'

Luke feigned interest in his cigar, which had gone out.

'Oh, I get it. You just put two and two, right? He's got something to do with this pill business and now he's done a disappear, yes? You've got a bad mind, Luke, a lousy bad mind.'

It was coming on. First the blank screen, then the message 'important announcement'. Then the voice, warning, informing, asking you to pass it on. Then the repeat, with the whole thing written on the screen for the hard of hearing. Then a few more words about what to do for the poor sap next to you that just swallowed his Phenthanol. How to make him honk up, that kind of thing.

George had gone from white to something beyond white, to something akin to transparent.

'I bought some of that stuff,' she said, almost inaudibly.

Luke went bolt upright.

'You *what*? Have you taken any?'

'No. I don't think so. Well, maybe.'

'Well, did you?'

'Yes,' she said quickly. 'Yes, I have taken some. But it didn't do any harm. I mean I don't think so.'

'How many?'

'How many what?'

Luke forced himself to be patient.

'How many did you take?' he said, spacing it out.

'I don't know.'

'Get the bottle, George,' He stood up. 'Just tell me where the bottle is. Bathroom? Handbag?'

'Handbag. Under the phone. Listen, Luke, I feel fine, really.'

'Shut up, George.'

He came back with the brown bottle in one hand and the box in the other. This was a small bottle of twenty, so she couldn't have swallowed many.

'How many'd you take?' he said again.

'Two or three. Whatever it says.'

It said two or three.

'Give any to anybody else?'

'No. Definitely.'

There were something like seventeen inside. Maybe she was lucky. Maybe this bottle wasn't from a bad batch. He eased off inside. Part of him was marvelling at how concerned he was for her.

And he went on reading the label.

That was some list of ingredients all right. Some names were short, others so long they were unreadable, with more syllables than an Aztec god. Others were common things that even he could recognise, such as chalk. That would have to be the base material, surely. Without knowing why, because it was his habit, Luke counted them.

Twenty-two.

Uh? Luke grabbed the book again from the floor where he had put it. *Twenty-two?*

'What're you doing, Luke?' She seemed to be settling again, drinking her coffee.

'Just a minute.'

He was comparing the numbers scrawled on the flyleaf of Steve Maringelli's book with the numbers against the ingredient list on the bottle. No resemblance, apparently. For a few seconds he hung up, but he was too quick, too long in the game to be held off it for long. The numbers on the bottle were exact weights. They were just a list of how many milligrams of this or that you get in a tablet. They meant nothing if you didn't know the weight of a tablet, and to get that you had to add them up. If you did that, and then you divided that number into each of the twenty-two, then you had the percentages by mass of the ingredients.

'Got a calculator?'

Luke flashed through the arithmetic, scribbling his calculated numbers into the book, alongside the numbers there already. One thing Luke always had was a pen, usually several.

They weren't in the same order in both lists, but he could match them now, almost but not quite exactly.

Because two were different. From his own list, Luke could say what they were. The base material, chalk or whatever it was, was down on what the bottle said by quite a bit, but the other one, the Trinax ingredient, well that was way over the percentage claimed on the bottle. Orders of magnitude over.

'Is this your brother's writing?' Luke was pointing to the first list of numbers in the book.

'It's his book.'

'We know that. Is it his writing?'

She looked, squinted, shrugged.

'I guess so. Why?'

So he explained it to her. Very carefully, that this list of figures her brother had written in his book, and left in a car, *before* the thing became public knowledge, was a description of the very pills that had slain an unknown but growing number of innocent people.

He explained that as steadily as he could. Then he said, 'You tell me. Did he or didn't he know, the night he came here, what I say he knew?'

George swallowed and said, 'Yes.'

Luke said, 'Now tell me. Why do *you* think he's disappeared?'

'You mean, did he *do* that? Are you asking me if he's guilty of something? Shit, Luke . . .'

'Easy, George,' Luke warned, 'I'm asking you to help me with your knowledge of the kind of man your brother is.'

'He wouldn't hurt anybody,' she said.

'Would he run away from a mistake? Would he go and hide if he'd done something that would hurt people by accident? Even if by admitting it he could prevent more people being hurt?'

'He wouldn't run away,' she said definitely.

'All right,' Luke told her gently, and in his mind he wondered if Steven Maringelli had indeed said what he knew to somebody. That meant certain things that George shouldn't hear. Not now.

'What're you going to do, Luke?'

He thought for a while. He could just turn this stuff in to OTC or he could get involved. Getting involved was something he owed to George, but it was not easy via OTC. They'd tell him to stand back. Not your case, they'd say, especially that creep DeJohn, who was waiting like a vulture for some kind of crumb to come out of the AX–9 case.

There was always a way though.

Luke started using her telephone, as he had before.

'Who're you ringing, Luke?'

'My computer. I want it to do something for me.' He kept knocking in codes as she waited for him to go on. 'I'm going to get it to interrogate another computer in the OTC department in Lupus Street. They're my government watchdogs, right?'

'I know.'

'It'll take a while. It may not work at all. There may not be a name yet.'

'What name?'

'The name of the man who's working on the Measons case. Sooner or later there's got to be one, and he'll either come from OTC or he'll be like me, one of their untouchables. Only I still might not screw it out. My program doesn't always get through their traps.'

She smiled faintly, for the first time in a while.

'What you're doing is sneaky, isn't it?'

'Everything I do is sneaky. I'm a sneaky person.'

Something appeared on the screen. A message, saying obscure things about correlations. It seemed that the word 'Meason' had correlated, as had the word 'Phenthanol'. Luke's finger continued playing over the screen. It formed a word. Was it a name, George wondered.

'Wyke,' Luke said, grinning hugely. 'Well I'll be . . .'

'Is that the man? Is that the man who's on it?'

'That's him.'

'Who is he?'

Luke gave her another big grin and said, 'He's a genius. He's also a very old friend of mine that you'd have had to meet in the end. I had a message from him the other night when I used your TV as a monitor. A message about a pig. Remember, George?'

'So what about it?'

'It's time we replied.'

George said, 'Who's we?'

Luke grinned his sneaky grin.

'Me and worm.'

George went, 'Shhh . . .'

Luke contemplated the screen, wondering.

'I met him ten years ago. We stay in touch. We've got this game we play.'

'If he's your friend I should meet him. You don't have many friends, Luke. Neither of us does.'

'He's crazy,' Luke said. 'He lives in the East End, the bit of it that's still a frigging slum. He's got a machine makes mine look like a toy. Saved up a year's pay to buy it. Doesn't believe in bank loans.'

'So he's nuts. Sounds like fun.'

Fun! Luke snorted at it. Was Douglas fun? The man was a renowned weirdo to nearly every TI in town. Most of them were scared shitless of him, but none of them knew him like Luke did. If knowing was what you could call it.

Finn and Wyke had come into the TI business about the same time and worked on a few early cases together. They had prejudices in common and that had been enough to form a friendship of sorts. It was a strange one though, because Douglas Wyke was something else.

He was brilliant all right. He did things on his computer that were as far out as any research lab's efforts, and a lot of it he published. More than once he'd been offered an academic post, though he had always refused. There was a Wyke model of something or other, Luke couldn't just recall what.

Douglas had some pretty deep interests in life, most of which left Luke arctic cold. Music was one, strictly classical, strictly live only. Hifi he had none, but he'd spend two hundred on a first-night ticket at the Festival Hall, turning up in his one faded suit with a worn-out jumper under it and boots on his feet. Sculpture was another. Once, when the National Gallery had David on loan from Florence, Wyke had dragged Luke to see it (never get another chance, man, *please*) explaining how Michelangelo had used this piece of badly cut marble to create the famous twisted stance. 'See how he looks to his left,' he had said. 'The left is sinister, Luke. Evil comes at you from the left.'

How would Wyke think of this thing then? How would he spot the evil here?

Luke keyed in one more longish number, and then George's TV screen went blank. Then a white patch appeared in the middle of the screen and bounced off the bottom as if taking a bow. Luke lifted the receiver to his mouth and started to talk to his computer.

'This is a message for pig,' he said slowly, and his words appeared on the screen. Behind him, George ran her hands over her upper arms as if cold, though the room was warm. 'So is worm,' Luke said after a pause, and then, after a second pause, 'Message ends.'

Then he dropped the phone, fingered in some more stuff to put his computer to sleep and turned to George again. He was smiling, but only for appearances' sake.

19

Day: minus 5

The technicals pranced about among the cables like those south sea dancers who hop around between ankle-high poles that the rest of the troupe use to try and cripple them with. Sixty metres away. McEwen stood with his hairy arms crossed, gnawing a spanner. George noticed a couple of things; firstly that her own technicals seemed to be sustaining their enthusiasm, and that was a thing that pleased her troubled mind, and secondly that there were other people here, other technicals who undoubtedly hailed from the firms they had used, the laminate people and the laser people and what not, and their presence here at the demo meant they'd have to know the plan, and though that was possibly unavoidable it had been done without her sanction being sought, which meant it was going to cost somebody their left ball.

Right, so get on with it, George told them silently. While she waited, she looked around because somewhere high above, a pigeon clattered across the ceiling.

The old Palace was gutted now, and had been for years. They kept saying they were going to rip the place down, but it hung on somehow. The decrepit old shell had its uses still, as a place to do large things in. It was what they wanted for today. She was getting brassed off with waiting, though.

'You ready yet?'

'Nearly,' Technical pimply leader said. 'We're powering the lasers now.'

The lasers had to be the two things in big white metal

boxes with what looked like gun muzzles on one end, pointed at the huge scaffolding arrangement a hundred metres away by the end wall, whereon were mounted a hundred laminated screens in a ten by ten, edge to edge array. Nowhere near as many as they'd need on the day, but this was just a demo. This composite screen wasn't as high as it would be on the skyscraper either, but as they'd told her already, the lasers would be further away then, so the angle of elevation would be the same.

McEwen had already shinned up the scaffolding to examine the fixing arrangements behind the screen sections. He'd need a few minor mods to those was his conclusion, to lock them to Centre Point (he'd shinned up *that* already).

Technicals of one shape or another had tried to explain the laser system to George, when she'd asked, but not a hundred per cent of it had gone in. They'd had the side of one of the white metal boxes off and showed her. See those glass wheels? Well if you look edge on you see they vary in thickness. One spins vertically, the other horizontally, but one goes about a hundred times faster than the other. What they do to the laser beam is just what the electrical fields across the deflector plates do in the TV sets. They swing it up and down and side to side, right? Right, George had said, just like in a TV set, and in her mind she's saying to herself, don't knock it, you work in television so you must know how the damn things work.

As long as they got it right, that was all.

This demo was going to be live. They'd arranged for a radio camera to be hauled around Oxford Street and the flics piped up to a van on the hill outside.

'We're ready now,' pimply leader announced. 'You might like to stand behind the lasers, just as a precaution.'

'Fine,' George said.

'I think Mister McEwen might be well advised to move over a little too.' McEwen was standing in what he clearly imagined was going to be a position akin to that of a cinema audience, just under the projector beam. Evidently, he had not considered the prospect of being decapitated by it. Though the truth was, the lasers weren't that intense, they wouldn't have done his retinas a world of good, however.

'McEwen can look after himself,' George said.

'Right,' Technical said, and then he waved to the man by the door about forty metres on the right and he in turn waved at somebody in the van outside, who in turn radioed the man on the hoof in Oxford Street with the radcam. Then the man on the door closed it and threw a big lever switch that lowered all the lights in the place.

Technical brought on the beams with a couple of red buttons.

George couldn't believe it.

A live picture had appeared on the giant screen. A thirty-odd by thirty metre moving image was cavorting before their eyes. People walking up to the street camera, waving to it, peering into it, laughing at it and making the cameraman shake it about. As it swung left, the whole of Oxford Street suddenly whizzed across right, in instantaneous perspective. George wondered why everybody wanted to leer into the lens today, showing their goddamned fillings. Then she remembered she was only seeing the central one twentieth of the picture that the lasers were transmitting, because of the limited screen, and the radcam operator naturally centralised on faces when there were faces about. And then she realised what a sight it was going to be on the big screen. You were going to get the Australian Prime Minister on Centre Point, the size of King Kong.

'Far out,' George breathed.

'What do you think?' Technical asked loudly, over the buzz of the deflector drives. 'You like it, eh?'

'I think it's heavy,' George said. 'It's really heavy.'

She was smiling again. Oh yes, George was back online again now.

20

↑ SS BATTLECODE SIMULATOR PROMPTING BS

'Loaded,' Luke said. 'Which corner you want?'
'Blue,' Douglas said.
'Then I'm red.' Luke held his hands up by his face and wiggled his fingers like a safecracker. In went the commands. For a second, nothing happened on the monitor, then:

↑ BS BLUE PIG VS REDWORM – – – STARTING

'Here we go,' Luke said. 'This time your boy gets really screwed. You just watch.'
'I am watching,' Douglas said. 'We're both watching. There's nothing else to it but watching.'
And there wasn't. There really wasn't anything else to this game but watching, not from this point on anyway.
Luke Finn and Douglas Wyke both sat back in Luke's easy chairs, one with his feet up by the VDU screen, the other in a half-lotus, and settled down for a longish wait. If they were lucky, that was. The last few encounters had been mainly long, and getting longer, but there'd been the odd swift kill here and there.
This had been developing for years on and off.
Way, way back in the mid-eighties, a few men and women in a very clued-up computing department in the USA suggested this kind of game. They in turn based their idea on an old chestnut of a yarn that had been around in software lore for years, even then. According to this fable,

there was once a certain firm that had a big computer on which its big system of programs ran all the time. So heavily dependent was this firm on this system of software magic, that they just couldn't afford for it to stop working. If it ever did, they'd go belly-up within a day. Now they had this programmer working for them who got a bad case of the hump following a disagreement with his employers. So the kid went, but before he did, he left them a present: a little program that he loaded in the machine and set it like a time bomb to start running a couple of hours after he'd gone. When it did run, it ran for just a few micro seconds and then it went to sleep again for a couple of hours more. And the sole thing it did when it ran, its one and only function, was to create a copy of itself. So a couple of hours later, you got two of the things waking up, and of course, being exactly the same, they both did the same thing and so you got two copies more which made four. A couple of hours later, four went to eight, then eight to sixteen, and so on every couple of hours.

The kid that lit this fire called his dumb but nasty little program Creeper, and before long Creeper clones were beginning to fill up the system though nobody realised it yet. And the system was beginning to feel the strain. First off, the big, not-so-frequently-run programs started getting missed because they couldn't fit into the machine any more. Daily stocktakes didn't get taken. Midnight printout reports didn't get printed. The company staff wondered why, and Creeper just went proliferating. Then the smaller programs started suffering, the fast, efficient realtime modules that kept the company responding to clients' orders and the flow of cash. Pretty soon, hardly any of the software was getting any kind of bite at all at the CPU, because every damn thing on the scheduler queues was coming up a Creeper.

At this point one illustrious member of the system staff figured out the problem, though God knows you'd have thought they could have found it before then. But what to do? According to the tale, they couldn't afford to shut the system down and reboot because firstly they couldn't be without it (though they were losing it anyway) and secondly, they'd got no guarantee that Creeper wasn't also lurking on the system disk, waiting to kick the whole thing off again. What was needed was a cure. And the cure, as the heroic staff programmers realised, was to fight fire with fire.

It wasn't hard to dump out a hunk of memory and by checking the repeating hexarrays, figure out what Creeper looked like. Having done that, they wrote Reaper. Reaper was a program whose sole function was to keep on scanning the memory areas looking for copies of Creeper, and whenever it found one, to zap it flat by zeroing out the bytes. Reaper was a Creeper hunter, turned loose to nail Creeper for them. But of course, there was no guarantee that Reaper was going to make it. It could get a Creeper when it found one all right, but as long as there were Creepers left they kept on multiplying, so a chance existed that sooner or later, Reaper itself would be squeezed out, just like the system. It all came down to whether Reaper could nail Creeper before Creeper nailed Reaper. What they had was a battle, and the outcome was both unpredictable and out of their hands. All they could do was let Reaper get on with it and hope for the best.

Of course, the story went that Reaper prevailed in the end and all was well. As a story it had a certain popularity but its accuracy was more than doubtful, because for a number of good reasons, nobody was ever so helpless that such a thing was possible (though plenty of people got almost as dependent on their machines without really knowing it). But as an *idea*, it seemed like a new generation of computer game. Not one of those crummy little man eats ghost or ball breaks wall things, but a real game, a *war* game. It wasn't a game you bought, nor was it a game you even played. It was a game with but one law, to kill or be killed, and what you did was write the players.

Programs that fought against programs. The battle-ground: the memory of the computer. The rule: each program tries to write garbage into the code of the other, so the other can't be understood by the CPU and gets wiped out. The techniques: whatever the programmer can dream up, offensive, defensive, you name it. When the notion of battle programs first came up, the techniques were elementary. Each of the two warring programs would run under the control of a battle master, an environment simulator. Each would take turns to have one of its instructions executed by the CPU. They would do simple but nasty things like lobbing non executable instructions at each other, moving their own locations in the memory and so on. There was a great deal to learn about these things to begin with. It was a game for the aficionados.

Things had come a long way since then.

Lucius Finn and Douglas Wyke had got into this a long while back. Douglas had developed his fighting program, called *pig*, over a period of years, and Luke's champion, elegantly named *worm*, had a similar pedigree. Each man guarded the details of his binary warrior jealously.

The game was on. According to *battlecode* (the referee and arbiter of doom), *pig* got first move and did an immediate shift, sneaking off to some other part of memory from where it had been loaded. Luke found this jump interesting. Obviously Douglas thought Luke had figured out a way of getting *worm* to wangle *pig's* loadpoint from *battlecode*. He hadn't, that was probably beyond him, but something in the last game must have made Douglas think he was able. Hmmmmm . . .

↑ BS REDWORM SCH 2

'That won't work,' Douglas scoffed. 'I'm telling you that's not on.'

Luke bit a lip. Shit, if he said it wasn't going to work then he was wise to the two small programs *worm* had scheduled to report back every time they ran to a couple of secret locations in memory. They were scouts. Expendable and cheap. If either of them didn't report, *worm* would know that *pig* had nailed them, and then it would figure out, by sending more sacrificial scouts, what *pig's* movements were. Exit *pig*. But Douglas had seen the move and recognised it. That meant *pig* could either nail a scout without leaving a trace, which was surely impossible, or it could tell the difference between *worm* and one of its worthless scouts. That could mean it knew what *worm* looked like. Hellfire . . .

↑ BS BLUEPIG RD ALL

Douglas smirked. Luke boiled deep in his belly. The rotten thing was scanning. It was using all its CPU cycles just to read memory. It knows, oh fuck. Oh fuck, *pig* knows what *worm* looks like . . . Aaarghhhh!

↑ BS REDWORM MV

Aha! *Worm* had moved now. That was cute. Luke was surprised and pleased. There was randomness built into his code. Sometimes he played a wild card. He knew Douglas looked down on wild card techniques. Douglas was a general of the old school, a lover of algorithms, a hater of heuristics. Anyway, *worm* had done the safe thing for now.

'You jammy sod!' Douglas snorted. 'You jammy rotten sod! That was a pure fluke.'

'No it wasn't. You underestimate my expertise in the field.'

'Propaganda!'

'Suit yourself. But a good commander doesn't underestimate his opponent. My boy's fighting my rules.'

'Hurrrr.'

They laughed and poured another drink. Through the silent labyrinth of the memory of Luke's computer, through the million pathways of its semiconductor maze, *pig* stalked *worm* with logic bomb and binary bullet, and round random corners of its myriad tunnels and gates, *worm* coiled and hid and laid ambushes and booby traps of recursive zerowriter code and trap functions.

The conversation began to roam.

'So what do you think of those numbers?' Luke asked casually.

Douglas glanced at *Stereochemistry of Monoclonal Enzymes*. 'What am I supposed to think? It's a plain fact. He knew about the duff batch. He had to.'

'So how do you read it, Doug?'

'You mean him not being here any more, this Maringelli bloke?'

'Yeh. You reckon what I reckon?'

'You mean he's been and had something nasty done to him? Yes, I think that, if that's what you reckon.'

'He's not implicated?'

'In what?'

'In screwing up the pills, dammit. Making the bad batch?'

Douglas yawned and slurped his whisky and soda.

'We're assuming it was deliberate and not an accident, but I think that's right. Also I think your bird's brother wasn't in on it. If he was, why write those figures on his book? And why not disappear more – uh – elegantly?'

'Right,' Luke said. 'Agreed.'

'You've told her all that?'

Luke shook his head. Hard.

Douglas just pursed his mouth and said, 'Suit yourself,' as if it was all the same to him, which it probably was. He lurched forward to look at the VDU screen.

```
↑ BS BLUEPIG RD 10 WZ 10
↑ BS REDWORM MV
↑ BS BLUEPIG WZ 20
↑ BS REDWORM RD 5
↑ BS ***BATTLECODE: WT REDWORM ***
```

Douglas pointed triumphantly. He spilled some whisky in the process.

'Your thing's requesting an adjournment, Luke. You've been hit. Hoho.'

Luke grunted. 'Not so fast. We ain't down yet.'

'Give it up. You lose again.'

'Naw. Not yet.'

They both stared. Luke knew he still had a chance. It looked like *worm* had caught one all right. A write zero, one of *pig's* last spread of twenty, had struck home. Now it was weighing up the alternatives. It could repair itself, which swallowed cycles and would leave it in the same place for another sideswipe from *pig*, and that one might floor it for good, or it could cut off its damaged portion and jump away what was left, like a lizard leaving behind its tail. *Worm* wasn't called *worm* for nothing, it could do that. It couldn't regrow its tail like a lizard, but it could function in separate bits, because that was Luke's latest secret weapon, section re-entrancy.

↑ BS REDWORM MV

'Huh?' Douglas nearly came out through his horn-rims. 'It can't *do* that. It's not possible. Batcode doesn't allow that.'

'It just did.'

'How? How did you do that?'

'Figure it out,' Luke purred.

Douglas Wyke grinned like a sly old weasel. 'I will,' he said.

On went the war.

As it raged, Luke leaned towards Douglas and rolled his glass between his palms. His feet were off the desk by now.

'Listen, Doug. I want you to let me in on this case of yours. You know why now.'

Douglas just said, 'Sure. If that's what you want.'

'I know you can handle it. I just want to know what's going on. She wants me to do it and I want to do it.'

'If OTC find out they'll get shitty.'

'We can stuff them, can't we?'

'Right.'

Luke poured again.

'So what's your next move?'

'Obvious isn't it? Whoever's at the back of this wants people to think that your bird's brother has just skipped

134

as the guilty party. We don't let on we know he analysed some of the bad stuff and we wait to see who slips up at question time.'

'I'd like to help,' Luke said.

'Pleasure,' Douglas said.

'What about your *nark* stuff? Going to use it on this case?'

'I wouldn't think it was necessary,' Douglas said. 'Anyway, it's a real bind, using that.'

'I didn't think so, last time I saw you run it.'

'Aw, it's a whore,' Douglas said demurely. 'It's just like OTC's thing. It never cuts up with anything without you break your balls.'

Douglas was just being modest. Luke knew that. He had this piece of code he'd written that fell under the general heading of artificial intelligence; *nark*, it was called, and it helped you to solve crimes. Home Office had fancier versions they'd developed on bigger databases, and OTC had one of their versions in research, where the smoothy DeJohn ruled. Douglas Wyke's effort didn't have the encyclopedic knowledge base of the government software, but at least it had been written by a genius. Given data to chew on, it could make some very nice deductions. A regular mains voltage detective was *nark*.

'It's better than OTC's version,' Luke offered.

It looked like the end of the converstaion for now. Things seemed to have come to a dead stop at the VDU.

'Aw, shiiiiiit,' Luke bawled. 'Aw . . .'

↑ BS ***BATTLECODE: REDWORM DOWN ***

It was the final message. And he'd been doing so well this time.

21

Day: minus 4

Centre Point, nine a.m. on a lousy morning, and George
was riding a lift. She wasn't happy. It wasn't as if she
didn't have other things to do, right?

There always had to be one, George was thinking
sullenly. You rang all fourteen firms in the place and thirteen said OK. The other one wanted to think about it. The
other one wanted to see you.

The temperature had dived during the night and stayed
on the deck at minus two. The sky was flat white, with an
air of unpromising finality so you knew this was the best
daylight you were going to get all day. Cutting right into
people was a nasty northern wind that made your tear
ducts run, and your ears ache, forcing folks to scurry along
with their faces buried in their collars and their eyes slitted
against it. As a day, it stank meteorology-wise.

By the time the lift reached the relevant floor she'd
undone her fur collar (not real fur, George thought real fur
was a really bad news trade) and let her coat hang loose,
but the heat in here, coming on top of that ice-razor out
there, was making her cheeks flush and her nose run.

The lift gave out with its cheerless little bell. Doors slid
back, revealing a foyer adorned with luxurious divans and
enormous tropical flora. Signs suspended from the ceiling
invited the newcomer to consider various possible
destinations.

All the possibilities had a common theme, for this floor
was occupied by one firm. What visitors were

recommended to do was go to reception. George went to reception.

'Good morning,' sang the incredibly expensively coiffured and couturiered female within, her voice reverberating like a door chime. 'Can I help you?'

'Yes,' George said. 'I have an appointment with Mister Constantine.'

George remembered the name easily because it had struck her as unusual. She remembered that the man had asked to see her personally, making a point of giving her his name so she wouldn't end up with somebody else, like a PR hack or something. There shouldn't be any problem, he'd said, but if you wouldn't mind coming along just to reassure me. . . we'll have had time to discuss it by then. . .

What George hadn't caught in that earlier phone call was the pause. The tiny little pause that came just after she'd mentioned *her* name to him. George hadn't picked up on that little pause. Come and see me, he'd said, because I'd like to see you.

George signed the visitors' book, observing that every page of it had the company name on the top. 'Tekniks Consultants' it said simply, which didn't exactly tell you an overwhelming amount. The name was embossed on the leather cover too.

The receptionist led her off down a plush carpeted corridor with big glass-fronted abstracts on the walls until they halted outside a big teak door. The receptionist opened it after a perfunctory knock. It was like she knocked it open.

'Miss Maringelli,' she announced, and then departed in the manner of either an experienced butler or gaoler.

'Good morning, Miss Maringelli.' The man at the end of the long room was on his feet and coming towards her. George advanced to meet him. As he approached his hands came out together as if a hug was on the cards, only one of them seized hers in a handshake, while the other took her by the elbow and steered her towards a pair of armchairs. The hands were huge, she thought instantaneously, long and thin, with fingers that wrapped around her own completely, like a shell.

They sat down side by side and started to talk, without any kind of preamble. A deeply reassuring smile, not too earnest, not too schmaltzy, seemed to have settled on Constantine's features. Interested was the word, George's id started telling her, he's actually interested. Looks-wise, she decided right off, he wasn't what you'd call wolfman either, in fact he was a very marketable piece of male gender. Standing up he must have been six one, and tightly proportioned, with a great shock of blond hair which came back from his forehead and temples on either side of a high parting, like the bow wave of a ship. His face was almost aquiline, with an imposing nose on either side of which steel-blue eyes took in anything that flew, walked, hopped, breathed or slithered, and below which his sincere smile was built upon a clean-shaven mouth framed by the squarest of jaws. Not the sort of head you could sport on top of anything less than a double-breasted charcoal suit, and one of those slick shirts where the neckband is white and the rest of it something else, and a major public-school tie. Bottom end you had black silk socks and very fancy black shoes with tassels. Everything by way of accessories looked like gold, including the massive bracelet which dangled loosely from his left wrist. Some might have called it vulgar on account of its size, but not George. The way she saw it, you considered the fact that there was enough nine carat in it to brain a horse and you had to think class.

You'll do me, George thought. Boy, I could have some fun bringing you to heel. She now realised that she wasn't all that sure of all the things he'd said. It seemed to have been a while.

'Pardon?' she realised she'd said.

'I meant a kind of dry run,' Constantine presumably repeated, 'surely you'll want to do something like that?'

'Well yes. Yes of course,' George flustered. 'Yes, well I haven't scheduled it that closely of course, but obviously we'll have to test it out.'

'Except for the date of the actual event of course.'

'Uh?'

'Your schedule? That particular date is fixed, surely?'

That looks like your little joke, George reckoned. That was worth crossing town for.

'Oh yes,' she laughed, haha, 'yes of course.' Get a grip, she told herself. Or leave.

Leave, she decided.

'Gosh, is that the time?' she announced, after an impossibly quick glance at her digital. 'I hope you don't think I'm rude if I run along. I, er, really wanted to underline our assurance that we are concerned to respect your cooperation in allowing us to use your premises.' She said just the same claptrap to them all. Covering the windows with laminated boards, running cables through a couple of their offices, it wasn't exactly an invasion for any of them. She headed for the door, escorted by Mister Marvellous.

'No trouble at all,' he answered her sincerely. 'Please feel free to contact me again at any time up to the event.' He put his left hand on the doorknob, strangling it with his looping digits, twisted it, pulled open the door. 'And, may I say how fascinating I think your idea is. I certainly look forward to seeing the result.' His right hand was out for the shake.

'Thank you,' George oozed, allowing herself to be grasped again. 'Please get in touch with me personally if you want to know anything else. No doubt we'll be in touch over something. Your secretary has my number?'

'Of course,' Mister Constantine said.

They were shaking hands all the time through this last sugary exchange. This time though, George's fingers escaped total encirclement by Constantine's great hands, and the tips of them found and felt the large ring on the small finger. George just had to look, because she hadn't seen much of the right hand during their conversation.

It was a huge ring, of solid gold, with a big black stone set into it. Jet-stone at a guess, but George wasn't all that clued up on gems and that.

22

Luke had lots of theories for the AX–9 disaster by now. Well, perhaps we exaggerate; he had a few. Several.

They varied in quality, depending on how far your credibility stretched. There was the lunatic driver theory for a start, which he'd briefly entertained at his first reunion with Sandell, but had soon dismissed.

Luke still didn't want to buy a mad pilot, though.

There was airframe failure. Now that one was very attractive when you recalled the punishment taken by the external hide of this huge liner as it scythed through the stratosphere for hours on end at Lord knows how many degrees and under terrific expansion strain. At high cruising speeds the frame went up to such a temperature that it was centimetres longer than it was on the ground. What if it did develop a crack, Luke had enquired of the system and the experts at Schaum. Well, they'd find that before it flew, they said. Suppose they didn't? Then that could be bad news. That could be like (he had had to grind it out of them) a stretched sheet of rubber getting slit; it could go all at once, in a veritable trice. In his mind's eye he had seen those tiny figures tumbling out and down, their screams lost in the icy stratos . . .

They had gone purple over that idea, the Schaum emergency council. That wasn't sabotage, they'd said. Give us some fucking sabotage. Hell's bells, man.

Fine, so there was always Sandell's small bombs, right? No, really, Luke had given it some thought and now it wasn't all that far out in his opinion (an opinion formed under pressure? He didn't think so). You would need, not a pattern of charges but one. A single powerful device in the right place was the way to do it, the right place being somewhere that would immediately cripple the aircraft and simultaneously silence her. Somewhere in the ceiling of the main fuselage, about twenty metres aft of the geometric centre, just under the flat outboard antenna which rose up and back at that point like the fin of a shark. A shaped charge would be ideal, a coned blast going straight up and out.

That one they loved. That was them, the innocent frontier-technology plane builder, striving for a better and faster and safer and cheaper aviation service, under attack from a mindless anonymous bum with a grudge (or a fee). That was a better scenario all round. That kept them in the aerospace business.

But it would need supportive assumptions, Luke had smoothly pointed out. The device would need to be detonated. That implied a timer of some kind. Then the whole thing, explosive and timer, would have to be got on board and fitted into place. That has implications for security, *huge* ones.

That was a dampener all right. They had averted their garrulous gaze whilst they eyed each other. But if it was a trade-off between looking like clowns on security and looking like lousy plane builders, they had it decided already.

All in all, Luke came back to his personal favourite every time. For him, the control system theory was the front runner. It could be a design fault, but it was just as likely to be some kind of software patching.

Some *what?*

Software patching. Sabotage, in other words.

Ah, *right*. They nodded gamely, though not as hard as they had for the bomb theory. If he was saying sabotage then that was one thing and it was fine, but there was still a hidden comment in there about their plane. After all, if you *could* do that, wasn't it a criticism that it was capable of having that done to it, so to speak? It was their control system, wasn't it? It wouldn't have been their bomb.

Can't you find *anything* to push the bomb theory?

What's anything? I can't prove any of them.

You mean, like *yet*.

Well, yeh, I guess so.

You could see them practically choking on it. *Make something up*, their eyes beseeched, *name your price, you hairy, bushy maned, bearded . . .*

Fuck you all, Luke had declined to say. Never took a touch yet. Not starting now. Forty dead men in the Bering sea had to stand for something.

Luke reeled out of the report meeting with Sandell in tow. They looked like they were emerging from a courtroom, still free but smarting under some scything personal remarks inflicted by the judge. Throughout the proceedings – which had taken place in the style of a military tribunal, with Luke facing a row of brass and Sandell over to the side – Sandell had spoken about four words, give or take, which made Luke wonder what the hell he was there for. Still, Lucius Finn was well used to treading water.

'Sorry it was rough,' Sandell offered. 'As you know, they're rattled.'

The poor miserable fat pricks.

'Right.' Luke was following the route to the front entrance. He wasn't obviously in a tattling mood.

'They're anxious to find out exactly what happened to their plane,' Sandell tried again. 'Just like I am.'

Luke stopped. 'What they want,' he said evenly, 'is for me to make up some fancy *evidence*, which makes their plane look good after all. That's what they want. Right?'

'That's strong,' Sandell said. 'That's not true in my opinion.'

'Have you ever heard of a joker called DeJohn, Sandy?'

'Who?'

'DeJohn. Mister Carl DeJohn. He's my boss in a very tenuous sort of way.'

'You mean he's OTC?'

'I mean he's very much OTC. He's a bigshot inside OTC, or at least as big as shots get in OTC. He's also a shit, but as fate decrees he's got me by the short hairs once a year when I have to check that I can still prosecute my chosen profession.'

Sandell looked hurt by Luke's indignant fury.

'Why don't you ease off, Luke?' He smiled. 'I don't know what you're talking about. What does this DeJohn have to do with anything?'

'You *don't* know him?'

'Should I? No, I don't.'

Luke softened. About one tenth of a degree.

'Listen, Sandy. What do they tell you, your bosses? Those fat clowns in there?'

'They just tell me to keep your nose to the wheel. They tell me to keep on seeing you get everything you want, day or night.' He paused, looked at the ground. 'What else do they tell me?'

'Weren't you even listening to them in there?'

'Sure, but . . .'

'Yeh, sure.' Luke was still easing off. 'All right, Sandy. You were always a little unworldly, did you know that? A little too innocent.'

'Luke, for God's sake . . .'

'All right, all right.' Luke was actually smiling now. 'It's like this: your bosses got on to OTC, in the person of this DeJohn bloke, and they've put it to him that they want to come out of this, them and their plane, looking like the victims of a sabotage, and not the designers of an airliner that crashes on its own, without help. The general idea is that I arrange for that to be true. DeJohn tried to twist my arm and now your bosses have tried as well, and I'm getting very uncool about it because it goes against the grain. You understand me, Sandy?'

'Would OTC do that?'

'Why ask about OTC? Why not ask about your own people?'

'Well, I . . .'

Luke patted a shoulder.

'They'd do it. I'd say they've done it before.'

Poor old Sandy.

Luke left him standing on the top of a stair in the main Schaum foyer, and headed for the giant glass doors. He took his time crossing the large, heavily carpeted area with its giant rubber plants and its stone fountains and seating areas. When he reached the other side, by a bank of payphones, he paused to feign a glance at his watch and in doing so sneaked another one behind him.

Sandell had gone. Disappeared back into the labyrinth. Sandy wasn't likely to notice he was using a payphone, let alone enquire why, when they'd practically offered him a hotline to the Kremlin and beyond, but one couldn't be too circumspect these days.

Luke slithered into the one in the corner, out of the light, merging into it like a bat on a cave wall.

'Hello,' the voice said sleepily.

'Douglas?'

'Of course.'

'It's Luke. You get the stuff?'

'What stuff?'

'You know, the other cases. You said you might need some fresh from OTC's machines.'

Douglas seemed to rack his brain for a second. You could almost hear it down the line, being racked. It took a considerable racking, Douglas Wyke's brain. And it had a lot to give.

'Yeh, I dipped in for some more. I got about another two hundred. You'd be amazed what's going on, Luke. It's a flaming riot out there. People getting into people all the time.'

'I *am* out here,' Luke said. 'Have you run anything yet?'

'Not yet.'

'Want to give it a go?'

'What the hell did I get it all for if I don't? Of course I'm going to push it through.'

'Wait for me,' he said. 'Give me an hour. Give me an hour and a half.'

'Bring some booze,' Douglas said. 'And I'll give you two.'

23

Bruno and Constantine had not spoken for a quarter hour before the other car arrived. They saw it slide into the underground park with sidelights on and park facing them, deep in shadows between the pillars. Its headlights flashed once and then went out. By the time the two of them had walked over, its single occupant was out and skulking in the blackness against the wall.

Constantine leaned on the pillar. Bruno did the same only facing the other way, so he could watch the deserted expanse of tunnels, ramps and parking bays for any sign of movement.

'You seemed concerned on the phone,' Constantine said casually. 'I thought we should meet.'

'I am concerned,' said the voice in the dark.

'Well then. Here we are. Why don't you start by telling me about Mister Finn?'

The shadowy figure did not move for a moment. Then it seemed to nod its head a couple of times.

'He's found it. He knows how it was done on the AX–9. He can't prove it but he's guessed it. He'll have to be got rid of.'

'Obviously. All in good time. What else?'

'I'm worried about him and Wyke getting together. What the hell's happening?'

'It's because of his woman, that's all. It's not a problem. It's a nuisance, that is all. We could not have anticipated these links.'

'Why not?' snapped the voice of the figure by the wall. 'What about our man in OTC? Is he asleep or what?'

'OTC files don't go too far on their investigators,' Constantine said. 'They're secretive people, they don't trust their employers.'

Constantine let it lie there, waiting for a response. He glanced at Bruno, who was slowly quartering the car park. Bruno sensed it and looked over his shoulder. He had a sarcastic grin on his face.

'She came to see him at the office,' Bruno said, and that made the other man snap up again.

'She did what?'

Bruno sniggered. 'She's a TV producer. They want to use Centre Point for that big thing next week and she's in charge. She came to talk about it. Ain't that right?'

'Correct,' Constantine said.

'Is there a connection? I mean, with . . .'

'Of course not. I checked. She went into every firm in the block.'

There was a long pause then while Constantine waited for the next thing he had to field. Nothing came. That was it then. His turn now.

'Have you considered my suggestion concerning our French client's requirement?'

'Yes,' the other man said. 'It's insane.'

'Insanely impossible? Or insanely original?'

'It's possible. In fact it's easy. It can be done from your machines and equipment at Centre Point. All I need is the command set.'

'But?'

'Don't you realise how crowded the place will be on the night? You know how many people are going to die when that thing goes down?'

Constantine considered a guess.

'Twenty perhaps. It's not so many. No doubt there'll be time to get out of the way.'

'They won't be able to get out of the way.'

Right, Bruno thought. They won't.

'Thirty then? Fifty? It's an average day on the roads.'

'Probably come down on a roof,' Bruno said. 'What's the odds?'

Constantine let Bruno have his say and then went back to watching the other man. 'You remember the Hindenburg?' he said gently. 'People got a syndrome about it, but now they've forgotten. They need to be reminded. Don't they?'

The other man didn't say anything more, but his head was bowed, as if he was sleeping.

24

Day: minus 3

'A what?' George got ready for a fight.

'I said a hanging mike, dear.'

'What the hell are you giving me?' George wanted to know.

'A microphone,' one of the Technicals said. 'On a chain. We can trail it behind the dirigible.' George glared, Technical winced. 'It's no problem technically,' he added. 'We can use one of the mooring winches.'

Artistic strove for forbearance. If it was a matter of life or death he could tolerate the most beastly of life's troubadours, but it could be tiresome to have to do so. Unfortunately, with Maringelli it came close to being a matter of life or death.

'It's a directional microphone,' he stated with gargantuan restraint. 'That crowd is going to make noises that have never been heard before. I'm appealing to your imagination.'

'We can get the mike,' Technical said. 'It's a terrific thing. They use them for underwater prospecting. They dangle them down into the ocean and listen to the seabed moving. You can hear whales and things from miles away.'

'OK, OK,' George said. 'Do it.'

George was feeling pretty good about Artistic now. This hadn't been his first suggestion since George twisted him by the gonads. He had come up with a few nice-sounding ideas for colour displays between features, as a kind of crowd amuser. You could get incredible visual effects with multilaser displays.

'Right,' George said stiffly, peering about. 'Let's hear some more nice things. What about the PM and the other comedians we've approached? All keen I suppose?'

PR's job was to dish out air time on the coming phantasmagorium to interested parties. Naturally he'd had more takers than he could use, all wanting to be wiped across the Centre Point fifty times a second by a beam of photons.

'The Prime Minister's agreed,' he confirmed. 'Also the Leader of the Opposition. I suppose we should include the also-rans?'

'Yeh,' George said. 'We'll have to give 'em a word or two. What about human beings? Got any human beings decided on?'

'One or two from upstairs,' PR said, meaning TCTV's brass.

George went, 'Uh. Right. Well, we can get them out of the way early.'

PR said, 'We'll have to have some kids for the link-up.'

'Sounds good,' George said.

'And animals?' PR said.

'Fuck animals.'

Artistic showed his disgust. Was there ever a more ghastly woman in world history?

'Right,' PR said. 'No animals.'

'Suppose the other countries put animals on?' a voice enquired.

All eyes turned to the speaker. This was a new face in the team, and already ensconced with his label, Production Two. George of course was Production, but she had decided that her function required the services of an assistant.

'What?' George said.

Production Two sensed the danger. He coughed nervously.

'I mean, suppose they all put animals on their transmissions. You know the kangaroos from Australia and . . .'

'Suppose they all stand on their heads,' George said.

'Suppose they all pick their frigging noses. Does that mean we do the same?'

'Well, no. It's just that, when you said about the others all putting kids on, I just thought . . .'

'That was a good idea. This isn't.' George allowed him a cannibalistic smile, to add a touch of finality to the point.

'Oh, right,' Production Two said. 'Right.'

George returned to PR, who having become seasoned to her by now, was enjoying a sadistic grin with the rest of them. 'Well, that looks to be going all right. What about the King?' she asked, as if it was an afterthought. Goddamn, she nearly forgot.

'No reply yet,' PR said. 'It's been a little while. You think they got the letter?'

Hoots of mirth from all present.

'Did you get the address right?' some rotten comedian wanted to know.

More guffaws. Nothing like a spot of gay badinage.

'Of course they got the bloody letter,' George hissed. 'They're considering it, see.'

'Should I send a reminder?'

'For crying out loud, you dumb fucking dope. You don't send reminders to the King. What the hell are you, a PR man or what?'

'Well we've got to know. I mean if the King's going to speak on the thing it needs preparing, doesn't it? It needs a spot.'

'He'll do it,' George said. 'My guess is the Palace'll go for a local spot. Just the King talking to the people. It might not be going out over the link. It depends. That's a Palace decision.'

'Why not? I'll bet he'll talk to the Yanks. He likes the Yanks.'

'Maybe,' George said. 'That's a big plus for us if he does. Meanwhile we can bank on the local spot. Anything else?'

'Lots,' PR said. 'We've got the whole world and his brother lining up for this. I've just touched on some of the obvious ones so far. What we need is something unusual, too. Something cute.'

'Cute?' George looked suspicious. 'What's cute?'

'Well, I don't know. Something that none of the others will come up with.'

George looked even more suspicious. What was this cute thing? A public hanging perhaps?

'If we could find a kid who spoke all the languages of all the countries we're joining to, that would be something cute,' PR said, showing all the symptoms of terminal inspirational genius. 'There must be some angelic five-year-old can speak in 'em all.'

'Oh right,' George said, beginning to marvel at the depth of PR's latent lunacy. 'There's bound to be some five-year-old who can speak French and German and Hebrew and Urdu and Malay and Japanese. It's a racing bloody certainty. Also, his mother's going to love us dragging him on the air to say hello to a bunch of foreigners every hour on the hour from midday till midnight.'

George turned to the technicals.

'Right. Which of you has sorted that split-screen business?'

Technical Number One owned up. 'I had a look at it. It's no problem. We can put our own local stuff up alongside the incoming stuff from Transworld Satnet.'

'So politician to politician live is on?' George asked. 'That's a sure and certain fact?'

'Definitely.'

'It's your balls,' George reminded him. 'What about beam on to the States? I want us to be the main European sender to New York. They'll take it from there to the West Coast, but we get most of the European out time. I've seen to that, but you've got to give me technical guarantees.'

'You've got them,' Technical One said. 'Count on me for the nuts and bolts. What you send is your affair.'

'Come back to you on that,' George told him. 'I want that very clear to me. Right?'

'Right.'

George rolled on to International, who had thus far been attempting to hide by remaining immobile in the manner of certain ground-nesting birds.

'So who's going to be the main linkers?' George enquired.

Transcontinental TV had offices and production facilities and all necessary hardware and personnel just about everywhere. Where it didn't have a main office it had a 'presence'. If you fell out of a plane into the wastes of the Gobi desert, you'd be most likely to meet either an IBM salesman or somebody from TCTV, in either order.

'More or less as we agreed,' International said. 'Starting with Auckland. Then Sydney, Tokyo and Singapore. Then Bangkok, Delhi and – er – I'll come back to that.' He paused, as if considering a pain in his teeth. 'Then Nairobi, then Tel Aviv, if they ever get themselves sorted out, and then we run Europe in together, with timeouts back for the others and lots of feed to the States.'

'What's up with bloody Israel?' George growled. As if she didn't know.

'Usual crap,' International said. 'They want a straight through to the States for one.'

'They can shove that,' George snarled. 'Tell 'em that, any way you like.'

'I will,' International said, 'I will.'

'So come back to it then,' George prompted, after a pause.

'Uh?'

'You were coming back to something. What was it?'

International sucked his top teeth.

'Tbilisi.'

Silence fell.

'What?'

'It's a town in Russia.'

'Terrific.'

'In the far south of Russia, in Georgia.'

'Oh really.'

'Yes,' International said. 'It's between the Black Sea and

the Caspian. It's very mountainous around there, with lots of forest all around. They have wolves and . . .'

He shut up, noting that George was drawing breath and rolling eyes in an effort to maintain control.

'Go on,' she said finally. 'Just go on.'

'Well the thing is,' he explained, 'there's this big gap between Delhi and Nairobi. Longitude-wise it's a fair old hop.'

'You mean we're stuck for a song?'

'Kind of. If we stick with Delhi until it's Kenya's turn to click through, we could end up having India on too long. We need something in between.'

'Fair enough,' George said.

'So I reckoned, after the big thrash from Delhi – they'll have some of the biggest crowd scenes I should think – and before that bunch of shits from Tel Aviv, maybe we could get something from Russia. Something quiet. A kind of interlude.'

'Maybe we could interview a peasant.'

'Uh?'

'Or a wolf?'

International sniffed in a way which showed he was suitably offended.

Silly twat, George was thinking. What the hell was he about? If they wanted the Russians in then it was best coming from Moscow, not the middle of sodding Siberia, or wherever it was.

'Any other brilliant notions?' she enquired.

'Well, if you don't like that we can get a transmission from a ship in the Indian Ocean.'

'Might one ask what ship?'

'A warship would be best. They've got all the hardware for going up to Satnet.'

'Fine,' George said. 'So we either go down to the arse of Russia or we rub it with the navy in the Indian Ocean. That's how we handle the gap between Delhi and Nairobi?'

'Maybe I should think again.'

'Maybe you should,' George said. 'Except there isn't time.'

International lapsed into catatonia again.

George wound it up then, with a few very muted compliments and a heavy dose of admonitions regarding the passing of time. Then she let them go.

For a short while she contemplated the prospect of watching McEwen and his men dangling like lemurs from Centre Point, since he'd said he would be fixing some screens up today, as a check-out on his mods to the bracket clamps. But it was getting late, and for the last hour or so there had been snow moving across her office window, flurrying in the turbulence that the building caused in the north wind. No, McEwen would not have stayed up there for long in that.

Instead she tried to ring Luke. As she punched his number, the bad feeling came back about Steve, pushing through again, after being buried by work.

There was no reply. George decide to go home and sleep, if she could.

25

Douglas Wyke wasn't shit hot at everything, by any means. One thing he was lousy at was inventing convincing acronym phrases for the fancy names you give new lumps of software. Some people were absolutely ace at this kind of thing, and of course this is the way round it's done. You want a name for a program. What you *don't* do is write down a sensible phrase describing what it does and then form an acronym from the first letters. You start with the clever name and work back from there.

Douglas had this program which he called *nark*. A *nark* puts his finger on felons, and that's what this program was meant to do as well. Wyke's problem was that he couldn't think of a phrase which described what *nark* really did, and which also generated the word *nark* as an acronym. The best he could come up with was 'notification and analysis by recursive key correlation', which was enough to make you throw up in itself, and which didn't tell you a damn thing about what *nark* did.

Actually, *nark* was a very sexy piece of software indeed. It was based on a system of programs used by OTC on their Lupus Street computers. Their code was called *corrina*, which wasn't an acronym at all, at least not a very obvious one, but being civil servants, that wasn't their kick. Douglas had been so taken by *corrina* when he first heard about it and saw it at work, that he had immediately started work on a version of his own. It had taken a long time for Douglas to write it, and he had taken a lot of trouble and time with research into IKBS and fuzzy algorithms and whatnot. But Douglas wasn't in a hurry; he had approached the job with care and patience (as rare as hen's teeth in the software ethos), he had discussed fine points of design with various devious people like Lucius Finn, and the result was *nark*. Without a doubt, *nark* could do a respectable takeoff of *corrina*, and nobody, hardly, apart from Douglas and a few of his more trusted TI colleagues, knew of its existence.

For all that though, *corrina* was also a very advanced piece of work, and OTC were known to use it constantly. Which was why Douglas had designed his *nark* software to have the same data interface as *corrina*, after a few sneaky looks at *corrina*'s source code and purloining some case files to check the format.

Any program of this type had to be fed with data. In the case of *nark* and *corrina*, it consisted of details of suspected or known technocrimes. Douglas had simply ensured that *nark* made the same assumptions as *corrina*.

Just like Lucius Finn and many others in the techno jungle, Douglas Wyke was well versed in the cult science of systems security penetration: the science of stealing data from target computers by using a computer of your own. Douglas had found the way through the various landnets into OTC's computers a long time ago. Sure, every so often they changed the encryption coding of the password sequences, but that never kept DW out for long.

He wasn't without restraint, though. All he ever lifted was case details, and that, he sincerely believed, was in order to improve his own efficiency in holding back the flood gates of technocrime. As for other data he could have laid his hands on – people's salaries, promotion prospects etcetera – he never even peeked.

Nark was driven by inputs called keywords. How fast you made progress with it depended on how you dealt your keywords from the pack. Luke and Douglas had *nark* in full flow. Luke had stayed overnight on Wyke's floor. And they'd been at it most of the day already.

Pushing . . .

Pushing four p.m. and nothing yet.

Douglas cracked another can of lager. Luke went for pale ale.

'How long is this fucking thing going to take, Doug?' Luke yawned. 'I mean, what's it now? Eight minutes. That's a lot of mill time, Doug.'

Mill time, Wyke thought. He'll be talking about *cores* next, and maybe even *paper tape*.

'We wasted our time on the other runs,' Douglas said. 'They never work, long shots like that.' Luke always played that game, though. Whenever he ran *nark* on his system (Douglas had given him a copy) he tended to use it as a guessing board. Sometimes it worked. Always it was fast. Douglas didn't like that approach at all. As he rightly pointed out, that wasn't the idea of *nark*. That was almost an insult to it. You had to let it do the work. 'What you've got to do is what we're doing now. Give it all the gen you've got with a few really general keys, and then pare it down from there.'

'You start with a big correlating set,' Luke argued. 'You're there till for ever.'

'What you're doing is making progress,' Douglas insisted. 'Anyway, my machine's faster than yours. It won't be long now.'

Wyke was right, of course. Wyke was usually right. You could waste a lot of effort with *nark* by trying to outguess it, as they'd proved when they'd tried Luke's approach first off. They'd kicked *nark* off with commands to lock on to the Measons case and to correlate others for 'chemists (human)'. That got them an answer in less time than it took to set up the question. There was but one other in the whole dataset, and it was the now celebrated AGF case of six months or so ago. AGF was a pharmaceutical firm, about one thousandth the size of the mighty Measons, which had set itself up to cash in on this terrific discovery one of its people had made. It had been fouled up somehow, people had been hurt, some were dead. The product had been sound, but there'd been a bad batch that got loose on to the public. The firm had folded. Luke and Douglas had tried a few expansion lines with *nark* to see what else could be found in common about the two cases, but nothing had come out. Fast but fruitless. Could be just a coincidence.

Luke's next shot had been with the Schaum case. Keyword 'aircraft (civilian)'. They got two other suspected technocrimes that time, a Boeing that had gone down in the Indian Ocean, and a Russian jet that had 'stalled' climbing out of de Gaulle and gone tail-down into a Paris suburb. Commonalities there were unknown due to one plane being lost and the Russians making such a thing with the French that investigative results had been withheld.

None of it had been leading anywhere, so they had started doing it Doug's way.

First he had ignored the caselock. No case was to be special, it was to be a global correlation on the key 'computer (software)'. *Nark* was being told to come up with all cases that could potentially have resulted from a software attack. That was going to be most of them, they both knew it, maybe as many as eighty or ninety per cent, but the others needed to be eliminated. Without waiting for *nark* to get through that, Douglas had followed up with instructions to sift the cases found in the first pass on the key 'microprocessors'. That would eliminate a lot of the commercial targets like banks and credit houses and insurance groups, who did most of their in-house work on big mainframe machines. However, it could still leave in any cases involving their non-mainframe operations such as their communications systems and their dispenser point networks. Douglas had let it ride there, and had sat back to wait.

Luke knew that Douglas had a theory really, but he hadn't said anything yet. Instead he had contemplated the inspiring view from Wyke's second-floor office window. Depressing would have been one word for it.

The evil corner in which Douglas chose to abide lent a new dimension to the concept of urban decay. Situated at the downriver end of the late eighties dockland renewal zone, it had been foul enough by ninety-two when they admitted things had gone bad and blew up the new slums and the not-so-old high rises and put up in their stead the so-called low complex. The low complex (origin of term unknown, originator long since withdrawn to well-deserved obscurity) was an anthill-type arrangement of hundreds of small maisonettes and similar dwellings. Nothing went over three floors. Numerous small 'gardens' had been installed, and lots of brick walls and alleys and walkways of one kind or another. The idea was to make the whole thing more personal whilst preserving such vital necessities as defensible space. It was to serve the end of defensible space that every unit in the low complex was independently accessible without encroaching on the topology of any other. On the face of it, the low complex had been a great idea.

The reason it hadn't really worked was, the current belief went, that it had been made too big. At least that was the best excuse for a reason they had been able to come up with. In any event, the low complex was now just a high-rise slum that didn't rise all that high, and a thriving nest of iniquity wherein every conceivable depredation known to man was practised relentlessly, from one swing of the clock to the next.

Douglas had a two-storey maisonette close to one edge of it. His TI business was conducted from the upper floor, where he had an office containing his computer equipment and his lunatic filing system, and his living quarters were at ground level. From his office windows (one front, one back) you could admire either the scenic beauty of the old dock, a half kilometre distant, or the multitude of marijuana patches in the gardens of the neighbours. Immediately below Wyke's small domain ran the boundary of the low complex, bounded by the fragrantly named Slaughter Road, which right now provided, by the minority of its lamps that functioned, the only external lights in the area.

Luke kept watching one of these lights, though he wasn't sure that what he was watching was worth his attention.

There was this black car, that was all, and it was parked, with its lights off, just beyond the watery pool of light that this particular mercury lamp was casting on to the glistening wet, snow-dampened surface of Slaughter Road. Luke could just make it out, down there in the dark, though he couldn't have named its make. He knew the car was occupied because it had moved once. In fact, that was why he was idly allowing it to hold his attention. It had drawn away towards them, disappearing from his field of view below, only to return from the opposite direction and park again in the same place less than five minutes later. Why had it done that?

'We're in business.'

Luke snapped forward to watch Wyke's monitor screen. He was just in time to see the end message disappearing off the top of the screen as the results began to flow up.

God, but there was a lot of it, though.

'We'll be here all night again,' Luke despaired.

Douglas didn't seem to be hearing him. He was too busy watching the rolling mass of data pouring up the tube.

'There,' he said, stabbing with his finger. 'That's the Measons case it's picked up.' He kept on glaring intently at it, his eyes piercing right through his horn-rims. Luke could see his owlish face reflected in the VDU.

'There's mine,' Luke said, observing the details of the AX–9 whish on by.

'Bound to have got them both,' Douglas said.

'There's a hell of a lot of others, though,' Luke said, trying to get Douglas to appreciate the fact. The cases had stopped rolling now. The message 'end datafile' was on the screen, static below the tail end of the results.

'There must have been a couple of hundred there.'

'That's our starting set.' Wyke sniffed. 'We drive it now, using these alone. You want to go with this or not?'

'Play it out, pal.'

Douglas turned to the keyboard. His fingers flew over the buttons, hieroglyphs flashed to the screen. There was never anything user friendly about Doug's software, you either knew how it was handled or you didn't. Douglas wasn't into all that human factor garbage, which to him just meant eye-hand-screen and bypass brain.

'OK,' he said as he went along. 'Here's what.' His hand went to the screen, pointing. 'What that command there means is it's going to scan all these cases that we've got here and it's going to look for those which have been done by a patchmod to existing machine code.'

'I knew you had something in mind,' Luke said slyly, stopping Wyke's finger in mid stab.

'What?'

'You think whoever spiked the Measons pill did it by getting into one of the chips in the process controller for the production line.'

Douglas smiled. 'They're downline loadable,' he admitted. 'I found that all on my own. Also the autoassay system. It takes samples off the production line as they're made. Analyses them on the fly. That would have to be spiked too.'

'Well, bully.'

'Shall we proceed?'

Luke grinned like Caligula. 'Go ahead,' he said, and Wyke's finger turned *nark* loose again.

Response was quicker now, with the scan set down to a couple of hundred cases and the correlating keys becoming more specific. *Nark* came up with a total of thirty-two cases. Patching a complex program in its machine-runnable state requires an expert, especially when the program is part of a big, intensely interactive system of programs, which nearly all industrial systems are. With a system like that, you can change one word of machine memory, one byte, one *bit*, and if it's the wrong one the thing can fall in a heap. If you want your modified memory image to actually *work* and do that new and nasty thing you had in mind, then you have to know your business.

And here were thirty-two luckless organisations who had been hit by somebody who knew his or her business.

What was more, both the Measons case and the Schaum AX–9 case were among them.

'Told you we'd pick 'em up,' Douglas said.

'So what? So we've picked them up.' Luke found it just as obvious. His own pet theory about what happened to the AX–9 was exactly the same.

'So now we lock on these two, or maybe just one, and we start some really detailed key searches on this collection here,' Douglas said. 'If we find anything, then we've got a clue on our own cases that we couldn't have got without *nark* here. If we don't then *nark* couldn't help because our two cases are one-off jobs. At least we know where we stand.'

Finn was beginning to feel just a smidgen confused. Was it actually possible that he didn't *grasp* this technique? Had he, all this time, been kidding himself? Professional panic blossomed in his breast.

He gave it a cough. 'Like what detailed keys?'

Well that was the question. From here on was where the human helped the machine.

Luke Finn and Douglas Wyke tried all kinds of ideas for about the next two hours or so. By agreement they started out on technical keys and tried to exhaust those first. They tried pcb layouts, they tried processor types, operating systems, downline loadable designs, reblow designs, assembler sourced, high-level sourced, the combinations were legion. Many beers later they moved on to the less technical, starting with personnel. That key got you into the liveware side of the cases. Personnel could be in-house or it could be contractor. It could be examined at the salary level, the previous employer level, the *all* previous employers level, and so on.

They hit something at about ten o'clock, or a little after.

'What's that you say?' Douglas said, poised over the buttons yet again.

'Contractors,' Luke said. 'Try it.'

Douglas put in the commands. It happened very quickly. When they saw it, both men paused, wondering.

'Well, well,' Luke said. 'Look at that.'

'Best yet,' Douglas agreed.

For a few long seconds Luke just let it confront him. He was counting, his gaze clicking down the screen from one to the next.

'Who the hell is Tekniks?' he said finally.

26

'Seems to me I heard the name some time,' Douglas said. He was reaching up to a shelf over his head and grabbing a huge year book, fat enough to form a drain cover. He slid his thumb down the notched edge of the pages to the letter C. Opening it he found the section entitled 'Consultancies'.

'Tekniks Consultants,' he announced. 'They're not big but they're specialised. That's what it says here.'

'Meaning what?'

'Meaning they're about forty strong, including admin staff. The consultants bit is just a catch-all. What they are is a software consultancy specialising in highly skilled, very technical stuff. No stock control rubbish or anything like that. They employ only the ultra-best people and they pay big bread for them. Personally I take all that crap with a pinch of salt.'

'Where do they hang out?'

'Centre Point.'

'What?' Luke's bells were going. Coincidence?

'What about it?' Douglas asked. 'Somebody's got to inhabit that fucking concrete virus. Why not them?'

'Never mind,' Luke said. 'Just a thought. You think eight cases is significant?'

'Within the last ten months,' Douglas reminded him. 'You notice anything else?'

'Yeh,' Luke said. 'We've lost the Schaum case.'

It was true. What they had here was a list of possible or actual technocrimes, involving sneaky things done to the microcomputers of organisations which had been employing subcontracted staff from Tekniks Consultants when they were hit. Measons was one but Schaum wasn't. Luke didn't like that.

Nark had also found that other subsets of technocrime had yet other contract agencies in common. In one case, a second contractor was involved in the personnel search of some six crimes. Two further contractors each turned up in five crimes. Numerous agencies occurred in four or less technocrimes. There were thirty-plus in all. But Tekniks was out in front.

Tekniks? Luke couldn't fathom why he'd never heard of them.

'Who's the Tekniks person at Measons?' Luke said softly.

Douglas keyed in a query.

'Man called Pruett,' he read off. 'Speciality is process control software. Pharmaceutical production line control systems, that is. Like I said, the micros in it are downline reloadable.'

'That's interesting.'

They continued studying the list that *nark* had found for them. It came up in screenfuls, with lots of gen on each case.

Some of them were really big events. With others you couldn't be sure whether they were big or not. They already knew the seriousness of the Measons case. That was big all right.

Then there was AGF again. Well there was a thing.

What some smart cat in AGF had discovered was a cheap way of producing a protein known as an autogenesis factor. Certain roving human cells called macrophage cells produced this protein as a kind of secretion. The trick was to find a way of making that natural process work on a commercial scale. The anonymous AGF genius had cracked it and AGF (named after the autogenesis factor) was set up to reap the rewards. These had promised to be immense because what this particular protein did was to accelerate the regrowth of capillaries and other small blood vessels in the region of a serious wound such as a large burn which upped the healing rate by a mile and prevented scarring. Potentially it had been worth a fortune.

What actually happened when AGF went to market with their product had turned out to be a nightmare. Somehow they'd got another substance into the bottles, and this substance not only neutralised the protein in the bottle, it also destroyed macrophage cells in the patient when the stuff was injected, so he ended up without even the natural healing factor he would have had anyway. There was no doubt it had been sabotage. Probably done in the mixer control system of AGF's highly computerised and as then unpaid-for production facility. They couldn't locate the precise point of the sabotage because the software was erasable throughout the processors in use. AGF had to withdraw the drug, never recovered from the loss in confidence, and went to the receiver about four months later. Shortly after that, a consortium of Swiss and German drug outfits began marketing a replacement drug with huge success.

Uncanny was what Luke thought.

There'd been a man working for AGF then, a very fast character from a consultancy called Tekniks. His name had been Keogh and after AGF went under, Keogh went into thin air.

All very fascinating, Douglas opined. For AGF you could almost have read Measons. And for Keogh you could almost read Pruett.

Come back to Mister Pruett. Oh yes.

What else?

There was a comms hit. Very cheeky, that was. The mighty British Telecom wanted this swanky new all-singing telephone exchange up in Birmingham. Half a dozen of the big utilities went for the job, and BT had finally selected a pair of finalists. Both the exchanges on offer were good, both fully stored program controlled on powerful computers, both modular designed providing guaranteed one hundred per cent up time, both as fast as

167

hell. Spoilt for choice, BT has girlishly announced it would field trial both in separate though comparable cities, and then award the plum order to the better of the two on the basis of experience. No doubt other orders would follow. Both contenders greedily went along.

Contender number one, who might as well remain in painful anonymity, had it bad after about a week. Something went so wrong with their system it was embarrassing. Calls were lost, charges didn't get made (BT frowned on that so hard their eyes got stuck), people were misrouted, cut off, wrong-numbered, overcharged, undercharged and God knows what. Contender number one withdrew its system in disarray and held an enquiry. It found the memory images of many of the software modules for the exchange computers had been 'manipulated'. It went crazy, it had a witch hunt, it offered rewards for information, it screamed to the police, the OTC, BT and God. In the meantime it lost the tender.

A Tekniks employee, name of Goodman, acting as software consultant to contender number one, left the company about a week later and vanished into the mists.

Well now.

And there was the TCTV thing! Luke had clean forgotten about that one. Fancy it turning up here of all things. Of course, he hadn't even met George when this event occurred before the eyes of the nation, so there was no reason for it to stick. It was coming back now though.

In the past couple of years there was a sudden flurry of activity over speech recognisers. It wasn't a new idea, but the applications seemed suddenly to come to fruition.

The machines at last got smart enough to distinguish the clever stuff like 'that's a tanker' from 'that's at anchor'. They did it by context recognition. At the same time the simpler problem of synthesising speech was being smoothed out, so when the micro talked back to you it didn't sound like Donald Duck. This had led to a number of new products, notably the automatic translator machine.

The UN had been using theirs for years and were pleased as hell about it.

Then somebody thought of the 'mini-interpreter'.

The market was crying out for it. Imagine the UN monster, cut down to size so it just translated from English to French say, and back again, and all packed into a little box with an earphone and built-in mike.

As usual, one firm got there first. Like lots of quick-fire outfits, it called itself after its product – 'Mini-interpreter Ltd'. Where TCTV came in was with the feature. It made for a nice little spot, a twenty-minute thing, dropping the name of the product a few times by way of a free push in return for using it to amuse the multitudes and maintain ratings. The spot consisted of a reporter footing it around remotest Gascony assailing assorted French peasants with a mini-interpreter box, under the lenses and mikes of a much-entertained camera crew and sound team. The company logo was well displayed on the product, and unhappily the programme went out live using TCTV's famous resources, to viewers all over the UK, potential buyers every one.

It's a scene from something they used to call vaudeville.

The French farmer obligingly dismounts his tractor and stands grinning, Gitane in mouth, beret pushed back in the heat, his little puckish eyes glittering in his brown, leathery face. The purpose of the magic box has been explained at some length to the viewing millions, but not to him.

'Good morning,' the reporter says, poking the mike into the farmer's face.

Not a tweet comes out of the mini-interpreter.

'Good morning,' the farmer replies, delighted to be able to air two of the three English words he knows.

The reporter seems ruffled. Neither device nor rustic peasant are behaving to specification. He decides to go for something a trifle more challenging, in an effort to force the dirty-looking sod to revert to his native tongue.

'I was wondering if you'd like to try this wonderful new

169

invention for translating conversations immediately from English to French and vice versa,' he streams out.

'Yes.' the farmer says immediately, hopefully trying his other English word. The smelly cigarette has never left his mouth.

Suddenly the box emits a garbled squawk. Its few recognisably French words constitute a sentence which lacks practically all grammar, and alludes to Wales.

The Frenchman stares at it in muted alarm.

'Qu'est-ce que c'est que ça?' he demands, pointing with a calloused digit.

The machine barks an announcement in clear Oxford English, complaining that its gums are swollen.

A million homes collapse in laughter from Scotland to the Scillies, except for some of them, where Mini-interpreter Ltd executives stare in sick disbelief at the sight of their product publicly emasculating itself, unassisted and unstretched.

Mini-interpreter Ltd never did make it with their fabulous device. They sold about a hundred before they collapsed and laid off all their staff, with contractors leaving first. One of the consultants came from Tekniks, and according to *nark*, returned there. His name was Pinetti. Where Mini-interpreter had failed, a competitor thrived. But such is life, the FT said.

There were others, four further cases, but the pattern was similar. Some firm would be in the lead, holding an edge, and suddenly it would slip up hard. Its edge would be lost, sometimes its life. Sometimes, nearly always, people were hurt. They were either hurt directly, killed or maimed or God knows what, or they lost their jobs and their prospects and were scattered like confetti in an industrial or commercial disaster.

Tekniks, Luke thought.

'You beginning to think what I am?' Luke said to Douglas.

'They've got to be checked. It's a *statistic*, right?'

'How the hell we going to do that?'

170

Douglas curled his considerable beard with forefinger and thumb. 'Well, we can go mad over it, right? We can assume a model density function . . .'

'Of a random variate . . .' Luke said, grinning.

'Denoting probability of a personnel link between a given contractor . . .' Douglas said.

'And a given incident . . .' Luke said.

'We can integrate . . .'

'Take a null hypothesis . . .'

'We can . . .' Douglas couldn't hold it any more. He wheezed into a laugh. 'Shit.'

They both took a few swills of beer. While Douglas Wyke recovered his composure, Luke just sat and forced his last mouthful through his teeth, filling his mouth with froth.

'Tell you what we do as a shot,' Luke said.

'What's that?'

'We do it on technical staff.' He leaned forward, gathering earnestness.

Luke's hairy Afro-head peered over his shoulder like a gargoyle as Douglas Wyke stabbed yet more buttons, calling up his graphics package. For such a sophisticated piece of software plotting this little graph on the screen was going to be nothing at all.

Bright yellow lines swept out in a blink of axes, then the points came up like a row of tiny bullet holes stitching up the screen. Apparently insulted by the trivial nature of the task just allotted to it, the computer loftily demanded the opportunity to try a few regression analyses of the data. Wyke ignored it.

The bigger a consulting outfit was, technical staff-wise the more jobs it got, the higher the chances of it being involved with a firm hit by a technocrime. That was what came up on the graph. A smooth increase in involvements, with increasing technical staff number. With a single exception, all thirty odd of *nark*'s list of consultancies were on the curve, within ten or twenty per cent either way. With a single exception.

Guess who?

'Way off,' Luke said. He slapped Wyke gently on the shoulder. 'Tekniks isn't on that curve at all.'

'Got to agree,' Wyke said.

The Tekniks point was high above the general run of the curve, clearly atypical. Put another way, the firm seemed to get involved in a hell of a lot more technocrimes than anybody else, size for size.

There were other names by now, like Keogh and Goodman and Pinetti, but they were just names because they weren't locatable in quite the same way. Whereas Pruett was. You kept coming back to Pruett.

You could find Pruett.

He was real.

'Want to try for this Pruett bloke, then?'

Douglas went, 'What?'

'Pruett,' Luke said. 'The Tekniks man at Measons. We could fork him out, just to see which way he jumps.'

'What's this "we", Luke? Whose case is this anyway?'

Luke recoiled one point three millimetres.

'What the fuck does that mean?'

'What it says.'

'I already told you my interest in this.'

'Right,' Douglas said. 'Only you didn't say anything about a partnership. What you seem to have forgotten, Luke, is that we haven't mentioned Schaum for a while.'

True enough. Schaum wasn't figuring in any of this. One or two of the other consultancies had people into Schaum, but neither hair nor hide of Tekniks. There was this gap between Luke's immediate employment, and their whole line of enquiry.

'I can spare the time.'

Wyke didn't say anything. Luke knew what was up his tail, probably. They cracked the Measons thing early and then Douglas was seeking alternative employment while Luke went back to getting bread from Schaum. From a certain point of view, you liked a case to last a while, because then you ate for a while.

'Listen, Doug. This Schaum thing is getting heavy. I

mean there's lots to think on but nothing you can put facts to.'

'I know the feeling.'

'I could use some help is what I mean.'

'Yeh?'

'Definitely.'

Well you never knew. Fucking hell, Luke was saying inside his skull, the things I do for George.

Douglas gave it a little more thought. Certainly he wasn't dumb or naive enough to be wheedled by a hard like Luke, but then again he had never intended to give Finn the elbow anyway.

'OK. We'll spike this Pruett person. It'll have to be me up front, and you in the outfield.'

'Done,' Luke said.

Oh yes. Oh yes.

That was as far as it went that night. They stayed on a while in Wyke's office, finishing the beer and whisking off a couple of games of lightning chess against the machine. It murdered them easy. Luke was relishing what they were going to do with the man called J. Pruett. It was more than a year since he had done such a thing to anybody, and in the guidelines of the OTC for TIs it was considered unprofessional.

Entrapment, it was called, at one extreme. Surveillance, wiretapping, eavesdropping, all kinds of things at the other. You had to be guilty to be really uptight about it.

Outside, in the dark, beyond the mercury lamp, Bruno sat and watched the window from his black, snow-dusted car. It was still lit, there had been no movement across it the whole day and evening. What the hell were they doing in there? Playing fucking Scrabble?

27

Day: minus 2

Despite everything else, of course, it *was* still the festive season, more or less. You had all the usual stuff dangling over West End thoroughfares, all the usual light-speed routine in the stores. The robot in Santarobes had long gone from Selfridge's window though, slain by popular demand. He had been replaced with the exact opposite, a near-naked human female whose only concession to season was the colour and fur trim of her incredibly scanty attire. With true thespian detachment, the young flesh and blood robot replacement went through her bargain highlights from Selfridge's Sale of the Millenium for nigh on three hours at a stretch while a leering crowd gaped from point-blank range at her silk-slung pudenda. Warmer in the window than out, was what you found yourself hoping.

Temperatures stayed down all day, not usually making it up to zero. Snow it didn't, not much anyway, what there was coming as flurries of tiny, pinhead flakes that caught you right under the eyelids and stung like hell. Nose and ears could be protected by layers of wool, but short of going around like an eskimo with a pair of slit whalebone goggles, you had to get it in the eyes.

The fact that in a couple of days time it would not just be a new year, or even a new century, but a new millenium wasn't exactly *lost* on people. God knows every human in the land had got the fact jammed down every orifice that led to the brain about a million times already, but it wasn't until now, with just over forty-eight hours to go, that people actually seemed to be *moving* on the event.

174

The capital was filling up. The regular post-Christmas mini-tourist peak this year was way off scale. Hotels normally still taking bookings were full up for the duration. Every train hitting the main-line platforms was standing room only. Peak traffic hours became smaller peaks as the times in between became busier. Car park 'full' signs glowed on every street. Walking down pavements in the city centre became a slow business, as the crowds thickened. And you got the silly season. Every major event pulled a little silly season along in its wake. This one was no exception. In fact, this one was a record breaker. Barring possibly the coronation, that was.

There was this guru type who had shinned up a flagpole in Horseguards with a saw, a hammer and nails, and a small piece of blockboard, constructed a small platform, divested himself of all clothing bar his loincloth (home-made according to expert commentators from various fashion magazines), and assumed a full lotus. The cops had announced early on, with some recklessness, that cold, hunger, and lack of 'facilities' would soon bring him down, so they hadn't put a sniper on him or sawed the pole in half yet. So far however, the cold had had no effect other than to freeze him immobile, which only added to his buddha-like appearance, and the lack of food intake appeared to have obviated the need for 'facilities', at least so far as the current nonstop observations seemed to indicate.

On a more organised level, you had the endless stream of 'let's-have-your-views-on-it' from the press, the competitions, the features, the special reports. Every TV company had its interviews with schoolkids and grannies and jail-birds and priests. The BBC had a song contest for it.

Then prophecies staged a comeback. After ninety-seven, when the pope that was supposed to have been the one in whose reign we all got creamed, came and went, nobody had a lot of time left for prophets. If old Malachy flunked it, the general feeling went, then who the hell *could* get it right? Why, they even started flogging computer programs that could take in any amount of current news and analyse you up a prophecy on any subject you named, be it men's fashions or limited nuclear war.

But with a new millenium, you had to get a new resurgence in the art. According to one bathead, we were going to get visited, yet again, by intelligent beings from another star system within the next year. The Russians would finally opt for the capitalist road some time soon, though not yet. Furthermore, there was going to be a major fast-breeder accident very soon, which was great news and a merry yuletide for all those dwelling within fallout radius of fast breeders. President Richardson was going to walk back into the White House again, so the polls just happened to be right on that. And we were in for a lousy stinking cold winter.

If you sat back and just looked and listened and read and heard, you could see millenium fever catching hold. You could feel it taking a grip on people. You could see them walking around, looking up and round and side to side, as if AD 2001 was peeping over the rooftops, getting ready to pounce.

And when the screen was up on Centre Point, they stopped in crowds to look at that as well.

It was vast. It covered the top two thirds of the entire west face of the skyscraper. By day it sat there in midair like a huge piece of paper, waiting for some mighty hand to come along and scrawl cosmic graffiti on it. By night it manifested as a great black gap among the patchwork towers of neighbouring buildings, like some massive open door to a nameless region of dark and unknown space. People were gathering to point up at this massive screen. A TV picture *that* big? Was it possible? Why yes, TCTV had promised it. What was more, it would be a worldwide linkup, it would last all afternoon and all night. Well my oh my, would say the passers-by. Isn't science wonderful?

Of course, the folk in the streets couldn't see the preparations on top of Selfridge's, where technicals and various other members of the production teams laboured over the

176

steadily growing mass of equipment. Inside their weather-proof shelters, they checked their lasers and their targeting equipment, power supplies, cameras, cables, items beyond numbering. Already they had hurled pictures to the screen, using lower power beams invisible to the crowds below, but visible through the intensifier optics of their calibrating rigs. Already it was looking very smooth indeed.

Overhead, the crowds had seen the big balloon a few times, the slender airship with Pureflite emblazoned on the side. It had something to do with the big screen, that was everybody's bet, but what exactly none could guess.

Inside the gondola, Artistic reigned in splendour, demanding first one angle of the skyscraper, then another. Many times he had lowered the wide-angled microphone on its massive, chain-enclosed cable. No doubt about it. He would capture sounds on that night that had never been experienced before.

28

Wiretapping was just the old-fashioned term for it.

In fact, since the nineties rolled up, nobody actually tapped anything. There weren't usually any wires.

It was the long-awaited fibre optic technology that changed all that. Instead of your python-thick cable with its sheaths of metals and plastic, you had this thing the width of a pencil. Inside, it was mostly cladding, but *right* inside you had these sixteen or so ultra-flexible glass tubes, each no more than a fraction of a millimetre in diameter. The glass of which these fibres were made was so pure and clear that if you shone light into a block of it as wide as the UK, you'd still get twenty per cent of your photons out of the other side. So you put a spot of light down one of these tiny fibres and generally it came out of the other end, even if the other end was very far away.

That's how the information travelled these days. What started off as a digital message in a computer or as a complex sound in a human voice-box ended up being fed to a laser, which turned electrical signals into matching light pulses and fed them down the glass fibres in streams of sixty-four million per second. Different sets of data became interlaced in this avalanche of light. Thousands of conversations, hundreds of thousands of computer to computer transfers were jumbled together. Magic software in the computers at either end sorted them out, each machine sifting out those intended for itself from the many others.

There was no way to break into a fibre optic link halfway. You had to catch the message you wanted to intercept either before it went down the glass chute, or when it came out. It went in from the memory of a machine, and it emerged into another one. And to hunt around in there you needed software.

Modern wiretappers didn't use crocodile clips. They used programs.

'You want me to do *what*?' George sounded really blown by it.

'It's easy,' Luke soothed. 'Anybody can do it. Lots of kids do it all the time.'

George, not surprisingly, seemed less than convinced. 'Look lover, I don't know anything about computers, see. I don't know anything about computer programs either. TV programmes yes, computer programs no.'

'You don't have to know a damn thing.'

'Balls.'

'No, honest, kid. It's true. You just plug in the box I give you in the place I tell you. That's it.'

'That's all?' George made plugging-in motions with one hand. The other she flapped in Luke's face, kosher style, as if to say tell me another. 'That's all there is to it, right?'

'Well apart from a couple of commands. Just little tiny commands. Nothing much.'

'Forget it.'

Lucius Finn knew it was going to get like this. George wasn't exactly the leader of the pack when it came to technological awareness. It wasn't that she was stupid, though admittedly most of her cunning was animal, it was just that she distrusted anything that had buttons, or hummed or flickered, which left George at odds with most of the accoutrements of modern living.

Just now George was curled up in Luke's antique, seventies-vintage velour sofa, gripping a brandy glass between her bare thighs.

She'd buy it in the end. Luke knew how he could be sure of that. There was an easy way.

Lucius Finn had been manipulating the mailnet system. He'd done it before and so had a few other people, Wyke included, though it was naturally as illegal as hell. With its fibre-optic technology the system was supposed to be secure against tampering. It was meant to be a super-service, where you paid your subscription and hooked in your computer with whatever software Telecoms said was compatible and you became a bang up to date participating member of the age of electronic mail. You weren't supposed to end up getting screwed by it.

It looked right now as if Tekniks actually believed that.

Luke had put a lot of effort into getting the Tekniks mailnet computer to talk to him without knowing who the hell it was talking to. Its conversation so far had consisted only of an acknowledgment of his existence, together with a standard ID-string which gave Finn a few basic though vital facts about itself. He had to decode a twenty-digit alphanumeric string to get them, but they were all there. Its type, hence its operating system and a few other things. It was all Luke needed to know.

Knowing that, he could write a program for that Tekniks computer that would merge unobtrusively with the many other programs resident in its brain. Also, he could arrange for it to be easily loaded into the computer from a standard peripheral device which, from knowing the machine's type, he knew could be connected to its front panel.

This was the box that he had been telling George about. It was a tiny disk drive. In it you had a flat square plastic container with a microdisc inside that held Luke's program. Coming out of it you had a jack-pin array which locked into a hole array on the Tekniks machine's chin. You could plug it on in one second, less with practice. From here it was a couple of simple instructions on the keyboard, and the program was off the disk and into the computer. Out with the jack and there was no trace. Meanwhile the program was scuttling into the id-segment area of the computer locating resident program names, picking a typical one and renaming itself in the local idiom so to speak, so any curious system hack scanning the file lists wasn't easily going to spot the interloper.

All that was fairly standard trickery these days. Pretty low-key stuff, in fact. What mattered with Luke Finn's program was the job that it was going to perform.

It was a bug, an eavesdropper. *Bug* was Luke's name for it.

Bug was a rewrite of programs that Finn had used before, on similar exercises to this. *Bug* was software's answer to the little things they used to hide in the mouthpieces of telephones, just after they invented fire. Once running, *bug* would listen out for any mailnet messages coming into the Tekniks machine from any source. If any such message arrived, *bug* would relay it down the mailnet to Luke's fictitious address, where it would appear on his office computer. *Bug* could do other things too, if it had to. It could open a back door for other spy programs if necessary, and if it needed to fight, it could fight. Right now Luke just wanted to do some eavesdropping.

All it needed was to get loaded on to the Tekniks machine. All that needed was George.

Luke decided to stop pussyfooting with her.

'Look, these Tekniks people are involved somehow in that Measons thing with the pill and with whatever happened to your brother.'

George eyed him with alarm. There was that troubled, sick look she kept flashing however much she tried to hide it. And it made Luke feel bad, in a sudden switch of emotion that came on him like the dimming of a light. Call it empathy? Luke was in love with George.

'What did happen to Steve?'

'I don't know yet. He may have just gone somewhere. But somebody somewhere must know, and I think this Tekniks firm might be the place to start getting some answers.'

'But what's their connection to Steve?' George groaned. 'I don't get it.'

Luke wanted to be patient.

'The connection with Steve is just the connection with Measons. The connection with Measons is complicated.

You've got to understand the software industry, the computer industry. It's the game I used to be in, remember.'

'I remember,' George said. 'Before we met, right? Don't give it me again.'

'Fine,' Luke said. 'All it comes down to is they've got this man working at Measons. He's a Tekniks guy but he works at Measons. He's a specialist in a certain kind of computer program. He was close to your brother, functionally speaking. He could be involved.'

By now George knew damn well she was going to go along with this manic scheme of his. If he wanted to don rubber and perform some act or other on Marble Arch, she knew damn well she'd go with that too. George was in love with Luke.

'You say he's *involved*,' she moaned. 'What the hell is *involved*?'

'It means he's bad, kid,' he stated very quietly. 'It means he does bad things. Very bad things. For Tekniks. Why, we don't know. We think we might know, but we aren't sure.' Luke hesitated. 'The truth is we aren't sure of any of it. I'm just telling you something that maybe you need to be told. I can't make you believe what I believe.'

George just stared. Well get that! Straight from the heart, was it? Reach out, brother, it's easy to do, just reach out.

'What do I have to do, then?'

Lucius Finn gave Georgina Maringelli his best hair-framed dazzling smile, normally reserved for those of whom he required more than favours, and started to lead the way to his office. That was a walk of about twenty metres through a couple of rooms, and it did not require George to put on any clothing.

'I'll show you,' he told her when they were both standing in front of his machine. 'You ready?'

'Yeh, right.'

'OK. Now imagine you've got to their mailnet computer and you're standing in front of one of its VDUs, right?'

'I can't imagine that.'

'I'll show you photographs of the exact thing. You'll find it, even if they've got others, which they probably have.'

'Suppose they've got others of the same frigging type?' George said. Which was a most germane observation, considering.

'We can handle that, don't sweat.' He pointed to the screen of his own monitor. 'Look, see that funny little up-arrow? That's its prompt, see. Whenever the computer wants you to tell it to do something, that's what it puts on the screen. Now their mailnet machine is an STA G700. That's not the same as mine, but the only difference it makes as far as this is concerned is the prompt symbol. Instead of an up-arrow, it's a colon.'

'A colon. OK,' George said, trying hard.

'Fine. So key in the word mail.'

'Male? Like in female?'

'No, mail. That's m-a-i-l. On the keyboard there.'

George did it.

'Hit the key marked *return*. Always do that as a kind of full stop.'

George did it.

Immediately the screen whipped up its mailnet message. George smiled to see it, because she'd seen it before. It announced the service, asked you what you wanted to do, and so on.

'That's all you have to do,' Luke said. 'Just type in mail, and you get the old mailnet start-up message. That's how you tell it you're dealing with their mailnet G700, even if they've got other G700s around. If you're lucky, they'll have a piece of rotten cardboard on the VDU stating the fact. Most outfits do that.'

'OK, then what?'

Luke produced the box, as if by legerdemain. It was about the size of a paperback book. It had no visible controls save two flat touchsensor pads on the front. From the back end protruded a wire with a pin-jack on the other end.

'This is a very nice bit of kit,' Luke told her, in the

manner of a salesman. 'You can keep it in your pocket, if you like, and just have the cable coming out in your hand. All you have to do is press those two pads one after the other. That's *power on*, and *online*. OK so far?'

'So far,' George said.

'Now watch,' Luke went on. 'I place the jack into the hole in the front of the VDU marked *remote disk*, OK? Their G700 VDUs have one just like it. It says the same thing. Nothing happens on the screen, OK?'

'OK.'

'Now you type *rdload*. Go ahead, type it.'

George tapped it in on the keys. After a second or so she followed where Luke was looking and remembered to follow up with the return key.

The screen said, '↑ rd unit online, local.'

Luke said, 'Now type *bug*.'

'Just *bug*? That's all?'

'That's it.'

George did it one-fingered. Click, clock, clock, return. This time the screen said, '↑ bug loaded, 128 blocks.'

'That's it,' Luke said. 'Now just hold down the return key till you've cleared the screen, and haul out the jack.'

George held down the key and watched everything that had just happened on the screen roll up and away. The jack plug came out without any reaction, just as it went in.

'All there is to it,' Luke said.

'No kidding?' George was converted. Any kid could hack this. What made these software hicks such hot stuff anyway?

'Just one thing,' Luke told her. 'On their machine you don't type *rdload*, you type *rdload 1*. Can you remember that?'

'Of course I can damn well remember that. What happens if I screw up?'

'Nothing. You can't break it. You can't cause a rupture. It just won't play.'

'Suppose it doesn't play and I *haven't* screwed up?'

'Then forget it. Just lean on the return key to clean up and get out.'

George reached out with her right hand and pushed her forefinger through Luke's goatee, round his chin and up behind his ear. Her breasts moved to accommodate the action. She began to push her knee up the inside of Luke's thigh. She was smiling in a totally different way.

'Sounds easy,' she purred.

Luke smiled right back.

'You'll murder it,' he promised.

29

Day: minus 1

George and McEwen and Technical One went plodding up the stairs. It was stairs and not lift because they'd been visiting other firms on the floors below, and legging it up a couple of flights was less time elapsed, albeit more exertion.

Still as that klutz on the other channel kept on saying, it flushes out the arteries. George always watched the be-healthy klutz on the other channel, because he was better than the be-healthy klutz TCTV had on theirs. Their be-healthy klutz looked like a victim of the palsy. He looked downright ill. He made you *feel* ill.

McEwen made it up like a racing ape. He could probably go up and down stairs all bloody day and night if he had to. As for Technical One, death's door was what it looked like. Next to him, George felt like a high-jumper.

Technical One was around because he was necessary. The whole wiring *had* to be checked. What strictly didn't need checking was the fastening. My left ball on it, McEwen had avowed, they're secure. But George needed McEwen as an excuse to forage about the Tekniks suite in every office facing west over Oxford Street, because she didn't know which one they kept their computer terminals in, and that meant McEwen being just a very little in the know on this caper.

'What's *he* going to be doing?' the big Scot whispered, referring to Technical One. McEwen whispering sounded like a force nine.

'Checking the cabling,' George said. They both contemplated Technical One's corduroy-clad behind, about six steps up as he led the way off the stair landing and into Tekniks' tropical foyer. The only thing that was different about it since the last time George was in here was the lengths of heavy power cables that came out of the air-conditioning ducts and snaked around the walls and down to the western-facing corridor. From there they branched off into various office doors, whose occupants were not only obligingly leaving them ajar, but also working by permanent neon as the screen outside blocked all daylight.

The receptionist gave them the usual patter and led off down the corridor. When she reached the first office she stopped and leaned into it, one leg pointing out towards them. A light shone from inside, finding its way out over the corridor floor and on to the opposite wall. While she spoke to the incumbent of the desk within, McEwen enjoyed a long uninterrupted view of the leg, which he observed with satisfaction was adorned in the traditional 'suspender' style of which so much was said but so little seen.

'In you go,' she honked.

For the next five minutes George watched as Technical One and McEwen clambered out of the window and inspected various parts of the large laminated screen attached to the outside.

One man resided in this office. Throughout the check of the equipment – which was McEwen yanking on things like a trapeze artist and Technical One connecting up a box with dials on and reading things – he attempted to maintain the illusion of carrying on regardless. Even when McEwen's boot arrived by his suited arm, he politely moved the arm and said nothing. What he seemed to be doing was some kind of design. It had boxes on it, and arrows and circles and diamonds and small pictures of various types of computer equipment.

He's a programmer, George decided.

George came on with her 'call-me-out-the-numbers' role for a while, but since he didn't seem to notice what she was supposed to be doing, she let it go and strolled out of the room, leaving the door open so people passing could see what a real fucking nuisance this was, so hopefully a few of them would vacate for a minute or so and get a coffee or something. It was worth a throw, Luke had told her, anything was usually worth a throw.

Four doors down, on the opposite side of the corridor, she found a door labelled 'Mail'. She slid in, pushing the door to behind her but not closing it.

George was in a dark room containing what seemed to be a minimal quantity of equipment. But beyond it, visible through glass panels, was a much bigger place like something out of a space movie, reached through a pair of larger doors labelled 'Computers'. George didn't want to go in there, but she peered fascinated through the glass.

It was deserted right now, and it stretched all the way to a far wall with yet another door that must have come out beyond the corridor somewhere. George had not seen a mainframe room before; she stared in at it uncomprehendingly.

There were big cabinets with switches on standing side by side opposite rows of smaller ones with plastic domes on top. Processors, disk drives. Here and there she recognised a magnetic tape unit from its big vertical reels which now spun spasmodically. In the corner a pair of lineprinters kerked erratically, spitting paper up in bursts. There were work tables dotted about, with half-open heaps of listings, and yet more monitors winking and flashing. It was as if the whole thing was alive, functioning on its own.

It was clean in there, George thought dully, like a hospital. On the wall she could see the air-conditioning units with paper streamers blowing from them to reveal the airflow. The floor was sectioned into tiles, covering the cabling, whose conduits snaked neatly up the walls to the partition ceiling from which hung fire sprinklers and halon gas inlets.

George pulled herself away from it and turned.

She put on a light from the waist-high switch by the

door and saw four VDUs, all the same shape. None of them looked like Luke's VDUs. These things sat up on stalks like robot heads. Their keypads were below, on the ends of cables. They all had STA, in stylised slanting letters along the bottom edge of their cases.

One of them had a large card standing on top of it. On the card was the word 'Mailnet'.

Hellfire, thought George. Oh hellfire.

George backed off a pace and looked up the corridor. People were approaching, official-looking people with identity badges on their lapels. Technical One and McEwen were entering the next office along. Down the corridor, a couple of women were standing talking to each other. They seemed engrossed.

George decided on minimum risk. She strolled back down the corridor and hung around outside the second office until McEwen and Technical One came out. Technical One knocked on the third office and then went on in, but George got McEwen by the arm.

'Now,' she whispered, 'in this one.'

'Sure?'

'Of course I'm bloody sure.'

McEwen pursed his lips and went into the office after Technical One while George strolled casually back towards the 'Mail' door.

It happened almost immediately.

There was a whooping yell trailing off into an anguished wail of fear from the third room. Everybody within earshot turned to the sound. A youngish man, on his way down the corridor, dived into the office without breaking his stride. A second later he was out again, followed by Technical One.

'A man's fallen out of the window,' he announced to all. 'Where can I get a rope?'

'What's happened?' another voice enquired.

'A bloke's fallen out the window,' the young man said again. 'One of the TV people. He's tumbled down behind the screen.'

'How far down?'

'About a floor or so. He's safe enough, but he needs a pull up.'

'What about the fire brigade?' another spark suggested.

'He isn't on sodding fire,' the youngish man said. 'He just needs a hand up. Now where the hell is a rope?'

'What about a fire hose?' somebody said.

'Right! Right! That's good. Get the fire hose.'

Between them, the young man and others dragged many feet of red rubber fire hose through the office. The crowd followed, forming a hubbub at the door.

George faded into the mail room and went straight to the mailnet VDU. There was nothing on the screen but a single green colon in the top left-hand corner, followed by a letter-sized green rectangle, which pulsed regularly, as if panting.

George put her hand into the deep right-hand pocket of her leather hip-length jacket and drew out the tip of the jack-plug cable, made double sure the disk drive buttons were on, found the remote disk connection on the VDU by peering under its chin, and slid in the jack.

It's easy. Don't worry, she told herself, it's easy.

She keyed in the *rdload* command and hit the return key.

The VDU wrote up, 'Command not recognisable.'

George froze.

What in hell was the damn thing on about?

What in God's name was wrong?

George thought, don't panic. Yet.

Voices approached from the other end of the corridor. They were talking about the TV people. One of them mentioned the woman in charge.

Suddenly George remembered. She keyed in *rdload 1* and returned. The VDU responded with 'rd unit online:1', which was close to what Luke's had said.

Close enough for jazz, George thought, and typed in *bug*.

'bug loaded: 128 blocks' it said, just as she'd been led to expect.

George hammered the return key and cleared the VDU

screen. She tore out the jack, pocketed it, left the room. She put on what nobody would have been fooled into thinking was a relaxed, what's-the-fuss-type air. In fact, nobody even looked at her.

They had McEwen out by now. He had struggled dutifully like a trapped fly, down behind the giant screen, until they lowered the fire hose and rubber-banded him back up to the window whence he had surreptitiously leapt. He was bruised and scuffed in places, but George would soothe all that with a timely payment of best malt. Professional to the end, McEwen didn't even give George an awkward glance. He just laughed at everybody and said what a fool he was and sorry for the fuss. Technical One told him he was a clumsy twat. McEwen told Technical One to go and jerk off.

They finished the pseudo check without any further ado. On their way out they thanked the receptionist who glued on an extra-special ivory-clad smile for them. Halfway down in the lift, George remembered that she'd left the light on in the mail room.

30

Luke wrestled through the crowds that were pouring into the capital, taking maybe four times longer to get to Schaum than usual. They were like ants on the march, the way they were pouring in. Cops were everywhere. The day was glittering bright and cold, under a blue sky with no clouds from end to end. As he rolled through the security post at the main gates, he thought he could hear a band somewhere. Today there were bands everywhere.

The techlibrarian nearly swooned when Luke turned up. Every time this bearded son of a bitch appeared it meant strife. Today the man had intended to get away prompt, but if this swine wanted help till midnight, the Olympian directive was that he got it. Shit and more shit.

'Yes, there's a list,' the librarian affirmed. 'All test flights have a list.'

The AX–9 flight list made a total of thirty-seven individuals, including the aircrew. That was thirty-seven dismembered corpses feeding the arctic sharks at the bottom of the Aleutian trench. Against each name were some brief details, not many, but enough to link them to mainbase files, such as personnel.

Sandell came around like a pilot fish, like he always did, just as Finn settled into the cubicle. Luke figured it was either Security or Techlib who had the standing word to tell him.

'Why them?' was the obvious question. 'What's to find, Luke?'

'Something, maybe nothing.' What he wanted to say, he

couldn't. What he wanted to ask was whether or not these thirty-seven had been on the technical personnel lists that went into OTC inside the technocrime file when the incident occurred. Since he wasn't supposed to have seen that, he couldn't ask. But maybe it was so. If it *wasn't* so, then *why* it wasn't so could be an interesting question.

Luke found all of them in the personnel stream. One by one he let them slide up on the VDU screen. One by one he examined their sections, their areas of expertise. Sandell looked at them too, without seeming to know what was being looked for.

Still no contractors, Still no Tekniks.

'Dead end,' Luke said ruefully.

'*What's* a dead end?' Sandell said. 'Try me, Luke. What was the hunch?'

'Just a thought, that was all. Maybe one of them was a control system man.'

'Well definitely,' Sandell said. 'I can confirm that.' He pointed to the very bottom of the screen. 'This guy here. He was one for sure. So what?'

'So nothing. It was only a thought.'

'A saboteur? In the crew?' Sandell seemed blown by the idea. 'He'd have to have committed suicide, no?'

'Yes,' Luke said.

Finn flicked off the VDU and stood up. He folded the piece of narrow output listing paper into a fourfold triangle and turned for the cubicle door.

'Happy new year, Sandy,' he said wistfully. 'Maybe we'll get stoned tomorrow.'

Sandell watched him go, watched him toss the flight list back to the techlibrarian on his way to the exit. The techlibrarian was puffing with some kind of relief.

Bruno was growing observably more restless. He needed to be allowed to hurt someone again, and soon.

'Get rid of them,' he said bluntly. 'Kill them, kill all of them.'

'When we know what's going on. Then we'll get rid of them,' Constantine said.

Constantine felt his hair rising behind his ears. It felt like the caress of some small hand, brushing upwards.

'We know what's going on,' Bruno said. 'You've got your coincidence explained. The woman is Finn's bird. He's looking for her brother because she fucks him. Finn and Wyke are old pals. They're swapping notes. Now she's been snooping around here again. How much do you fucking need?'

Bruno's rasping tones didn't put Constantine in a well-wishing mood. It cramped his psychoanalytic style, which generally rested on the psychiatrist not getting pissed off with the nutter on the couch.

Not that Bruno was any ordinary nutter.

'There was that light in the mail room,' he growled on. 'Maybe she did something in there?'

Constantine smiled. Bruno thought in black and white, that was the trouble. To him, facts were like building blocks, and what passed in Bruno's reptilian mind for a thought was just a pile of facts, with square edges and no fuzziness or probability or significance or interpretation. If they fitted together, that to him was reason and cause. This new fact, this new business with the Maringelli woman, was all Bruno needed to turn his helpless struggling with disjointed facts into a solid, unbreakable immutable superfact, a megafact that demanded action and effect.

'She hasn't the capability,' Constantine said. 'She was just snooping, that's all.'

'The man who fell from the window, then? It wasn't a diversion?'

'Of course. She had a peep round the place. Probably looked in a few drawers. But there's nothing to see, is there?'

'We'll settle with her soon enough,' Bruno assured him. 'She goes out shortly.'

Constantine pointed at Bruno, a new, commandeering manner in his attitude.

'Tomorrow, Bruno. Everything will happen tomorrow.'

'I can have them, then,' Bruno stated, a kind of claim.

'Wyke, probably,' Constantine said. 'I want Finn and the woman here. We'll have a little party, I think.'

Not finding Tekniks in the Schaum case file had been making Luke fret some. There had to be a link, and if one wasn't visible there were a couple of possible reasons to go or. One of them was that somebody took Tekniks out of the Schaum case file before Wyke got to it. If that was the case then it had to have been done in OTC somewhere, and wouldn't that be a thing, oh my yes.

But there was another place to look, right? What consultancy didn't keep a file of its clients?

Luke had a program that scoured a computer's files, just like he had programs for most of his dirty tricks. This one he called *hacker*. Getting *hacker* loaded was *bug*'s job: *bug* was the one that gave *hacker* a pull-up into the enemy camp.

Of course, he could have made *bug* a file hunter as well, but that made *bug* a little too big and a little too visible. Luke preferred to keep it simple. He kept *bug* as a mailnet keeper with just enough intelligence to load up another program on demand and wipe it afterwards. That way the main interloper kept a low profile and temporaries like *hacker* went in and out as fast as they were needed. A lot of TIs did it that way; though the variations were legion.

Luke had got *bug* to load *hacker* into the Tekniks mail machine after a couple of tries. Right now the pair of them were giving him lists of file names. Luke tried to be quick. If they started to use their mailnet now they'd likely spot the activity.

Cs, thought Luke, try the Cs. There were maybe twenty files starting with C. Clients started with C.

Hurreeee . . .

Luke keyed in a list command for a file called *cpsupp.a* Immediately addresses swept up his screen, tabled against

195

names like IBM, DEC . . . He killed it. They were cpu
suppliers. Again he scanned the file list. What about
condr.1? Luke listed it and found himself reading a draft
contract. Damn!

Luke started to sweat. Maybe they didn't keep a client
list on the mailnet machine? But hell, they'd have to,
wouldn't they?

Then he saw it, right there at the bottom. Luke banged
in the call for a list of the file names *currcl.1*. Had to be
current clients, *had* to be.

Just for a second, he sat back and grinned. There they
were, the current clients of Tekniks. Already he could see
Measons about halfway down.

Luke didn't waste time reading the screen, he just
reached over and flicked on his printer and keyed in the
print line. Right away the information on the screen started
to chatter out on the paper roll to his left. In less than a
minute it was finished and Luke sent in the order to stop.
The screen went blank. Miles away, *bug* took control of the
Tekniks machine, wiped out all traces of *hacker*, relinqu-
ished the processor and faded back into its lair to wait for
incoming transmissions.

In his office, Luke tore off the listing and started to
read. He was breathing steadily again, but the smile was
dropping off his face.

No Schaum still. He went down the list again to be sure
and then accepted it. Schaum just wasn't one of Tekniks
clients. Not even Tekniks' own files said so. Luke folded
the list very slowly and neatly and slid it absently into his
pocket.

31

Day: zero: 31 December 2000

By just after midday, central London was starting to creak, audibly. From Marble Arch eastwards, Oxford Street through to Holborn was sagging under the weight. Traffic was down to one lane each way, and half the time that was blocked by drifting mobs of folk welling off the pavements in droves. The pulsating swarms continued down Regent Street, Tottenham Court Road, Charing Cross Road, Piccadilly, Park Lane and beyond. Baker Street and Portland Place were filling up. Bond Street and South Audley were going under fast. Along these thoroughfares the Metropolitan Police battled to maintain access. Wherever you looked there was a cop yelling at a herd of pedestrians to keep back. What they were keeping back from was anybody's guess.

The battle on behalf of automobiles was already lost. Mayfair and Soho were jammed solid with human flesh. Within this one area, the police were estimating at least two million souls on the move. For pickpockets it was the day of days.

As for the cops, they were at their wits' end already. Every scrap of leave was cancelled, every blackhat in the Met and City forces was out slugging non stop, with no shift breaks or breathers. The stations were empty, bar the duty officers, and they were breaking new ground in control and command. Muggers and thieves they tossed uncharged end over end in cells to await the new millenium. Drunks and whores they chucked back out in the street. Those complaining of dogs fouling footpaths they just laughed at. Lost kids stayed totally and tearfully lost.

Over it all, senior officers in the communications centres in Vauxhall and Marylebone yelled advice and instructions to each other about how bad it was *really* going to get in the next few hours. Nobody even tried to imagine what it was going to be like in the dark. The coming night seemed beyond dreams.

'Far out,' George said, looking down over the Selfridge parapet. 'I never saw crowds like that before.'

Technical One turned away from the laser he was twiddling with to join her for a second.

'I saw something like it in Saint Peter's Square once when they were choosing Pope Leo. Remember that one? It was hot as hell, as well.'

'I wasn't on that one,' George said. Popes were not George's metier. She was more into kings and potentates, coronations of. 'The coronation was a big crowd,' she said.

'Not as big as the Pope,' Technical One insisted. 'The Italians go ape over a new pope.'

Technical One went back to his equipment. He had one crew with him, another being up in the dirigible which at the moment was heading their way from its lift-off point in Hyde Park. King of the scene up there was Artistic, who had a camera crew, video crew and various idiot commentators, together with a sufficient supply of scrumptious food and wine to last them all well into the next millenium.

Here on Selfridge's roof the TCTV Real Features team had been swelling all morning as various engineers, presenters, newstypes and Lord knows what else came and stayed and got briefed in. Bolts-wise it looked OK. Technical One and his tame eggs kept running checks on every bit of kit strewn across the roof, no doubt with an ear to George's stated threat to personally castrate with her fingernails anybody having any connection with any piece of gadgetry that failed to function one hundred per cent when switch-on time came.

George watched the big silver cigar come up and over to the west and then lifted the handset she was carrying.

'What's it like up there?' she said.

Nothing happened. Then a hiss and a crackle came out of the thing in her hand and a voice said, 'Pardon? Is somebody on the air?'

George had no mind for procedures. Shitfuck, she thought. Then she said, 'Ground to balloon. This is Maringelli. How's it look up there, over.'

'Balloon to ground,' came Artistic's unmistakable warble. 'Absolutely disgusting, over.'

'Ground. We're ready to take some video.'

'Balloon. Any time. Just some crowd scenes?'

'Ground. That'll do. We won't put it out yet. Checking the system.'

'Balloon. Stand by ground.'

Up in the gondola, Artistic gave directions to the cameramen on either side. They flicked on their minicams and started gunning triggers. On the two ancillary viewers, Artistic could see what they were seeing below. 'Send one down,' he said to Technical Two, who was sitting over the control panel, awaiting his commands like a robot.

Artistic was rather pleased to be up here in the air-conditioned gondola rather than down there on a freezing roof. It was more pleasant, and better for his hair.

Down on the freezing roof, George watched the video appear on their local viewers. Not bad, she decided.

'Looks good,' she said into the handset. 'How about some audio? Is the mike down?'

Aloft, Artistic supervised the lowering of the huge hanging microphone assembly. It was a big brute composing a cluster of directional mikes. Fully seventy centimetres across the array, and encased in a steel shell the shape of an enormous egg. It dangled from a massive chain with links as thick as your finger. As the mike went out and down, it began to sway about a mean tilted angle of a couple of degrees to the vertical.

When it was down by about ninety metres or so, Artistic told them to switch on.

It was amazing. A combination of sounds never heard before filled the gondola. The directional mikes each reached down to a different patch of streetworld, spanning an area of a half-kilometre radius. One grabbed a labouring police siren, another the calls of a newsvendor, others the chattering of individuals in the crowd. The separate noises were piped up through the cable and speakered out together. It was a sound picture, just as Artistic had said it would be.

'Balloon. Getting it?'

'Ground. Yeh. It's great.'

'I told you it would be,' Artistic said from his throne on high. 'Didn't I tell you, over?'

George watched the dirigible floating abreast of her now, with the chain dangling behind it like an umbilical. At the point end was a shorter mooring cable, but it was the big mike chain that you could see sweeping along behind.

'Yeh,' George said. 'You told me.'

32

Pruett was wearing a pair of green cords, a checked lumber-jack shirt and a long-suffering smile. He slouched behind his desk with his legs crossed and one booted foot on his knee. Both his arms dangled loosely behind him as if he was waiting to be tied up.

'Is this going to take long?' he asked. 'I wanted to be out by four along with the rest of the city.'

'Oh?' Douglas said. 'Why's that?'

'The place is closing at four.' Pruett said. 'It's the big night, or did you miss the news? So what did you want to speak to me about, Mister Wyke? What is it that's so important it can't wait for the next century?'

'The day he disappeared, Steven Maringelli ran a multi-analysis test on some Phenthanol tablets from the rogue batch,' Wyke said, stating it as a fact. 'I can prove that.'

'What makes you say that?' Pruett asked. His face showed nothing.

'I've seen the results,' Douglas said. 'They match numerous other results on multianalysis tests that have been performed here since then. The Trinax level is the same, the base levels are the same. Even the calibration errors match. His list was done in the main lab right here in this building.'

'Really?' Nothing else.

'Yes, really. I dare say I could pinpoint the very rig it was done on.'

Wyke kept his gaze right in Pruett's eyes, looking for the flicker of something.

'Fascinating,' Pruett said evenly. 'I presume you've told the management here?'

'Not yet. They'd only go trampling on everybody in sight. Some cockroach might scuttle out underfoot.'

'Meaning what?'

'Meaning I'd like to give them a stronger case,' Wyke said.

'And what is the substance of your stronger case, Mister Wyke?'

'You are, Mister Pruett.'

The consultant gave a small dismissive laugh.

'Please be so good as to expand.'

'You told him to run some sample tests on the market stuff,' Douglas said. 'It's a pretty routine chore. By that time all of the bad batch was out. I've checked the dispatch situation myself. If he'd gone to dispatch he'd have been given good tablets. But he must have gone to a shop somewhere and bought some and that means he found them too quickly.'

'Too quickly for what?'

'For your plans. By then they'd been in the shops for about half a day. Given a good effort – radio, TV, police cars with loudspeakers – they'd have cut down on the victims. You and your pals wanted a good few victims.'

'What the hell are you talking about?'

'Didn't you?' Wyke said.

'I asked you what you're talking about.'

'I'm talking about this conspiracy you're involved in. A conspiracy to hurt people and screw this company out of a lucrative and competitive market. Somebody is paying you to sabotage its product. And that's what you did.'

'At last, the accusation itself,' Pruett smirked.

'Didn't you?' Wyke said.

'You're mad,' Pruett told him. 'What you're saying is absurd. Of course I told him to run some spot checks. Everyone is aware of that. But he didn't. Also your sabotage idea is sheer fantasy. It couldn't be done.'

'On the contrary, it's not absurd. It's more than credible,

202

given the sophistication of the plant in this company. Given the fact that it's the most highly SPC'd drug production plant in Europe. Given that it's just been installed. Given that you're in charge of the mixing control software, and the autoassay control. You're about the only person who could do it. Now tell me about Tekniks.' Douglas changed tack deliberately. He wasn't too bad on the psychology.

'Tekniks?'

'Your pals,' Douglas said. 'Your employers. Tell me about them.'

Pruett started shifting his butt around on the chair.

'Tekniks is my employer. That's all there is to it. They're a consultancy. I'm a consultant. I'm one of many in this organisation, especially with the new plant and . . .'

'Do they tell you things?' Douglas asked softly. 'Do they tell you who's paying them for you to do this? Some continental outfit maybe? One of the big Swiss pharmaceuticals? Do you get told who's paying for you to commit murder, Mister Pruett?'

'I think . . .'

'Or do you just do it?'

Pruett stuck his hand up, signalling time.

'I think this has gone far enough,' he started to say. 'You have accused me of a serious crime. You have accused my employers of something equally serious. You'd better make this official, Mister Wyke.'

Douglas slammed his feet down on the floor and stood up. Without waiting for Pruett to go on with his claiming of civil and criminal rights, he turned for the door.

'That we'll leave till the next century,' he said on his way out. 'Enjoy the celebrations – Mister Pruett.'

Douglas Wyke came out of the Measons gate at precisely three twenty seven, walked towards his car, and passed within six metres of Bruno, who was sitting in his.

But Douglas didn't get in the vehicle. As Bruno craned around to watch, he crossed the street to a public call box on the opposite pavement.

203

Bruno swore a silent oath. This was one time where he could have used one of those old-fashioned little buttons. In the time that Wyke was punching up his number he could have slid over there and stuck one on the glass behind the coinbox, no problem. Bruno didn't have one, though. Also, he couldn't lip read.

In the box, Douglas kept it short.

'Luke? I'm just out.'

From his office window Luke could see the crowds milling towards Cambridge Circus. He was standing with the phone tucked under his chin, unwrapping a cigar.

'How'd he take it?'

'Well he shat himself, didn't he? He's our boy Luke, I'm sure of it. Watch out for your bug now.'

'Will do. You get back to a receiver and I'll get back when something shows.'

'Will do. I'll be at my place. Listen, Luke – '

'What?'

'What are we going to *do* with this character? I mean, if he bites. What's our actual move? OTC? Cops?'

'No, we collar the fucker. We pull him. There's no telling what Tekniks'll do if we leave him loose.'

TIs had powers of arrest, though few people knew it and they seldom used it. Those who had used it could usually show some scars. People were generally fussy about who they got arrested by.

'So who does that?' Douglas asked, sounding apprehensive.

'It's your case, Doug,' Luke pointed out. 'But I'll back you up.'

Bruno was still watching as Douglas came out of the box and started back to his car. The man had a weary look all of a sudden. Was that a knitted brow? Was the news bad?

It wasn't for Bruno. At long last he was going to use his hands again.

Pruett thought he should wait a while before making contact, but the problem was how to do it. Moving in person was out, that was for sure. It was too visible and the crowds would be too big. That cunning little creep could be skulking outside.

Pruett eyed the phone. Anybody could bug a phone. Holy shit, they didn't even have to do that. You had to *speak* to use a phone, with your actual voice, out loud. They'd only have to bug the damn room. They could do that from across the street. Pruett started to heat up around his neck.

It had to be the mailnet, he decided.

33

The dirigible was about five minutes late taking off for the second flight. The delay was Artistic powdering his nose in the mobile head they'd set up in the TCTV enclosure in Hyde Park. Artistic didn't fancy the pissbowl in the gondola. It looked downright uncivilised.

As it left the ground, Artistic and his crew could see the vast crowd below before they vanished in the gloom of the unlit park.

As they cleared the rooftops they saw the mighty picture on Centre Point. The huge prancing multicoloured oblong blazed out in the dark like a giant lamp, hanging over the layer of light and glitter from the streets. Several crewmen gasped again when they saw it.

'Get some,' one said gently.

'Don't get us too close for now,' Artistic ordered.

Then spake the voice of George.

'Ground to balloon. We're starting the intro any minute. Be ready to switch in, over.'

'Balloon, ready when you are.'

On Selfridge's roof, George watched it steer its way abeam of her. Behind her, laser banks were flashing out their multicoloured raining beams which vanished into the dark in the direction of the giant oblong eye. The whole roof was floodlit, so nobody would fall over wires or brain themselves on microphone booms.

'Get ready,' George shouted to the smoothie.

The presenter made final adjustments to his coiffure,

his lapels, his public-school tie. He cleared his expensive larynx.

George cued the lead-in music and up it came. From here it wasn't too loud, most of what they heard on the roof was from the monitors, but in the streets below it crashed out like thunder. TCTV Real Features theme music, known continent-wide as harbinger of all that's wondrous and new. On the Centre Point screen, TCTV's test pattern vanished, to be replaced by the Real Features logo, and the programme banner: INTO THE MILLENIUM, followed by: A WORLDWIDE ADVENTURE.

George decided she could have done better, bannerwise, given more of a shot at it.

A kilometre away, seven floors up the Pureflite Corporation building, a small number of engineers peered out of their window into the night sky. They could see the searchlight beams lacing about, picking out the dirigible in brilliant oval spots of white. Most of them chattered excitedly.

Only one of them sat by the monitor, fishing for his cigarettes. As he flicked a filter tip into his mouth he glanced at the others and shook his head. He was a little rankled at working up here tonight; on the whole he would have preferred to be out in the streets but the bonus had been too good to pass. It was just a watchdog job really. Nothing to do but keep tabs on the airship's status. If they had to control it they would, but they didn't expect to, not tonight.

The engineer froze, cigarette lighter poised, thumb on the wheel. Something was pouring across the monitor screen too fast to read. What the hell. . . ?

He looked to the others, started to speak, and then looked back. It was gone, replaced by the status messages announcing all OK, with the time stamp following. The engineer keyed a few buttons, interrogated it, ran a test routine, studied the screen again. Nothing. He leaned back again and lit his cigarette, eyebrows puckered. After a while he blinked and began to relax.

Sandell came out of the Tekniks mainframe room into the mailnet room. He waited until the hydraulic door eased shut behind him and then sat down across the table from the two men sitting there.

'It's done,' he said softly. 'It's responding. We're in control.'

Constantine looked impressed. Sandell was more at ease when Constantine looked impressed.

'When does it happen?'

'At midnight, as you said.'

'Why don't you go to my office and have a drink?' Constantine said. It was a hypnotic suggestion.

Sandell thought maybe he'd do that.

It was four twenty-five.

In the dark offices down the western side of Tekniks' floor the pitch black of the rooms was suddenly lit by brilliant multicoloured flashes as synchro'd lasers started their run-in sequences. Vast test patterns lit up the entire side of the skyscraper. Inside the building it was like being in an electric storm. First black, then instantaneous white, black, yellow, blue, black, red; vast bolts of light flooding rooms, leaving retinas with retained images of things in the dark.

Constantine's office was in darkness. John Sandell sat at one end of it with the drink in his hand, resting the glass on his knee, oblivious to the glittering and cascading colours from the screens beyond the windows.

Constantine sat in the mail room and stared flint-eyed at the VDU. He had another man with him, doing all the fingerwork. They watched the screen together, their heads not more than thirty centimetres apart.

The other man was nervous. Nervous of Constantine, nervous of Sandell, nervous of the whole scene. He was starting to wish he was somewhere else.

In the darkened room, the VDU glowed brilliant green. In its reflective surface the faces of the two men shone back, like two ghouls peering into an enchanted pond.

At four thirty exactly, the message came through. Pruett

had mis-spelt a few words here and there, doubtless due to his desire to minimise the time, but that didn't detract from the theme.

They were blown.

Constantine had this horrible pragmatism about what the other man could only view as a sprouting nightmare. He eyed the telephone by the machine. Its volume control was way down, so he could barely hear it burring.

'That'll be Bruno calling in. Get back to Pruett. Tell him to stay where he is. Bruno can take care of him there.'

'Bruno? What . . .'

'Do it.'

The man started keying in the response to the distant, sweating, shitless Pruett. Constantine picked up the phone as if he had all night.

'Bruno?'

'Who else? Have you heard from your person at Measons?'

Constantine knew Bruno was tasting blood already.

'You may act now, Bruno,' Constantine said softly. 'You can deal with the little one first. Is he conveniently nearby?'

'You could say that.' Kilometres away, Bruno had already reconnoitred the upstairs window of Douglas Wyke's place, where the light had been on about five minutes now.

Here, in the low complex, this crime anthill, this muggers' labyrinth, it was going to be too easy, especially with most of the inhabitants up in the West End for the pickings.

'Afterwards I want you to go and see our Mister Pruett. There will be guards to avoid.'

Bruno seemed to have said something like 'Aaaah . . .'

Constantine smiled indulgently.

'I wouldn't want to teach my grandmother to suck eggs,' he said with a chuckle, 'but it would embarrass us if you were careless.'

'Am I ever an embarrassment?' Bruno said. 'Leave it with me. What about the afro prick?'

'Oh, he's got to come here,' Constantine said, hardening his voice a fraction. 'That's important, Bruno. We need to question him.'

Bruno said he'd look forward to that and rang off.

For a few seconds, Constantine didn't realise that the man at the VDU was biting his kunckles.

'What's wrong?'

'I'm not sure. There's something else running. Some kind of monitor program.'

'Talk plainly,' Constantine demanded, turning to the screen. The mailnet reply to Pruett to stay put was no longer there, instead there was a list of mnemonic names, under a column heading that said 'active'. One of them was flashing from normal to reverse video and back again.

'What is that?' Constantine said. 'Why is it flashing?'

'It's a program, dammit. But it's not part of your operating system on this machine.'

There was a portentous pause as the man went looking for a way of putting it.

'It's a software bug,' he said finally. 'It has to be.'

'Stop the mailnet transmission. Stop talking to Pruett.'

'I already have.'

'Turn off the mailnet system.'

He stroked the button. The mailnet prompts and header lines vanished as the service went down.

Then they came back again.

The other man jumped visibly.

'Mailnet's back on,' he said in disbelief. 'It's that program. It brought mailnet back up. It's using it.' He gaped at Constantine. 'It's transmitting. Oh God, it's *telling* somebody what's going on. It's relaying everything we've said to Pruett, everything he . . .'

'Kill it,' Constantine said. 'Terminate it.' What the hell did they say? 'Purge it.'

The man on the keyboard broke in again. He rattled in the command to destroy the running program that was giving them both piles. The system responded, confirming the deed was done. Mailnet prompts went off, header line too.

Then they came back *again*.

The two of them started to go into warp.

'It's back. Oh hellfire, what's it *doing*?'

The program that had been killed was back in business. The OS showed it right there in the active list again, flashing like hell, hogging the CPU.

'It's a clone,' the man howled. 'It's a damn clone. There could be more of them.' He played the keys like a Russian concert pianist, all sweat and concentration without an overemphasis on precision. This time he went into the scheduler list to see what was waiting to run.

There were lots of things waiting to run.

'Dear God, there's hundreds of them.'

They both gazed in horror at the endless list of identical copies of the program that was running right now. They were all identical to it. Kill it and one of them would take its place. Kill that and . . .

Luke hadn't made *bug* as smart as *worm*, but then *bug* wasn't a fighting killer like *worm*, *bug* just had to fight for as long as it needed to survive. *Bug* had spawned, as soon as it started to run, enough progeny to win by weight of numbers once it was spotted. Chinese army tactics.

'We won't need any more transmissions,' Constantine said. 'Turn off the machine. Powerdown the mailnet computer.'

'But someone may want to contact us. We'll be reliant on the phone.' He made a phone sound like native drums.

'Turn off the machine,' Constantine hissed. 'Before I kick it to death.'

The other man reached down to the front console of the small suitcase-sized computer that was housed at floor level under the diskpacks. He grasped the small silver key that was already inserted in the bottom left-hand corner and turned it one quarter anticlockwise. The screen blanked off, leaving just the oblong cursor blinking in the corner.

'Who do you think it was talking to? Do you think it was Finn?'

'We both know it was Finn,' Constantine told him leerily. 'It doesn't matter, though. Soon we'll be seeing Mister Finn. He'll be able to tell us all about it. What you can do is bring in the woman. Now.'

34

Luke read the message again. He'd also picked up a reply, Tekniks back to Pruett. Stay there, it said, until contacted. Well he'd just leave old *bug* running; maybe they'd send something that could be used as evidence.

If bug was still running, that was. There was that suspicious chopped-off last word in the second relay which made Luke think maybe *bug* had been blown and dealt with. If so, they'd probably taken their machine off, because *bug* would have gone down punching.

Still, he had enough.

'It's here,' he told Douglas on the phone. 'Want to go get him now?'

'I was settling down for the great TV spectacular,' Douglas said from his pad. 'And you want to make an arrest?'

Luke laughed. 'It won't take long, Doug. Then you can come back to my place and watch the whole show from my office.'

He knew Wyke wouldn't want to do that. Douglas didn't care for the West End. Maybe it was because he had been born in that played-out rusty section of London in which he lived, that he had this protective dislike of the shiny bits.

'OK, Luke,' Douglas said. 'Inside the Measons main building. The big tower. Ground-floor foyer. We'll go in together.'

'OK,' Luke said.

Finn dropped the phone and looked out of his window

again. He drew on his cigar, the fourth in a row. It made his throat hurt. Then he decided. It had been on his mind a while.

He unlocked the drawer at the back of his antique desk and took out the little snubnosed revolver. He checked that the chambers were full and the safety was on before tucking it into the trouser band in the small of his back. Reaching in again, he scooped out the six spare shells and slipped them into the pockets of his waistcoat, three on each side. The tiny 5.56–millimetre bullets made no bulge at all. The gun was legal enough, but these vicious, tumbling hollowpoint rounds were anything but.

Douglas Wyke switched off his TV set, threw on his worn blouson and left his flat, leaving the lights on inside.

About ninety metres from his downstairs door, along various catwalks and through various alleys, lay Wyke's battered old ninety-four Volkswagen. Bruno had just returned to it, having used it as his starting point for a check of the environs, before calling on Douglas Wyke murder-wise.

Bruno smoothed back his fine, shiny black hair from his forehead and started walking to his intended's abode. The place was so perfectly deserted he could probably do it anywhere, really, it was just a question of making it look like . . .

Douglas appeared, dead ahead, strutting towards him like a chicken.

. . . a casual crime of some sort, Bruno thought on, as recognition dawned, and a warm glow ensued.

Wyke came on oblivious.

A mugging perhaps, Bruno mused, as the distance closed.

Douglas smiled at the big black-clad stranger as he started to pass. He didn't expect the gloved hand on his chest.

'Good evening,' Bruno said. 'Or should I say afternoon? It goes dark so early this time of year.'

'Pardon?' Douglas started. 'Who . . . ?'

214

'Death,' Bruno stated, feeling suddenly poetic. 'I am death. Yours, in fact.'

Bruno had this whimsical turn of mind which made him sometimes put things in a left-handed kind of way, so people just looked at him as if he were peculiar, rather than smart or smooth. Bruno was aware of this minor flaw in his character, and he had a feeling maybe it was part of the reason that Constantine thought he was a psycho. It was a real hoot the way Constantine took him for a psycho. At times, Bruno could barely keep a straight face.

This was going to be good, though.

Bruno moved his hand from Wyke's chest, raised it a fraction to cup the little man's bearded chin, and threw him by the neck against a convenient wall. Douglas arrived with a thud and a crack as his skull connected with the brick. Momentarily stunned he slid down to his backside and started shaking his head.

Bruno advanced grinning, his other hand drawing a length of stout piano wire from his coat pocket. Without taking his eyes off his victim, he wound one end around his left hand several times, leaving the other dangling.

Douglas tried to run. It was the only chance he had. He just got up to one knee and scuttled away. Or tried to.

Bruno let out a sporting growl of appreciation and bounded off in pursuit. But, he reminded himself as he closed in, he mustn't spend too long over this, he had other things to do as well. There was the little runt's place to scour out, then there was Pruett and his bits and bobs to take care of.

Busy night ahead, Bruno thought, as he pounced upon the hapless Wyke.

He seized Douglas by the hair with one hand, dragging him backwards with such force and speed that Wyke's feet flew on a pace or two ahead of his body, making him go over backwards into Bruno's waiting embrace. Bruno hauled upwards on his fistful of hair, stretching Wyke's neck like a capon's as it took the weight of his body. Douglas flailed about with both hands. Some kind of little screech came out of his mouth before Bruno's left hand whipped the wire around his neck and pulled hard to make it bite.

Douglas knew he was going to die. It was one of a number of small, disconnected thoughts that raced through his mind as it was being done. Would it hurt? What was all this to do with Pruett? With Tekniks?

He was distracted momentarily by a kick in the lower back, which broke his spine in two places. He sagged to his knees as his legs ceased to function. His hands grasped at the wire. His eyes rolled upwards to try to see his killer's smiling face. His mouth formed a silent reproach.

Bruno released the hair and lashed away the weak little hands with a couple of swipes of his fist. Then he took the free end of the wire and pulled tight with both gloved hands. The grip was excellent. He planted one knee between the shoulder blades of the runt to push against.

Douglas Wyke expired quite quickly.

Bruno let him drop with a faint crunch on to his face. Then he stood and listened very very carefully for a clear twenty seconds, in case somebody somewhere was moving, peeping, whispering. To maintain appearances, he extracted the few pounds in bank notes that he found in Wyke's pockets as he searched them for things to be removed (Bruno's rule was, when in doubt remove anyway). He stood up and took a final look at the Wyke character before starting to move off to deal with his flat. To further keep up appearances, he planted a couple of hard kicks in the dead man's face, bloodying the open eyes and mashing the nose. He decided to leave the wire since it was embedded in the hairy neck anyway. Wire was cheap. A mugger wouldn't worry about leaving the wire, even a mugger from this rat-hole.

35

Lucius Finn paced up and down the foyer like a caged ape. He had expected Douglas to make it here first, but already he had waited ten minutes.

From across the huge forecourt security guards came and went. Whenever one crossed in front of the entrance to start his periodic rounds of the now almost empty building, he would give the pacing Finn a curious but amiable stare. They'd seen enough of his credentials so he didn't rate a challenge.

Go on, Bruno urged mentally, go on. Get in there, why don't you? It's why you came, isn't it?

Bruno had watched Finn get waved through to the main entrance, only to be intrigued by the unexpected waiting act. For whom, Bruno wondered. It had to be the now defunct Wyke, did it not?

Well your pal's not coming, Bruno told the figure slouching back and forth. You might as well go without him.

Bruno wasn't exactly a moron in situations like this. What he had here, his agile predator's mind had realised, was a happy conjunction of paths. He had just done liquidating poor Pruett, and Finn had arrived to put the man in irons, probably. Probably they were both going to do it, Finn and Wyke. According to Constantine and Co., these jerks had powers of arrest, in a limited way.

Bruno's military training – which was one of the other things he figured Constantine got confused over in regarding him as psychotic – Bruno's military training

217

had taught him the value of action as opposed to reflection. Hadn't he been telling Constantine to act? Hadn't he? Ever since this thing started to *feel* bad, he'd been saying little else. That was what the training was about. Constantine didn't grasp that, he wasn't capable.

Bruno already knew what he was going to do. Sooner or later, Finn would come out and head back to his car, most likely. Only then would Bruno detonate the device. In the hellfire and confusion that followed he would take his man easily, as a soldier knows how.

When Lucius Finn disappeared from view Bruno grunted with satisfaction. In the gateway, a guard moved across the open door. Guards didn't bother Bruno.

The place was empty, like some great museum in winter. It seemed to brood about him. Something was starting to make Luke uneasy. He found Pruett's office from the nameboard on the foyer wall. The door was open.

He gazed about the deserted room, taking in the empty plastic cup, the coat on the hook and the briefcase by the chair. No sign of the man, no sign of Wyke. Further down the corridor a pair of swing doors signalled the entrance to a laboratory.

Try it then.

Luke's shoes knocked on the shiny floor as he headed for it, in a series of little snaps that echoed behind him as if he was being followed.

The rubber doors of the lab flapped shut behind him as he went in. Luke turned to look at them, noticing their size and the way they opened both ways. The place stank; like all laboratories it had its odour hanging in the air, a mixture of the latent fumes of the week's experiments impregnating the walls. And it was huge, bigger than any laboratory Luke had ever seen before, with more equipment than he would have dreamt of.

Somebody was sitting in the corner.

Luke stared, motionless. The figure was sitting upright with its back to him, completely still and with its head bowed as if asleep. Luke started to walk forward, with his hand sliding into the small of his back. Any moment he expected the man in the chair to lurch around and confront him. He started to sweat, his forehead prickling along the hairline.

He was almost standing over the figure before he realised.

The man's throat had been cut all down the left side. Vast amounts of blood had welled down the front of his shirt, drenching his hands and trousers. A great puddle of it had poured under the bench and spread along the wall. His eyes were closed but his mouth was wide open.

Luke reeled along the bench to his left, ending up by a window. For a few minutes he stood horrified, gaping at the bloody spectacle of Pruett's corpse, trying not to gag on it. He had a massive urge to run, to get away from it into the air.

'Fucking hell.' A whisper almost.

Luke's skin was trying to tell him something. From the way it was moving in ripples up the flanks of his back, something was getting said, instinct-wise. Look around, search, but don't stay here. This only just happened it said, don't stay here. He went around to the other side of the body to look at the big glass jar on the bench about twenty centimetres from the head. It was a lead glass carboy, fully a metre in girth. According to the label it contained acetylene gas under very high pressure. Luke bent to examine it, smelling the nearby blood. What had the man been doing here? What had Pruett. . . ? Luke stared at the face again. *Was* this Pruett? Hellfire, he didn't even know that for sure.

Out of the corner of his eye something caught his attention through the darkened window. Looking up he saw it was a searchlight, dancing across the night sky like a great white wand. It wavered about and then stopped, picking out the form of an airship. TV blimp, Luke thought, George's TV blimp. Another searchlight lanced up, and two pools of light hung on the long slim shape in the sky, as letter by letter the dirigible's name moved through the beams.

P . . . U . . . R . . . E . . . F . . .

Pureflite? In Luke's head, something was ringing. His gaze stayed on it as his hands tore at his pocket, feeling for the printout from his machine.

A hundred metres away Bruno watched the activity at the lab window. He had found the body, he could call the cops from in there. Bruno tensed, wondering if he should do it now and to hell with taking Finn alive. Bruno fingered the button.

Come out, come out . . .

Luke was staring at the list of Tekniks' clients. Pureflite was at the top, right at the fucking top, the first one. Frantically he tried to think.

That too?

An airship?

Tonight?

Then he looked down at the carboy again and saw the plastique. It was behind it, close to the bench, a thin, pink strip of putty with the prints of a thumb in it. There was a bigger lump in the centre of the strip with a tiny brass tube protruding from it. Attached to the top of that was a thin wire, and on the other end of the wire was a small black box with what . . . looked . . . like . . . an . . . aerial.

Luke went for the lab door like a madman. Crashing through it, he hit the opposite wall, fell, rolled, and sprinted for the foyer. He made the main entrance in four seconds flat.

Fine, Bruno thought. He pressed the button, dropped the transmitter and went for his car door in one neat move. Not before time, he was thinking.

Everything within a spherical radius of two metres of the centre of the carboy became atomised. The glass of the vessel, several cubic metres of bench and cupboards, a section of the ceiling, a section of the floor and all of Pruett from his solar plexus upwards got reduced to constituent carbons and sulphurs, hydrogens and nitrogens, oxygens and silicons. For about the next twenty metres beyond that, things either disintegrated at joints or if they held any expandable air, they just burst. Beyond that, for another hundred metres it was mainly a shockwave effect. It blew open the lab door, it sent the lab windows, with their frames, hurtling in pieces into the cold night air, followed by detritus of all shapes, from expensive counters and calibrators down to humble test tubes.

Across the courtyard, the single security guard manning the gate leapt out of his warm chair as the panes of his lodge windows came in. By the time he'd gathered his terrified wits together and bawled down his short-wave to his colleagues scattered about the complex, there were smoke and flames to be seen.

Also, there was this Finn bloke emerging from the building, alive, but not obviously in terrific shape.

The guard let him go, watched him stagger off down the street. They could catch up with him later. The thing first was the fire. He started hammering at the keys on his phone.

Lucius Finn was nearly at his car when he started to think straight. At first, he'd instinctively wanted to reach Douglas Wyke, because if what was happening to him was any kind of guide, Douglas was in harm's way. But then there was George, he'd suddenly thought. Dear God, what about George? She could be in the balloon . . .

Luke faced it then. This thing was beyond him. Whatever it was that was happening, he was out of his depth. Maybe he should have done this a long time ago, he thought as he lurched towards the phone box, like earlier this afternoon, which seemed a hell of a long time ago now.

Unfortunately, Luke had picked a bad day on which to summon the police. Today, the Metropolitan Police were a trifle busy. 'Someone is going to sabotage it, are they?' a patient voice on the other end said. 'That's about the tenth time today, sir.' It sounded like a full scale riot going on in the police station. There were frantic sounds of scuffling and screaming and the splat of truncheons upon bone.

'You don't understand,' Luke said.

'You'd be surprised,' the policeman said.

'Listen, I'm just guessing,' Luke tried to tell him, but he had this feeling of hopelessness already. 'You've got to get to them. I can't . . . I mean . . .'

'It's been a very good afternoon, I can tell,' the policeman said. 'Don't worry, sir, a lot of people started earlier than you did.'

'For crying out loud, you miserable stupid sod,' Luke screamed, his head aching slightly. 'I'm not drunk, I'm not a crank, I'm not a bloody flaming hoaxer. My name is Finn, that's F . . .'

Luke realised he was bawling into a broken line. He had been looking out of the phone booth down the empty street, in case somebody should come around the corner. Somehow he hadn't sensed the door open behind him; he hadn't seen the black-leather-gloved hand descend on to the cradle rest.

Luke spun around and looked Bruno full in the face.

36

Ninety metres tall and thirty metres wide, multicoloured
and suspended in the black void far above Oxford Street,
the Prime Minister was braying about what a momentous
night this was. His voice reverberated like a distant storm
out of the hundreds of giant speakers dotted about the
West End. Stand too close to one of those and you could
be stunned into a coma. The Prime Minister had an
operatic voice even without the damned amplifiers. It lent
him a certain charisma in the House, but on Centre Point,
boosted by TCTV's sound system he boomed out like an
ocean liner trying to berth. He sounded like a real goon.

After the big intro, they'd flashed up some replay highlights from the Auckland-Sydney-Tokyo stuff that had
been hosed into twenty-five million home sets earlier in
the afternoon. That was to get the live audience in the
streets back into the mood. Following that, diagrams and
animates reminded the masses what the hell was
happening timezone-wise, since as Artistic had been quick
to point out, the vast majority had no idea what time it
was in the UK, let alone anywhere else. While that was
happening, they cut in with the big live scene from
Bangkok. Numerous orientals danced, bowed and babbled
their regards to the people of Britain and the world.
Delightful Thai girls danced across Centre Point, their
jingling finger cymbals ringing out from Soho to the park.
After that, attention was drawn to the dirigible, in case
there was anybody who hadn't noticed it floating around.
Just to show the folks in the street what the folks at home

would be seeing, they sent the pictures from the balloon back up to the big screen, so Centre Point appeared on Centre Point, bringing massive exclamations of wonder from the appreciative herd below.

Delhi came through at six fifteen. A statuesque knockout in a sari provided their end of the link, making the English linkman-cum-presenter drool like a dog. More dancing ensued, this time by several thousand Indian children. The display was mesmerising. Whole sections of the West End horde stopped and stared upwards, listening to the resonance of the sitars at thousands of watts. On Selfridge's roof even George stopped and gaped at it, her expression melting to an open smile of pure enjoyment at the spectacle. In the dirigible, Artistic had the mike down and nearly went bald over the effect.

In his headset the directional mikes were catching not only the strains of India but the whole ecstatic reaction of a million listening individuals. Not just an integrated roar, but single voices, one upon the other, simultaneous but distinguishable. Here a woman let her voice go with the music, there a man sighed with the hugeness of it all, whilst between and below, children laughed and cops swore ragged curses.

India didn't waste their moment on politicians or celebrity bums. They stayed with the people as their capital struck local midnight and rolled into the next era. It was the best yet, by a mile.

George cut it on a high and pulled in the Americans for a comment. A grinning TCTV-NY man filled the side of Centre Point and made suitable plaudits about the Indian transmission. But something in his tone of voice said, 'Just you wait till it's our turn.'

George poured herself a beer from the stock they had on hand. Dwindling fast, she noted, soon be time to throw somebody off the roof for some more. Reflecting, she figured the whole thing was moving along OK so far. She told them to roll the music filler while the technicals geared up for Tbilisi.

In the streets it was party time. What with sweltering flesh rubbing together in such degree it was getting warm down there, December or no. Bands were out from every club in Soho, radios and cassettes screeched out, balloons and trailers and fireworks had begun to appear. More sounds for the hanging mike. Up in the big balloon they caught it all, piped it down.

Later there was going to be a hell of a fireworks display. George knew all about it, as did the trembling London fire brigade and numerous military observation stations around the city. That was going to happen at *the* moment, *London*'s moment.

Coming up towards eight and time for Tbilisi. To the inspiring strains of the Soviet national anthem, and a backdrop of a fluttering red flag with the hammer and sickle not quite in field, a number of coppery Russian faces loomed up with pasty grins.

'Intro,' George howled, lunging forward towards the transmission controller. 'Where's the bloody intro?' Behind her a specialist presenter fluent in Russian was waiting for a cue whilst being cordially ignored by all.

They scraped a voiced-over intro in the nick of time before the anthem finished and one of the Russians gazed expectantly into the distant camera and started talking. From there on it was all right, with the specialist presenter handling it pretty well expertly.

Deferring to the general worldwide bonhomie, the Soviet transmission spared everyone the usual display of two million tanks and a sky black with fighters. Instead it was a sightseeing trip of the Georgian city's Byzantine cathedral, vast university, churches and galleries, followed by cute Russian ladies in local silk attire conducting the perspiring, redeyed London pack on a tour of their local trade centre, mechanical engineering factories, food processing plants, textile and timber works. Pride shone in Georgian eyes at every turn.

Pretty boring, all said, though it didn't last as long as it seemed, rounding off at about eight thirty with panoramic views of the moonlit Kura valley and the rousing melody of 'Arise, Red Sun', which spawned some ten thousand or so Cossack dancers in Oxford Street alone.

Kenya was next, after a filler. It had to be more fun than Tbilisi. Rumour had it that Nairobi sported a most interesting meat packing plant, though on this occasion it was not on view. Instead it was a tribal treat, Kikuyu and Masai chanting and leaping all over the skyscraper's side in floodlit clouds of ochre dust, leopard tails waving, lion head-dresses shivering, drums crashing and spears glinting in the light. In the London streets, many responded with shouts to the images on the giant wall, and many danced to the music. In London it seemed, people would dance to anything.

The happy horde continued their alfresco jaunt. In Soho they consumed popcorn and hotdogs by the hundred ton. In Trafalgar Square naked women and men pranced by the score. In Mayfair they formed conga lines longer than any in recorded history. In various places, a good natured game of toss-the-constable took hold, until discouraged with the aid of german shepherds. Despite the close resemblance to a mass riot, police reports so far were encouraging. There had been only a five-fold rise in burglary, an even lower rise in muggings, barely three times as many rapes as usual for a public event, and hardly any increase at all in car thefts, though admittedly the congestion lent little stimulus to the trade. Confident they were holding this line, the brave lads in blue soldiered on.

Nine twenty-seven was when the hush fell. Up in the dirigible, Artistic and his crews were circling Centre Point with the mike lowered, and they caught the amazing moment on sound and vision. It was the sound that was the most impressive effect.

Starting with 'God save the King' the mood changed within seconds. Only a few bars were necessary before all the animal noises from below ceased, and it was just the music. When it finished, silence had embraced the capital like a glove. In the gondola the crews could hear the swish of air across the airframe, and the gentle crosswind against which the airship had been pushing all evening.

The King spoke, briefly, in terms formal to the occasion. As millions watched motionless from the streets, and scores of millions from their homes, he complimented the nations of the world on achieving this historic night. He commended to them the hand of friendship, the absence of war, and the sacred hope of another such night, one thousand years hence, to be cherished by generations as yet unimagined. Then he turned to his own people. At greater length, and with words from the heart and devoid of ceremony, he wished them well. He spoke of his own family, and of the millions of families in the land, with the same intimate words. He joked and told anecdotes, so you'd have thought it was an after dinner chat he was giving and he had the whole nation right there with him. It lasted twenty minutes, that latter part, and when he finished they cheered.

God, but they cheered. It started as a kind of rumble, coming up from the very bottom of the city's throat, and then it rose to a shuddering roar that rolled around and around, as if feeding on itself, for minutes on end. Only gradually did it subside to the resumed chatter and song and shriek and curse that had been there before.

By the time that cheer came, and the teeming swarm resumed their riot, Bruno had made it to the building. The crowds had stopped moving, more or less, when the King made his speech, so the struggling cops got their wind back and held the streets clear. Bruno had been labouring his car at a slow crawl till then, but at that moment he had seized his chance. He approached Centre Point from the south, and made it to the new underground car park by nine fifty.

By his side Lucius Finn was neither conscious nor unconscious. Nerve-shocked and hypo'd, he saw only fuzzy lights and heard only distant noises. The smells would have told him that he was in Soho, but he would have known little else. He sagged next to the driver, eyes rolling, mouth open like a fish. One or two cops had actually given him a sympathetic grin as the car crept by. Bruno had just shrugged knowingly. Overdone it, his smile told them, for him the party's over.

37

'Who?' George mouthed over the din.

'Didn't say,' the guard yelled back. 'Some kind of copper, I think. Or a government bloke. Anyway, he had this department.'

'Well, what's it about?' George said. 'I'm not exactly at a loose end here.'

The guard — one of Selfridge's own — gave her a patient sigh to show he wasn't paid to run messages up here for people who phoned in on the night lines. By rights he should have been patrolling the building.

'Listen,' he started again. 'This bloke is waiting on the phone. He wants to meet you at the side entrance. The one you people been using all night, yes? He says he's got to talk to you right now. To do with your brother . . .'

'My brother? Where's the phone?'

'I just told you. It's on the fourth floor. He's . . .'

'Yeh, right,' George said, taking off. On her way through the crew she got hold of Production Two.

'Can you handle this for a while? I'm just going to talk to somebody. I won't be long. Look, it's only the damned Israelis, right?'

'It's OK,' Production Two said. 'I can take care of it.' He cast a confident eye upon the struggling scrum on the roof. Maybe he could.

The voice was very restrained, with a clipped formality in it.

'Miss Maringelli, you don't know me. I'm a colleague of Lucius Finn. Let me just say that your brother is fine.

We've found him fit and well. But there's a lot to explain, Miss Maringelli. Could you come down to the street entrance? I'll explain everything to you there. If you could just pop down.'

George felt a big wave go through her, lifting her up on its swell. Of course she'd go down. For this bringer of glad tidings she'd go down, and then some.

'Hang on.'

George dropped the phone and headed for the entrance in question. When she got there and peered out, a mighty throng met her gaze, a solid wall of noise, and a truly vast smell of humanity.

Leaning by the entrance was a fairly well-dressed man. He stood up when she stuck her head out, and smiled.

'Miss Maringelli? It's a pleasure to meet you. I'm afraid this may have caught you by surprise.'

'Where's Steve?' was all George said.

'Not far away,' the man said. He was showing her a card, just like the one Luke flashed occasionally, but a different colour. She saw the letters 'OTC', and the man's photo.

'Actually, I'm Lucius Finn's boss in a manner of speaking. My name is DeJohn. I'm in charge of a department of OTC. Luke may have mentioned me to you.'

'I don't think so,' George said.

DeJohn shrugged gracefully. 'Would you like to see your brother? I'd like you to come right now.'

'*Now?*' George flustered. 'Look, I'm busy now. I mean very busy.'

DeJohn gave her another big grin.

'I know you must be.' He hesitated, looked around. 'It's quite a show, by the way.' Then he turned back to her with an earnest expression on his face. 'It's important that you come, Miss Maringelli. The fact is, we need you to talk to your brother right now.'

George iced up again.

'What's wrong?'

'Miss Maringelli, we know about Tekniks. We know

230

what you did for Luke in their offices in Centre Point and we need to act tonight. We need information that your brother may have. But he's in a state of shock . . .'

'What? He's in shock? What do you mean he's in shock? You said . . .'

'He's all right,' DeJohn assured her. 'We have doctors with him. They say it would help if you could talk to him.'

DeJohn leaned closer to George, his face oozing sincerity. 'We need your help, Miss Maringelli.'

'Where is he?'

'At Centre Point.' DeJohn pointed in the direction of Oxford Street, as if to remind her of the way. 'That's not far, is it? We can walk together.'

'Well I . . . Shouldn't he be in some kind of hospital? I mean if he's hurt?'

'He's not hurt. He'll be in hospital within an hour. But we must have information from him now. It's all to do with the computers at Centre Point. We have to know things and do things immediately. Otherwise the people responsible for what happened to your brother may never be caught. It's vital, Miss Maringelli.'

'I don't understand any of this,' George told him candidly, though God knows he was reaching her by now. DeJohn was a good liar.

'Luke's there, waiting,' he added.

'Well, it's got to be quick,' George said. 'If I'm not back on that roof within an hour and a half, I get boiled.'

'No problem,' DeJohn said as she came out and started to button her coat. 'It's not far. We can get you back in a hurry.'

She didn't see the look in his eyes as she walked ahead of him towards Oxford Street. She would have gone really cold over that look in his eyes.

In Paris they'd gone just as barmy as in London. Judging from the incoming stuff there were as many folks out in the streets over there, if not more, and the authorities had thrown in with it. There seemed to be a no-holds-barred situation over there, with everything hanging out all the way. Twice now the West End crowd had beheld gendarmes throwing a leg alongside cancan girls somewhere in the floodlit Place de la Concorde.

And as for the girls, hell's bells! It looked like the very choicest, and they were rising to the occasion. The French minicam boys on the scene were homing in on some rave material.

A strapping thigh filled the left-hand side of Centre Point, a dozen floors from frilly nether garment to black stocking top, its creamy expanse spanning forty metres side to side. Beside it, an equally monumental knee twirled its lower leg round and round.

In the gondola, yips of delight and appreciation greeted the sight. The whole airborne crew howled with glee, all except Artistic, who considered it vulgar.

'Of all the things they could send us,' he snarled, as another moustached French cop bounced into view between the bosoms of the danseuses, 'they have to hark back to *that*.' He hesitated to absorb a new feature of the outrageous scene. 'I swear that's a fireman. They've got sodding firemen at it now.'

The Gallic fireman in question was trouserless, though his helmet identified his trade.

The whole French scene was climaxing right now, with fireworks (*everybody* seemed to have thought of fireworks; ours looked like coming out as a keep-up), and general auld-lang-syne-type, grab-a-girl kind of abandon. The whole of continental West Europe was date-lining at the same moment but the one they'd decided to *be* with was France. All the way up to the instant – eleven p.m. UK time – the TCTV team had been cycling their responding units in Paris, Brussels, Rome, Madrid, Bonn, Geneva, Lisbon, Oslo, Stockholm, Copenhagen and Amsterdam. The crowd in the London streets had been treated to a mesmerising stream of greetings from a dozen capitals. One moment it had been a thousand Norwegian skiers lighting up a mountain with torches as they sang their felicitations, the next it had been a wild flood of Spaniards, complete with flamenco and prancing Andalusian horsemen. Too much, almost.

Aloft, Artistic didn't have much to do but let his cameramen follow it. His stuff wouldn't be getting much screen time what with the international traffic so heavy. So he just let his people pick their shots and concentrated on the racket pouring up from the trailing mike.

What he couldn't understand was why George Maringelli had absconded so close to the real event. This pimply youth to whom he was obliged to address himself had been standing in for more than an hour now. Highly irregular, as he'd not been slow to point out.

'It's eleven ten now,' Artistic said to the pimply youth. 'What happens if she's not back in fifty minutes?'

'She will be,' Production Two stated from the rooftop. 'She's bound to be.'

Artistic watched Centre Point with its huge rectangle of dancing imagery swinging around on his starboard beam.

'Of course she's bound to be,' he replied sarcastically. 'But suppose she's not. Are you sufficiently familiar with the plan we agreed to be able to drive that shower down there?'

'Plan?' Production Two said, fading a bit.

'For *the* moment, darling.' Artistic realised madly that they weren't following all that balloon-to-ground nonsense any more. 'The witching hour. We were going to inject our amazing shot from up here, remember?'

'Uh? Oh yes! Yes, I recall the plan.'

Dear God, Artistic thought to himself.

The plan was to capture the instant of midnight when the whole city crowd would count down the last few seconds, then draw a breath as Big Ben struck the hour, and then they'd scream like hell. At that moment, the dirigible would approach Centre Point from the east and pass right over it, mike hanging, to emerge with cameras blazing so to speak, on the screen-lit, crowd-bawling side. The visual would show the black face of the skyscraper like the dark side of the moon, looming up and suddenly bursting into dazzling light. Simultaneously the audio from the trailing mike would be nothing at first but the swish of air, suddenly transformed into cacophony as the sound-stopping bulk of the skyscraper sped past below.

The live event would go out to the nation as it occurred. This startling bit of footage from the dirigible would be injected about a half minute later, without warning, to catch them all while they were still breathless.

For Artistic, this was going to be his crowning moment. This was the part they'd be talking about the morning after. 'Did you see that bit where they came up from the dark side . . . ?' Artistic was solely responsible for the idea. It was his and his alone. The shot of shots. A golden inspiration.

What was more he was going to do it, no matter what. If George was going to clear off and not *be* there, well there'd be hell to pay naturally, but that aside, this whelp on the roof had better know how to drive it or else.

Artistic pursed his lips so hard he nearly welded them together. That damned woman plagued his every creative moment. He could see her now, sitting in some pub . . .

38

'Give him a few moments,' a voice said.

Luke's brain came on again, ganglion by ganglion. By the time Constantine had withdrawn the hypo, dropped it on the table and returned to his seat, Luke's eyes had jerked open and he was looking dead ahead.

Right into the muzzle of his snubnose.

Bruno let him register what he was looking at and then pulled the trigger. From right in front of his face, the hammer-snap came shockingly loud into Luke's mind. He bucked violently backwards in the chair as if punched in the mouth.

Bruno sniggered, tossed the empty weapon on to the table with a crack and then turned away to one side. Luke subsided again and started to stare about him.

The room was more or less in darkness, but laced with coloured flashes as if in an electric storm. Slowly he made out some faces. He was sitting at one end of a big office table. At the other were three men: DeJohn on the left, Sandell on the right. The one in the middle had to be Constantine.

'With us, Mister Finn?'

It was Constantine who said it. Luke ignored him and continued to study his predicament. His mind raced. All right, so he was in Centre Point, judging from the horror show at the window, probably in Tekniks' suite which meant a long way up. He wasn't bound, but how strong was he? Should he try to move?

In the next flash, he turned his head to squint up at

Bruno, recognising him this time. That big fucker who'd brought him here. The black-haired character who'd smashed him half to death outside Measons. Luke decided not to move just yet.

He felt as if he could move, though. He felt wound up like a spring. Unfortunately it was obvious that the way he felt was due to whatever they'd woken him up with, which meant that they'd be aware that he could move, too. Well, that was why the big cat in black was on hand.

Luke wondered if they could be fooled. He moved an arm and then let it hang in the air in front of him before letting it sag down wearily, as if he couldn't hold it up any longer.

This time it was DeJohn who spoke.

'He's still very weak,' he said. 'What did you put in him?'

'I just use what I'm given,' Bruno said, and that made Luke swivel his eyes around to look again at the big man, though he was thinking that DeJohn was fooled, oh yes, good old stupid DeJohn.

'You must have hit him rather hard,' Constantine commented. 'But he's all right.'

'What the hell does it matter?' Bruno said irritably. 'He just needs to talk. Let's get on with it.'

Constantine looked at Bruno in his usual veiled way. Oh yes, he knew that Bruno had some very nasty methods for making people talk. No doubt they were some part of his graduation requirements from that gung-ho special unit he'd been in. But Constantine knew there were other ways, which did not involve the questioner in becoming bloodied or vomited upon by the interviewee. Constantine would prefer that, if possible.

'Give him a while, yet,' he said gently. 'Mister Finn is probably confused. If we allow him to gather his wits and appreciate his situation, that will be to our benefit in the end.'

Bruno didn't look a hundred per cent sold, but then he didn't look that bothered either.

'Hello, Sandy,' Luke said.

His voice came up clear and steady, surprising everyone. His eyes, now bright and hard, were fixed upon John Sandell. They betrayed none of the emotions of anger or disgust that one might have anticipated, more of a kind of expectancy; a sort of anticipation was glowing there.

'Good evening, Luke,' Sandell said. 'You don't seem terribly surprised to see me.'

Lucius Finn moved a little in the easy chair. Not enough to make Bruno consider a counter of any sort, but enough so they'd notice the real effort he pretended to put into it.

'Let's say I'm only half surprised,' Luke said. He paused and then smiled drunkenly. 'Does that bother you, Sandy? As a concept, I mean. Can a man be half surprised?'

'A man can be many things,' Sandell said acidly. Now he sensed the rage in Lucius Finn, but he was sure he was the only one who did. 'Tell me why you're only half surprised, Luke.'

'You were always around, Sandy. Whenever I wanted some information, you had to be there. Whenever I ran a check on something, you checked on me. I began to wonder who was pulling your strings, Sandy.'

Sandell digested that.

'But still you were half surprised,' he said.

'I just hung on to your scientific integrity for you,' Luke said. 'I always admired that, Sandy. Your scientific integrity.'

Constantine and DeJohn both laughed quietly at this talk of scientific integrity. Behind Finn, Bruno wondered what it meant. Bruno was getting short on patience with all this balls.

Only Sandell did not show any amusement.

'But it was always you who said that science is corrupt,' he spat. 'By which you meant scientists. You, Luke, the one and only true and pure man of science. You're the one who always wanted to call the rest of us corrupt, while we worked and you made hay from looking under the beds.'

'I never thought you'd be part of anything like this,' Luke argued.

'Go to hell, Finn.'

Luke waited. A small thought came and went about bullets in his waistcoat. He forced it away.

'Who spiked the plane for you?' he said after a minute. 'Who did that?' He stared at Sandell. He felt something rising in his guts, like puke. 'It was you, wasn't it, Sandy? You did it, right there in the firm. You blew some software to kill the plane. Was it the control system?'

'Of course,' Sandell said. 'It's the obvious place, isn't it?' He hung on it a second longer. 'You're so obvious, Luke. You went to it straight away. And then you couldn't decide if you were there or not.'

'Who's paying you for this one then?' Luke barged on, wanting to hear it. 'Who's paying Tekniks for this service? Channing, is it? It has to be Channing. They have the only rival plane. So who pays for the Measons thing? Some Swiss conglomerate, is it?'

DeJohn stepped forward a pace, becoming more visible in the dancing lights from the covered windows.

'By now I should think most of it is obvious to you, Luke,' he snapped. 'You're a bright boy after all. The point is, nothing is provable. Nothing at all.'

Luke gazed at his former boss. Now he could see why OTC hadn't picked up the Tekniks correlation using *corrina*. The reason was DeJohn. And all that sly hinting DeJohn had been doing about how Schaum would be really appreciative if he could 'find' them a sabotage. That was just to put him off the idea of being bought, just in case Schaum tried to buy him. An obviously sabotaged Schaum was no good at all to Channing.

He let his neck revolve painfully from left to right, taking them all in one by one. He made it appear like a real effort to move, especially when he moved his shoulders as well. He put a couple of very quiet gasps into it, just loud enough for them to pick up whilst making it appear as if he wasn't aware of them himself. He had no idea if any of this feigned incapacity was taking them in, nor even if he could move fast when he needed to, but he hoped to hell. One thing for sure, he wasn't going anywhere after this conversation, not unless he made his own arrangements.

He made a slight point of looking at the gun. Not the hypo, the gun.

Constantine was showing a lot of patience, if you were stupid enough to see it that way. Little by little, Luke was letting it all out, not what he knew, but what he thought he knew. Constantine needed to know what questions to ask.

Later, that was. But soon.

Just enough. He had given Luke just enough.

'And tonight's the night for the balloon,' Luke blurted out. 'That's when it gets its moment, is it?'

Constantine sighed with satisfaction. On either side, Sandell and DeJohn let it show on their faces too.

Luke started gambling. He tried to give it all the triumphant, confident-sounding edge he could.

'Yeh, I know about it. I know who's paying you for it. It's not going to happen. Because I got to them. I told them. Ask your zombie here.' Then he balled it up. 'Your boy at Channing is blown.'

Constantine unfolded Luke's listing, dangling it from his hand without reading it. 'This is all he got,' he said to the others. 'Isn't it, Mister Finn?' He gestured to Sandell. 'Tell him. It'll help him to cooperate.'

Sandell stood up and went over to the window, blazing in the light from the screen.

'We found your bug, Luke. Very clever, but we found it. We know when your woman put it there. We know when you got that list. There hasn't been time for you to do anything.'

Luke started to say something, but Sandell cut him off. 'I know, I know, but you just rang the police, that was all.'

Luke said, 'They'll get your man. They'll . . .'

'Save it, Luke. You forgot to mention Tekniks. And our man is gone.'

'Gone?'

'We only needed him to tell us how, Luke. It's not a difficult thing to pull down. And it happens from here.'

Luke said, very softly, 'When? Tonight?'

'Tell him,' Constantine said. 'It will help.'

Sandell waited a second.

'Around midnight.'

'Like Cinderella,' Constantine observed.

Luke was running very low on nerves. 'What happens to your saboteurs? Your employees? Or is it a case of wasting them after they've done a job? Like Keogh? And Pinetti?'

'By and large,' Constantine said. 'It's neater.'

He gave it a couple more seconds and then added, 'You seem to have run out of questions for me, Mister Finn. It must be my turn.' Then he looked at Bruno and added casually, 'Bring in the woman.'

Luke's head came up as if yanked by the hair. He'd been wondering in the back plane of his mind about the other people who were with him in this. His main worry was on George, but immediate danger seemed to have attached to Douglas Wyke.

Till now.

George was hauled in without terrific deference on Bruno's part for her sex. She looked terrified. Her eyes were red-rimmed, her hair dishevelled. She stared at Luke first, started to say something and then stopped. Then she looked quickly at Sandell, who just grinned back at her like a gargoyle.

Luke shifted his elbows a little, imperceptibly almost, for the third time. He was fairly sure of the bullets now. But wait . . . wait.

Bruno sat George down in another chair, just like the one Luke was in. Suddenly she burst out talking.

'Luke! Oh Luke, what's happening? What have they done to Steve? Luke, I . . .'

'Calm down, kid. These are very bad people. We have to deal with them.'

'That's good,' Bruno said. 'They're going to deal with us.'

The big man produced, as if by legerdemain, a pair of medium-sized wire clippers. They had razor-sharp stainless steel jaws about two centimetres long. The kind of thing that electronic engineers take home to prune the roses.

Constantine stood over Luke again.

'I'll spell it out for you, so there's no misunderstanding.' He waited a second for Luke to give his undivided attention.

'Bruno here will execute any instruction given to him, as you no doubt realise by now. As you are also no doubt aware, your voluptuous lady has elegant breasts, each of which has an ample nipple, I'm sure. After that, there are many other useful appendages we can use as we proceed, to whatever extent is necessary.'

'Listen . . .' Luke said.

'No, you listen,' Constantine went on. 'Our requirements are straightforward. We know most of what you know, but not all of it. We wish you to fill the gaps. The technique is simple. I shall ask you a series of questions aimed at filling in our ignorance. Some of these questions will be traps, since I shall know the answers already, others will be for you to provide me with what I wish to hear. You of course do not know which is which. Whenever you fail to answer or give me an answer I know to be false, then Bruno here will remove part of her body with the wire cutters. To avoid any surgery at all, you simply have to stick rigidly to the truth. You will not find me an unsympathetic interrogator. I am not a savage.'

This was far better than what Bruno had in mind; Constantine knew it as a psychologist. Bruno would have worked on Finn directly, damaging the source of the information needlessly. But this was better. How much better

241

it was could be read all over Finn's face. How expressive was despair. How eloquent the face of anguish.

Ideally, of course, the best way was with needle and drug, and then more talking. Unfortunately, although the method always took effect, the time required varied with the subject. Constantine wanted answers quickly.

'Shall we begin?' he said. Then he turned slightly and said to eager Bruno, 'When I tell you, Bruno. But only a little at a time.'

Soon, Luke thought, any moment now.

'Firstly,' Constantine said. 'Please tell me how you came to be aware of the name Tekniks. Don't elaborate, just summarise. We'll fill in details when I have the overall picture.' He hesitated so Luke could absorb what he wanted. 'Commence.'

Luke watched the clippers, which Bruno held about a hand's width below his ghoulish, smiling face.

'We've got this program,' he said sullenly, not risking any part of George yet. 'A computer program.'

'What kind of program?'

'A data analysis system. It works out how things correlate with each other.'

DeJohn came forward slowly. He looked interested in this.

'A database system?'

'More than that. A lot more than that. More like your *corrina* code. It's an expert system.'

'Where did you get the data?' DeJohn asked quickly.

'Where the hell do you think? We took it from OTC's files.'

'We?' Constantine said. 'We means you and Mister Wyke, yes?'

'Yes,' Luke grated. 'What have you done to him?'

DeJohn's eyes glinted in the popping lights.

'What else did you take from OTC files?'

'Nothing.'

Constantine glanced at the cutters, weighed it up, decided to wait till he had a better reason. If he had her

242

ripped when Luke was telling the truth, he gave something away himself.

Bruno had his hands resting lightly on George's shoulders. He was standing directly behind her and about a metre to Luke's right. The gun was on the table still, just out of arm's reach to his left.

'You're going to pull out now, aren't you?' Luke said in a very matter-of-fact way. 'You're going to call it a day.'

'Really?' Constantine said.

'Yeh, really.' Now Luke turned his head coyly to the right and squinted up at Bruno. 'And I know what happens to you when they do. I bet you don't, though.'

Now Bruno was too cute for that kind of thing. But whatever he thought, he had to make some gesture, some comment however slight. He chose a contemptuous snigger and a flicker of a grin in Constantine's direction, during which moment Constantine and all the others looked straight at him, and Luke went for the needle.

Bruno took in the movement about one tenth of a second after it started. Then his mind took another half second to decide what to do, then his hands came away from George as he turned left, taking one step sideways and lowering his weight forward to brace his leading knee. The great hands came up and out as Luke turned into him, head down like a charging ram.

Bruno missed the hypo completely. Either because of the dim light, or because of Luke's body blocking his view or maybe just the speed of it, he missed the sweeping right arm that took the needle off the table in one fluid pass. As his iron fingers clamped on to Luke's head, the long thin sliver of stainless steel took him in the hip and snapped.

Bruno let go of Luke with a bellow. Whatever it was that had hit him in the belly (Bruno thought of his hip as his belly) had gone deep, deep to the bone. The big man recoiled, grasped himself instinctively. It wasn't going to put him out of things for long, Luke knew that for sure.

'Run!' Luke screamed at George. He nearly slapped her

head round as he pushed her towards the door. 'Run! Now!'

He had the gun, gripping it lock-tight in his hand. Already his fingers were touching the bullets.

39

Up in the gondola, Artistic was practically shedding his platinum rinse. 'Dear God,' he howled, 'it's eleven twenty-nine and forty seconds, mark, and *still* she's not to be found.' In exactly five minutes and twenty seconds they would start the run-in to midnight. Timed to the very last jerk of Big Ben's mighty black hand, they had the whole thing set down in a scheme. There was no room for error.

And the damned production boss was missing. 'Can you credit that,' Artistic beseeched of cameramen and sound techs alike. 'Can you?'

No, they admitted, we can't.

'Well I tell you this,' he railed as the great balloon tacked towards the south-east, ready to come up on the eastern point of the compass, 'I tell you this: we're going to do our run up and over the dark side, just as planned, whether she's down there or not, and if they spoil it for me, if they don't catch what we send, if they don't hook it in as planned, if they do *anything* wrong because *she's* not there or because that *pipsqueak* she's left in charge fouls it up then I swear to you all, darlings, as sure as I'm born, we're going to have a kamikaze balloon. I mean it, I do . . .'

George and Luke had crossed the foyer into the office corridor beyond. In the foyer George had veered for the lift but Luke had spotted that the key was missing, realised it was disabled and dragged her away. They'd never have made it down the stairs, not with Tarzan of the apes behind them. And anyway, what Luke wanted was down here.

'You sure it's in there?' he whispered.

'Through this door,' she said. 'You go right through the room. It's on the other side, computers and things . . .'

'OK, OK.'

There was no light at all down here. They were crouched against the mail-room entrance close to the floor, watching the open corridor doors and the foyer, twenty metres away. Two of them were in there waiting. The other two had gone down the stairs, though any moment they'd be back.

Luke kept still as a bird, arm straight, wrist on knee with the snubnose pointed dead at the doors. His free hand was clamped over the forearm like they showed him when he bought the damn thing. The big screen covered the foyer windows making it light up intermittently. One of the giant street speakers was suspended from the building right outside the windows. Every time the light flashed Luke could see the big tropical plants shuddering in their tubs from the ear-splitting noise of it.

'What're you going to do?' George hissed at him.

'Give them a reason to stay back,' Luke said. 'There's something I have to do in there, if I can.'

They were back. Luke saw a movement from the stairwell, then another. They were by the doors, close together. For a split second he heard voices. He squinted down his arm, waited for a flash, sighted the pistol waist high into the centre of the doors, tried to hold himself still.

Come on. Come on. Come on . . .

All of a sudden the flashing stopped. They were showing something less dazzling out there. Luke started to feel the panic coming up into his throat as he was robbed of the light. Seconds went by, his arm moved, it had gone quieter, oh . . . fuck . . . oh. Then he heard the voice, very clear but very quiet. Find the light switch it said, just as the blazing display came on again and the deafening crashing din drowned it out.

There were three of them framed in the corridor

doorway. Luke saw them for about one quarter of a second and maybe they saw him, maybe they didn't.

Luke triggered the gun three times as fast as he could work it, shocked by the brilliance of its muzzle burst. He hurled himself and George into the mail room before the return fire came.

There wasn't any.

Constantine took the first hollowpoint through his solar plexus, and the second bullet drove through his left pectoral, flattened itself against his sternum and went spinning jaggedly up into his throat. He tottered backwards with his hands clutching at his belly, consciousness draining from him, his eyes rolling up into his head. As he toppled into the foyer he fell over the tangled forms of Bruno and Sandell. One of them had taken the third round, but from the screaming and cursing and contorting they were doing, you'd have been down to guessing which one had been lucky.

There was enough light in the machine room to get around by. What had to be standby power was running the big computers. Luke had tried the phone both in here and in the mail room and found them to be on an internal circuit. There was nothing to tell him the dial-out code, and no time to play tunes finding out.

He made one tour of the equipment and then came back to George who was crouched just inside the mail room, peeping into the corridor. She had the snubnose in her left hand, but she was holding it like an ice cream cone.

'Two hands, dammit,' Luke told her again. 'It kicks. Hold it tight with both hands.' He pulled her by the shoulder. 'And keep out of the fucking corridor. That big guy's got to have a gun.'

Luke had seen the service door at the far end of the machine room, tried it, knew what it was. It led to the roof, to the air-conditioning tanks up there. It was a chance, if they needed it. But there was this job in here first.

He stared over his shoulder into the computer room.

There must have been a half-dozen processors in there, all running. He'd have to go around the monitors seeing which was hanging on which, interrogate them, try to shut down any non system code he could find. Luke knew he couldn't do it. He thought about depowering them, but he knew he'd have to do that one at a time. Back panel off, decouple the backup battery, find the power line, kill it, on to the next . . . forget it.

Luke read his watch. Eleven thirty-six. Maybe it was too late already, but he was going to have a small ball trying.

'I'm going to do something I always wanted to do,' Luke told George. 'I never thought I'd get the chance.'

He picked up a tubular steel chair from under the mailnet VDU and hefted it carefully. Too light. He dropped it, picked up a more solid wooden one and felt its dead weight in his hands. He went into the computer room.

George stood up a little and watched him through the glass as he went up to the first big cabinet with the row of square lights on it. Luke lifted the chair, held it by the top of its backrest with the edge of the seat horizontally touching the tellback panel, measuring the distance. Then he swung back the chair behind his shoulder and brought it across right into the computer's twinkling mouth. The thin sheeting of the panel cover went in like paper. Luke smashed it again, and again. The panel sprang back on a hinge, swinging bent and battered to one side, exposing the ends of circuit boards the size of lunch trays. Luke let fly again, hammering them off their slots. Sparks flew, chips flew, copper and plastic shrapnel filled the air, live wires ripped away and crackled against chassis, little gasps of white smoke curled up from the carnage. Luke beat the computer to a pulp, and then swung around grinning and aimed an overhead blow through the cover of a tape drive, sending one reel bounding to the floor and the other into rewind, spewing plastic ribbon high up over his head. Another swing and out went a diskpack, its cylindrical Perspex skull caved in from the top, its read heads and stack of brown Winchesters screeching around at a tilt. As an aside almost, he kicked in the face on a VDU, imploding it to a smoking black hole.

When Luke started in on the next computer along, George decided he'd gone insane. But of course there hadn't really been time for explanations.

Bruno lay with his back against the tub of a rather exceptional monstera deliciosa and watched Sandell and DeJohn like a lizard with two flies to choose from. The finger-wide trench that had been gouged across his left side by hollowpoint number three was aching monstrously. The needle tip buried in his hip grated whenever he moved his left leg. So far, Bruno hadn't felt anything going numb or rigid, which was a sign of heavy muscle damage, so he reckoned he was sound for the time being.

Constantine was pretty stiff, on the other hand. Bruno kept looking at his extremely dead body and shaking his head.

'He's probably stopped the machines by now,' Sandell said. 'It can't happen.'

They had all caught the tinkling sounds filtering through as Luke beat seven bells out of Tekniks' capital investments. They could hear it during the occasional lulls in the cacophony outside. It sounded like a thorough job.

Bruno studied the other two men crouching on the far side of Constantine's corpse. Look at you, he thought, feeling sick. You can't run because he knows you, but you can't take him. You're just waiting for me to do it for you.

It was goodbye to the financial arrangements, Bruno had already reasoned. The Americans and the Swiss would have paid Constantine through the banking system, firm to firm, but that was no use to Bruno now. Nor to these two here. None of them had a connection with Tekniks. The Americans and the Swiss didn't even know them. Why should they pay? Bruno knew it had been Constantine's insurance. No Constantine, no money.

Of course, Bruno was his own insurance. And as for

money, he could live in a world without money if he had to. Bruno liked *things*, and the things he liked, he could take.

These two had no insurance. All they had was Bruno.

I don't need you, he thought finally, as he brought up the magnum. You're a liability. You're two liabilities.

Neither of them caught the slow movement of the gun in the leaping light, because Bruno's arm didn't move, just the hand, swinging the long, black, silenced weapon around by the wrist. Sandell was dead before DeJohn realised what was happening, his head blown out at the back, brains spraying the wall. DeJohn felt them spattering his face before it registered.

They'd probably have done this anyway, Bruno figured. Constantine had never said it, but Bruno knew he'd had it in mind; it wouldn't have come as a surprise.

DeJohn died with his mouth open and his eyes bulging out like a frog's.

The big man flexed his left arm at the elbow and pulled it behind his head, stretching the lateral muscles across his ribcage. The pain ripped into him and made him gasp, but it cleared his head and prepared him for action. It was time to draw fire. Bruno considered his situation weapon-wise.

He should have gone over Finn more thoroughly than he had, that had to be admitted, though if he'd had his own way he'd have stripped the creep before interrogating him anyway. Still, that was water under the bridge, what mattered now was to draw whatever remaining firepower the man had and then take him. Bruno wasn't necessarily assuming just three bullets by now. There could just be more. The one that had caught him had spread out and gashed him like a spade.

Fucking hollowpoints. Bruno wasn't about to walk into any more of them. He unscrewed the silencer and slid it into a pocket, and without thinking anything else at all, he rolled out into the corridor doorway and fired from his belly.

The magnum crashed and lit up the black corridor like day. Bruno saw the figure in the doorway down there, saw the splash of his round above it, saw it duck to its right. He rolled again, further out, not back to his cover as they'd expect, because if they were good enough they'd have had his position guessed before and they'd know where to try for.

George wouldn't have been that good if she'd been fighting house to house since birth. She'd been rubbing her eye when the movement came, so she only half caught it. When the door jamb disintegrated into matchwood about ten centimetres above her head she practically fainted. The huge flash and the numbing blast barely registered. The prone man in the foyer she never even saw.

George just flipped. She stuck both her hands out from the door and let go, working the trigger of the snubnose with both her forefingers, her chin buried in her neck and her teeth clenched as it bucked in her grasp, three times, and then stopped. She yanked a couple more times and then gaped at it. Her heart was drubbing about one fifty a minute.

Bruno lay out in the foyer, tucked against the wall, and watched the kaleidoscope at the window. It had happened during a real shit storm of a row from the speakers but it sounded and looked like three all right.

Luke was rubbling the sixth and last computer when George came spilling in. The machine room looked as if a grenade had gone off in it. Every one of the big processor cabinets was disembowelled and twisted. A couple of them had shifted back on their castors to a drunken angle. From nearly all of them, mutilated CPU boards hung on their bus-straps like the guts of slaughtered hogs. The sprinklers had come on, soaking Luke to the skin and filling his shoes.

His feet crackled on ramchips and romchips, switches and solenoids.

'Luke, it's empty,' George yelled, waggling the gun.

Luke threw away the chair. Both its front legs were gone,

its seat in tatters. 'Leave it,' he said, grabbing her by the arm. 'Come on.'

He started hauling her towards the door to the roof.

A little more than four minutes to go. From where the dirigible cruised about a kilometre east of the skyscraper, the building looked like a giant monolithic slab, picked out by the glow of the West End on the other side. The big balloon was turning nose-on to the approach direction, the crew adjusting trim for straight-ahead flight. On either side of the gondola the big motors started winding up. The airspeed needles moved in the forward crew area.

Artistic yelled to his cameramen to start rolling, ordered his audio team to bring on the mike.

Far below, the massive steel ball hissed through the air on the end of its chain, recording little for the moment but the muted hum of the scene below.

Below and west, the struggling throngs stared up at the massive image of a digital countdown counter that was being lasered up as a superimposed feature on the display. It was counting down in seconds to midnight and right now it was going through two hundred and fifty-two. As it entered single figures the TCTV presenter would beam his twenty-metre wide smile and egg the multitude into a roaring communal time-out, just to ensure the crescendo of noise and cheering that would accompany the vast explosion of fireworks when the great moment approached.

Peering out of the front panels, Artistic rent his raiment. *Still* the bitch had not appeared. Oh boy, was she going to suffer for this. This time he just couldn't be browbeaten.

'Get going,' he said when his teams signalled that all the equipment was running. 'Now. Full ahead.'

They'd better get this, Artistic seethed, as the black slab began to grow.

Leaving the empty snubnose for Bruno to find had been an error. The magnum was half full, more than enough for what he needed to do. But for the burning agony in his side, he'd have been more than confident with just his bare hands. Bruno held his left arm clear as he stalked the roof. Every so often he stopped and waited for one of the many protuberances to move. There were a number of them up here: air-conditioning vents, skylight covers, aerial housings, generator blocks. Finn and the woman were hiding somewhere behind them, probably separately, hoping to sneak back to the stairs.

Not a chance. Not one chance in hell of it. Bruno kept the exit from the stairs in sight nonstop.

A starburst cracked off far above, followed by another, then a third, then a whole merging string of them, filling the sky above the lit-up face of the building with brilliant streamers of cascading, sparkling diamonds. Long, shrill whistles tumbled down, one upon the other. The roof was deluged in pure dazzling white, which faded slowly as the glittering display floated earthwards. Then more followed, scores of them, until the whole block of space above the West End was spattered with huge spiralling clusters of colour and warbling, shrieking, skittering sound.

And from below a new sound thundered up. It was the single voice of two million throats, all shouting the same thing. 'Thirty,' it clamoured, 'twenty-nine, twenty-eight . . .' More fireworks exploded into view.

Bruno saw the bent shape go scuttling between one vent and the next one along. That wasn't going to work either, he thought, grinning; potshots were unnecessary now. He went hungrily after it towards the hip-high parapet and the roof edge.

'Twenty-two,' the crowd bellowed, 'twenty-one, twenty . . .'

He was almost on top of her when George stuck out her foot. Behind the vent, George cringed in terror as she poked it into view, half expecting it to be blasted away. Bruno stopped, whipped up the weapon and lunged, just as Luke took him football style, head-first, right in the side.

The left side.

Bruno bawled like a bull. He buckled at the waist,

absorbed Luke's hurtling momentum and somehow stayed on his feet, using the terrific power in his legs. Luke kept his head down, gouging and punching, aiming for Bruno's testicles as the big killer twisted and shook, trying to bring the heavy pistol to bear.

'George! Run . . .'

But George wasn't running. She landed on Bruno's arm screaming, wrapping herself around it like a cat, heaving the gun hand away. The magnum cracked off, the steel-jacketed round clanging through the airvent cover, knocking a hole through it the size of a man's fist.

'Fifteen, fourteen . . .'

The dirigible came humming out of the black eastern sky like a gigantic bee, its throbbing turbines buried in the howling of the crowd below and the detonations above. None of them even saw it, let alone heard it.

'Nine, eight, seven . . .'

Bruno smashed George away from him with an elbow, sending her thudding on to her back, knees up to her broken ribs. One more massive lurch and he had his man clear and facing him, framed by the brilliance beyond the parapet. The magnum swung up.

Luke took one glance behind him and dropped.

Bruno knew it wasn't a trick, he knew *something* was there but he had no time to turn before the mike-ball arrived. Fifty an hour it was going, not fast because they wanted plenty of soundtrack up there, but weight-wise it came in just over the half-ton so it had enough momentum to do what it did to Bruno. Smack in the back it caught him, dead in the centre of gravity so he didn't flip over or tumble forward as he took off, he just launched out into space bolt upright with all four limbs outstretched, to a good forty metres clear of the edge.

Bruno got to a head-down position as he plummeted past the TCTV presenter's gigantic nose, diving like a fallen bat to the new millenium cheer. By the time he exploded off Oxford Street they were yelling even louder, so you wouldn't have known the difference really . . .

Bestselling Thrillers —
action-packed for a great read

__ $4.50 0-425-10477-X **CAPER**
Lawrence Sanders

__ $3.95 0-515-09475-7 **SINISTER FORCES**
Patrick Anderson

__ $4.95 0-425-10107-X **RED STORM RISING**
Tom Clancy

__ $4.50 0-425-09138-4 **19 PURCHASE STREET**
Gerald A. Browne

__ $4.95 0-425-08383-7 **THE HUNT FOR RED OCTOBER**
Tom Clancy

__ $3.95 0-441-77812-7 **THE SPECIALIST** Gayle Rivers

__ $3.95 0-441-58321-0 **NOCTURNE FOR THE GENERAL**
John Trenhaile

__ $3.95 0-425-09582-7 **THE LAST TRUMP**
John Gardner

__ $3.95 0-441-36934-0 **SILENT HUNTER**
Charles D. Taylor

__ $4.50 0-425-09884-2 **STONE 588** Gerald A. Browne

__ $3.95 0-425-10625-X **MOSCOW CROSSING**
Sean Flannery

__ $3.95 0-515-09178-2 **SKYFALL** Thomas H. Block

Please send the titles I've checked above. Mail orders to:

BERKLEY PUBLISHING GROUP
390 Murray Hill Pkwy., Dept. B
East Rutherford, NJ 07073

NAME_____

ADDRESS_____

CITY_____

STATE_____ ZIP_____

Please allow 6 weeks for delivery.
Prices are subject to change without notice.

POSTAGE & HANDLING:
$1.00 for one book, $.25 for each
additional. Do not exceed $3.50.

BOOK TOTAL	$_____
SHIPPING & HANDLING	$_____
APPLICABLE SALES TAX (CA, NJ, NY, PA)	$_____
TOTAL AMOUNT DUE	$_____

PAYABLE IN US FUNDS.
(No cash orders accepted.)